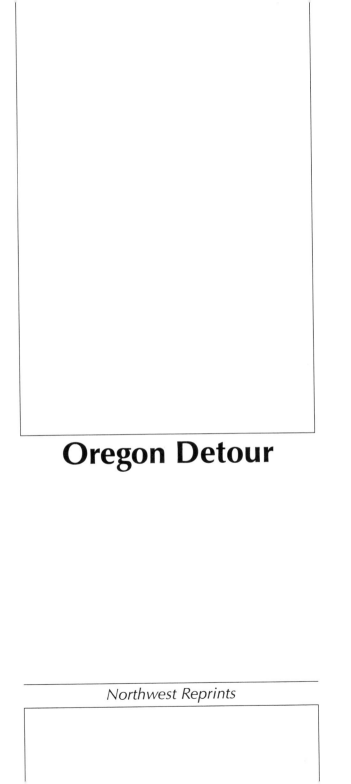

Oregon Detour

Northwest Reprints

Northwest Reprints
Series Editor: Robert J. Frank

Other titles in the series:

Oregon Detour

Nard Jones

Introduction by George Venn

Oregon State University Press
Corvallis, Oregon

The paper in this book meets the guidelines for permanence and durability of the Committee on Production Guidelines for Book Longevity of the Council on Library Resources and the minimum requirements of the American National Standard for Permanence of Paper for Printed Library Materials Z39.48-1984.

Library of Congress Cataloging-in-Publication Data

Jones, Nard, 1904-
      Oregon Detour / by Nard Jones; with an introduction by George Venn.
          p.   cm. — (Northwest reprints)
      ISBN 0-87071-500-3 (alk. paper).
      ISBN 0-87071-501-1 (pbk. alk. paper)
      1. —Oregon—Fiction. I. Title. II. Series.
PS3560.05225074   1990
813'.545—dc20   89-35452
                                     CIP

Introduction © 1990 George Venn
Printed in the United States of America

PREFACE

but there were things
That covered what a man was, and set him apart
From others, things by which others knew him. The place
Where he lived, the horse he rode, his relatives, his wife,
His voice, complexion, beard, politics, religion or lack of it,
And so on. With time, these things fall away
Or dwindle into shadows: river sand blowing away
From some long-buried old structure of bleached boards
That appears a vague shadow through the sand-haze,
*   and then stands clear,*
Naked, angular, itself.
*   from "Trial and Error," H. L. Davis*

People new to a region are especially interested in what things might set them apart from others. In works by Northwest writers, we get to know about the place where we live, about each other, about our history and culture, and about our flora and fauna. And with time, some things about ourselves start to come into focus out of the shadows of our history.

To give readers an opportunity to look into the place where Northwesterners live, the Oregon State University Press is making available again many books that are out of print. The Northwest Reprints Series will reissue a range of books, both fiction and nonfiction. Books will be selected for different reasons: some for their literary merit, some for their historical significance, some for provocative concerns, and some for these and other reasons together. Foremost, however, will be the book's potential to interest a range of readers who are curious about the region's voice and complexion. The Northwest Reprints Series will make works of well-known and lesser-known writers available for all.

RJF

Introduction

One January day in 1978, as students were
bundling up to leave my Western Literature class, a girl
who always sat in the back row approached me at the
lectern. She asked me if I'd heard of a writer called
Nard Jones and could she read one of his books for a
paper due in three weeks. I didn't know this student
well. She was a freshman. She'd done C work in the
course so far. She'd been absent a time or two. I asked
her which book she was interested in.

"Well, there's this one that people keep stealing
from the library at home," she said. I thought I saw a
kind of gleam in her eye. I must have looked doubtful.
"Really, it's true," she said.

"Where's home?" I asked.

"Weston. Over by Walla Walla," she said and
pointed northwest.

"Which book is it that people steal?" I asked.

"I don't know. My mother's got a copy, I think.
She's friends with the librarian."

"You grew up there?" I asked.

"Twelve years," she said.

"Well, it should make an interesting paper. Find
out as much as you can. Talk to the librarian. Let me
know if I can help."

"Oh, good," she said, and I'm still sure she went
out with a great smile on her face, as though something
about her life was suddenly worthy after all.

That was my introduction to *Oregon Detour,* Nard
Jones's first novel and the first "New Realist" novel
written in the Northwest. The student did read the book
and wrote her paper, but her project raised more
questions than it answered. For instance, she said that
the author had been run out of town, that he'd been

sued, that he'd written an awful book about the town's good people, and that everyone stole the novel. As I read this, something in me began to doubt. Was something being left out? I started to wonder how I might verify any of this.

To begin, I looked through my own research files for a survey of libraries in Eastern Oregon I'd done in 1973, to find what the librarian of Weston had, indeed, said in response to my question: "In your judgment, who are the most important authors who've written about Eastern Oregon?" The Weston librarian had replied:

DeVoto. Probably best known. Parkman. I think Nard Jones progressed into a good writer... I can't think of any more really important ones.

Given the student's paper, this was strange. I looked through the librarian's responses for more information. She had listed all of Jones's regional works except *Oregon Detour*. Something was being left out. That began to bother me. I'd clearly invited her at numerous places in the five-page questionnaire to mention any fiction about the region.

The more I thought about the apparent omission and the student's paper, the more I wanted to find out what had actually happened. To support that research interest, I wrote a grant proposal to the Oregon Committee for the Humanities, and they generously funded the project for the summer of 1981. To prepare myself for interviews in Weston about the novel, I read ten years of the town paper, the *Weston Leader*, and I dug into Nard Jones's literary past for weeks with the help of librarians at Eastern Oregon State College, Whitman, Umatilla County, and the University of Washington. With the help of Jones's sister, Audrey

Jones Baker, his son, Blair, his second wife, Anne Mynar Jones, and his daughter, Debbie Jones, I was given invaluable access to Jones's papers, biography, and Weston history. Thirty-five residents of the Weston area granted me interviews during the spring and summer of 1981, which allowed me to complete an intensive research project in six months.

That summary does leave out some notable facts: the specific hospitality of Cliff Price, George Gottfried, Hugh Gilliland, Wayne O'Harra, and Willmarth Reynaud—Weston people who treated me kindly as a wanderer; the wild-eyed fanatic who walked into the Umatilla County Library in Pendleton and said to the librarian, "You're not fooling God with this library and all your books," then stomped out as I drew the only local copies—noncirculating—of *Oregon Detour* closer to me; my two-year search for a copy of the novel that was rewarded in the Green Dolphin in Portland one rainy night; the immediate sources of affection that sustained me: food brought morning, noon, and night by loving hands, the doe at the spring in the mountain dusk, the generous fertile country where I found wild strawberries...

Since the initial publication of this essay in *Marking The Magic Circle* (Oregon State University Press, 1987), I have received responses from Margaret Sutherland, the Weston public librarian whom I also interviewed in 1981, and from her pastor, Rev. Dave Cassel. Their responses provided new information which has been partially incorporated here. Hence, they have given this new version of the essay additional clarity and potentially greater accuracy.

I presented what follows at Concordia College, Umatilla County Library, and at the Pendleton

Rendezvous, but the project really culminated for me when, one April afternoon in 1983, I stood before the assembled student body of Weston-McEwen High School in Athena, the school Jones himself would have attended if he were growing up in Weston today. Waiting in that shining gymnasium for silence, I reviewed my notes and watched the energy and excitement in the bleachers turn to attention. I hoped I was ready. For about half an hour, I told them the *Oregon Detour* story as I'd been able to find it. At the end of my talk, I read them part of a chapter about high school seniors from Weston going to Pendleton after graduation for a night on the town. The bleachers began to whistle and cheer. I stopped reading, looked up, waited, then read a few more sentences. They laughed. I read on, stopping while they responded, then reading on again. They loved it. Only when the bell jangled at the end of the day did they let me stop. Busses were coming, cars waiting.

On my way out, the principal stopped me in the front hall. He was a big man who'd gone to school locally and returned to teach. "Nothing's changed," he said. "That part you read? I did that too. These kids will do it too. It's all still the same. Even graduation." As he spoke, students were streaming by with coats and books and packs—voices rich, magnificent, and opening to the spring outside. I hoped there was another novelist among them. At least, I thought, they now have heard that writing fiction was a possibility—even here. At best, if I'd done my work well enough, *Oregon Detour* might again be included as a worthy interpretation of its generative community.

Among writers who grew up in the Northwest between the world wars, Nard Jones (1904-1972) cast himself a complex career as a full-time journalist who also wrote seventeen books, published more than three hundred stories in popular magazines, and broadcast numerous radio programs. He published twelve novels, including his national bestseller, *Swift Flows the River, Evergreen Land,* a history of Washington, and *The Pacific Northwest,* a regional history co-authored with Stewart Holbrook and Roderick Haig-Brown. Still selling at the Whitman National Monument is Jones's popular history of the Whitman Mission, *The Great Command.* As a journalist, Jones edited for Miller-Freeman trade publications in Seattle and New York for nearly 24 years, then went to work for the *Seattle Post-Intelligencer* in 1953, where he held various editorial posts, including chief editorial writer, until his retirement in 1970. *Seattle,* a history and memoir, appeared posthumously in 1972 from Doubleday.[1]

While Jones's writing still waits for major critical attention,[2] his first novel, *Oregon Detour*, remains important as the first novel by a Northwest writer to use the aesthetics of the "New Realism" established by Sherwood Anderson, Sinclair Lewis, and Scott Fitzgerald a decade earlier. *Oregon Detour* is further distinguished because it has been the object of fifty years of censorship in Weston, Oregon, where Jones lived from 1919 to 1927. Like other New Realist novels across the country, from Hergersheimer's *Cytherea* banned from his hometown library in West Chester, Pennsylvania, to Lawrence's *Women in Love* banned by New York Customs officials, to *Elmer Gantry* by Sinclair Lewis banned in Boston by the local D.A.—not to mention a host of others—Nard Jones's first novel could not be regularly kept on the shelves of the Weston Public Library between 1931 and 1981. Some people said the novel was absent because it was out of print, others said the novel had been stolen during the l930s, others suggested the novel had been indirectly banned prior to 1955. Also, the novel was removed from the Weston High School Library shortly after publication. This essay attempts to document and examine the history of *Oregon Detour*, an almost unknown novel prior to this printing.

II

After graduating from Whitman College in 1926 with highest honors in English, Nard Jones returned to Weston, Oregon, to live with his family and to work in the family general store. During that year at home, he continued the literary career he had started at Whitman. He wrote fifteen stories for the popular pulp magazines, a New York market he had been quick to understand. He also wrote weekly editorials for the *Weston Leader*'s publisher, Clark Wood,[3] who was also Jones's literary mentor. Jones's weekly columns showed the major literary influences of his Whitman education: the polemic style of H. L. Mencken, the New Realism of Sinclair Lewis, and the small town interests of Sherwood Anderson.

Also, during that year at home, Nard Jones began to work on *Oregon Detour*, a project he'd started at Whitman when he learned from Professor Russell Blankenship that a realistic novel in the manner of

Main Street had not been written about any Northwest community.

In September 1927, Jones moved to Seattle to work on two Miller-Freeman trade publications, *Pacific Motorboat* and *Western Woodworker*. In a sense, returning to Seattle was going home. He'd been born in that city in 1904 and had lived there for the first thirteen years of his life, a time when he had enjoyed great personal freedom because his family had owned a hotel there. Now, after eleven years away—California, Eastern Washington, Eastern Oregon—he returned as a fast-rising magazine writer, recent college graduate, new editor, and budding novelist. He moved into a hotel, edited for Miller-Freeman during the day and, bolstered by shots[4] of whiskey which could make him dangerous, wrote *Oregon Detour* and short stories during the evenings. In June 1928, he married Elizabeth Dunphy, the daughter of Walla Walla's leading lawyer and member of a wheat-ranching pioneer family. In March 1929, he hired Brandt and Brandt, literary agents in New York, and sent off the *Oregon Detour* manuscript. Within fifteen days, his new agent had sold the book to Payson and Clarke for $500 plus 10 percent royalties to $5,000, 15 percent thereafter.[5]

Here, then, was a Northwest literary boomer. At 25, he was a veteran of print, a quick learner, a skilled amateur actor with a taste for whiskey, jokes, and self-dramatization. Short, dark-haired, quick, handsome, slender, ambitious, Jones was a compelling presence. To complete this picture of sudden success—comparable to none in the region—all Nard Jones needed to hear was the comment of William Rose Benet, Assistant Editor of *Saturday Review* and Payson and Clarke's chief editor: ''Your book seems to be one of the most promising first novels that I have read in some time."[6] After some correspondence between Benet and Jones about revisions, Jones's novel went to press and was released in early 1930. From coast to coast, *Oregon Detour* quickly attracted critical approval.

In Weston, Oregon, however, events had progressed toward publication somewhat differently. Clark Wood, the *Weston Leader*'s publisher, had been trying for nine months to prepare the Weston audience for his protegé's novel. Wood had published a letter from Jones in April 1929, in which Jones wrote:

The hero of this book is the harvest. And any of my friends who circulate the rumor that any of its people are such-and-such persons will be shot in cold blood—even though I have to do it myself. This will take months of time, as I am the most damnable shot in the eleven Western states (April 19, 1929).

In October 1929, Wood had reprinted a complimentary national review of the novel containing the statement that "There is no bitterness in the book. No sarcasm. In writing of his people, the author has not forsaken them." Just before the novel was released, Wood further noted that "Weston is [the] locale but characters are fictitious." This evidence suggests that both Wood and Jones knew controversy was rising like thunderheads over Weston Mountain.

On January 17, 1930, *Oregon Detour* went on sale in the local drugstore, just a few yards from Jones's home on Water Street. (His father was mayor of Weston, a leading businessman, and an avid community booster.) All copies of the first shipment sold immediately for $2.50 each. Those who couldn't afford to buy the novel rented a copy from friends at

25¢ and read it. The Weston librarian, Josephine Godwin, another of Jones's literary mentors, added the book to the public library. It was immediately checked out by a family friend, then by the doctor's wife who read the novel aloud to her husband at bedtime. They laughed over each page and considered the novel a "boy's look at his hometown." Many of the surrounding wheat farmers who did business with the Jones and Jones Mercantile also bought copies of the novel. They felt it was a good-humored use of risqué local events. Some snickered that the pious now appeared only sanctimonious. Young married couples in the community— Jones's peers—were especially anxious to read the novel because the word quickly spread that *Oregon Detour* contained "real people."[7]

Nevertheless, a segment of Weston's six hundred people were furious. They were reading *Oregon Detour* as reporting. They called the novel vulgar. They objected to its "hard-talking sloppy lingo," and to Jones's use of names like Fanny Breast and Rev. Alfred Horliss. They objected to his explicit use of sexuality. Those who protested were generally members of two socially powerful groups in Weston, the Methodist Church and the Saturday Afternoon Club, both dominated by socially prominent women who held formidable powers over cultural life in the community. For instance, the Saturday Afternoon Club gave monthly literary programs, reviewed proper books, encouraged musical events, controlled the library board prior to 1955, and at one time owned the city park—which they later gave to the city of Weston. Their membership was by invitation only.

According to Nard Jones's sister, who was still living with her family in Weston when the novel appeared, a Saturday Afternoon Club member approached her on the street. As she recalled the encounter,

This woman said, I'm not sure what her words were, but it was something like she thought it was terrible that Nard might have put people in Weston into his book. I remember I was so shocked. I was fifteen, I guess, and I turned around to her and I said, "Mrs. ——, I really think that people must feel terribly important to think that they're in somebody's novel." I turned around and walked away.[8]

Many women in this group refused to read the novel after they heard about its characters and language. It was publicly stated to this writer that there was also a mass book burning to rid Weston of *Oregon Detour*. It was also suggested that somewhere in a Weston attic lies a trunkful of copies waiting to be discovered.

Even though he lived several hundred miles away, Nard Jones immediately felt the tremors of outrage created by his novel in Weston. His response, published by Clark Wood in the January 24 edition of the *Weston Leader*, is worth reprinting here in its entirety as the only document of its kind in Northwest literature—a New Realist asking his subject community to read their lives as literature rather than as reporting:

It's Only Fiction

To whom it may concern: It has been brought to my attention that individuals are looking upon certain passages in Oregon Detour *as reflective of truth. This is regrettable and far from the real purpose of the author.*

Only three actual names appear in this volume: they are merely mentioned in one or two sentences and this mention is intended as a compliment. All other characters are fictional, though necessitating common

xvi

names which would naturally be duplicated in this and thousands of other books and communities.

It is perhaps needless to say that what happens in "Creston" may happen in a hundred other wheat towns. It is also needless to say that the writer would not intentionally speak in a derogatory manner of those toward whom he has the highest regard.

Authors are frequently confronted with this situation, and it is no new thing. I am sure that the great majority of my hometown people will read the book purely as a story, not attempting to weave into it any information which happens to be in their own minds—but which was not in the mind of the author as he wrote.

Very truly yours,
Nard Jones

Apparently, Jones's effort to encourage his Weston audience to accept his fictional masque did not succeed. In Weston, the novel was read in 1930 and is still read today as "about Weston" by the majority of residents. Trying to figure out or trying to remember who the "real people" were in the novel is still a local pastime. There is no evidence that the novel was ever understood as literature, as a statement by Jones that Northwest small town life is—at best—a dangerous idyll.

Biographical evidence also suggests that *It's Only Fiction* was as much a feigned professional pose as it was an effort to claim his innocent intentions. Jones was not afraid of controversy. In fact he sought it. At Whitman College, he scandalized the campus his senior year by writing and publishing an underground sheet called *Spasm*. His editorship of *Blue Moon,* the campus literary magazine he founded, was constantly under challenge for publishing "blue" literature rather than writing of the "sunny side." His *Weston Leader* columns were often pure provocation. Thus, the professional innocence projected here only conceals a part of Jones that was iconoclastic.

However, other evidence suggests that Jones was not invulnerable to the snarl of the Weston status quo. Most significant in this respect must have been his now lost letter to Clark Wood in April 1930, to which Wood responded as follows:

Dear Nard:

Have no regrets about your novel. It was a good yarn—the proof being that I was absorbed in it myself when usually I don't care a damn about anything except a detective story with a mysterious murder in the first chapter—preferably a double murder.

The sex stuff naturally caused some comment around here, but they ate it up. Those who didn't buy the book borrowed it. I realized that you had to put in this sort of stuff in order to sell the yarn and I thought you handled it with extreme skill.

Some of the descriptive work—notably the flood and the wheat harvest—was strongly done, and was almost as good as yours truly could have evolved.

Forget it, boy. You haven't lost any real friends around this burg.

Woodsy
April 16, 1930[9]

The tone of Wood's letter suggests that Jones needed to be reassured about his potential loss of popularity at home. Evidently, behind the young New Realist's mask lived a writer both sentimental and nostalgic about Weston—a town where he'd actually been given the impetus to become a writer, a town he would visit annually for most of his life, a town where he gave copies of his books to the library, a town he wrote about in both fiction and journalism for the rest of his career.[10] Private sources also confirm that Jones himself was "very, very shy . . . he was not a daring person." He hated flying and avoided autograph parties as much as possible.[11] Even though he could call on national reviews, Clark Wood, and New Realism to shield him, a part of Jones was still vulnerable to the possibility of local dishonor.

III

Of course, Jones tried to convert this furor into a joke for Northwest writers who read *The Frontier,* the region's leading literary magazine. In the November 1930 issue, Jones reported his recent news in this fashion:

Nard Jones, Seattle, is finishing a second novel, Sin of Angels, *for spring publication. He has two long stories and a short to* College Life: *"Hollywood," "Expatriates,"* and *"Please May I Have Another?" For the past three years Mr. Jones engaged in trade journal work. Recently he took the* Oregon Detour *by auto—"without being shot at, or hanged."[12]*

While levity here worked to preserve some professional dignity, more important adjustments were going on at the typewriter, where Jones had just finished his second novel, *The Petlands,* and was at work on his third, *Wheat Women.* In advance notices for *Wheat Women* published in the *Weston Leader* in November, Jones continued to respond:

*I am doing another wheat novel in order to show
the other side of the picture depicted in* Oregon
Detour. *That book showed many of the faults of the
wheat land; this new wheat story will show many of its
virtues. It will probably, therefore, be longer.*[13]

Is Jones attempting here to recover from what he's
decided were his excesses in *Oregon Detour*? Is he
playing to an offended audience with tongue in cheek?
Is this the final evidence that he himself was
unprepared for the implications of his first book? All
seem likely. He was also careful to add a disclaimer to
the front matter of *The Petlands,* in which he reminded
his readers that the "story of this book is fiction."

Subsequent events in Weston allegedly took
several turns against Jones and *Oregon Detour*, turns
which seem to have been dominated by the Saturday
Afternoon Club. Most conspicuous were those hostile
moves alleged in the local narrative about *Oregon
Detour* recorded by the student writer, namely that
Jones was sued and run out of town. There seems to be
no base in fact for either of those charges. No evidence
of a lawsuit exists in Umatilla County courts or in the
memories of more than thirty informants. Also, Jones
was clearly not run out of town, since he had lived in
Seattle for three years prior to the novel's publication.
Further, Jones returned to Weston in June 1930, for a
two-week summer vacation with his parents. According
to family sources, Jones's father, Nelson Hawk Jones,
would never have allowed the young novelist to return
for the Pioneer Reunion if there had been any threat of
violence against him. Jones also returned to Weston for
Christmas that same year, and usually made an annual
trip to Weston the rest of his life.

Thus it appears that those who faulted *Oregon Detour* attempted to honor their own opinons by literalizing the novel and defining the novelist as criminal and outcast. In fact, there was never unanimous Weston disapproval of *Oregon Detour*. Jones did not lose his rapport with the majority. There was no suit. There was no expulsion. Even today, Jones's novels can be found in many Weston homes and many Westonites remember him fondly—jokes, boozing, pranks, stories, and favors.

However, the allegation that the book was not kept on the shelves of Weston libraries has an apparently factual basis. Shortly after the novel was published, a student at Weston High School gave a book report to his English teacher on *Oregon Detour*. She immediately removed the book from the sophomore reading list and the high school library. Weston Public Library records show that the book was added to the Weston branch in 1930, but soon had to be re-ordered from the main Umatilla County Library in Pendleton. The librarian confirmed that this could only mean the book was no longer in the Weston collection. In 1935, the novel seems to have been restored to the Weston branch collection, but by 1936 *Oregon Detour* again had to be ordered for Weston readers from Pendleton.[14] Evidently the novel was being stolen, a conclusion supported by a retired Umatilla County librarian, who stated that she was told "not to send *Oregon Detour* to Weston because it would never come back." In a recent newspaper report the current librarian "concedes the novel was not on the shelves when she took over in 1955..." For a multitude of possible reasons—lost, missing, burned, stolen, misplaced, banned, worn out—*Oregon Detour* could not regularly be found in the Weston collection until 1981, when the current librarian's 20-year search for a copy of the novel ended successfully: three copies of *Oregon Detour* were suddenly given to the Weston Public Library.

This apparent popularity of *Oregon Detour*—as a book with a doubtful reputation—is matched by an equally durable outrage about the novel that appeared in various guises during this research. The angry were generally old "native" members of the Saturday Afternoon Club or directly related to them in some way. One interview, for example, contained these comments:

Why you going around trying to get the skeletons out of the closet? Looking for a nigger in the woodpile? I can't see any good in it. I'm not going to tell you anything even if you want me to. I heard you was going around doing this. Why stir people up again over something that happened fifty years ago? You should let well enough alone.[15]

Other members of that group refused to be interviewed. Still others feigned ignorance of the entire event and its consequences, even though they were recommended as highly informed sources. Evidently, the small segment of the community that initially felt it had been slandered by *Oregon Detour* still feels that their reputations have something to lose some 51 years later.

Whatever the causes of their silence, the Saturday Afternoon Club and the women of the Methodist Church have made their judgment about the novel and its controversial status a fact of community life. Only one opinion about *Oregon Detour*—the Saturday Afternoon Club opinion—seems to circulate in the community. Research at Weston-McEwen High School in 1982 revealed that no current students had heard of the novel or read it, and only a few of their parents had heard of the novel at all. The book was not housed in the high school collection even though the high school librarian had heard of the book herself.

Yet banned book status for *Oregon Detour* by the offended minority is qualified. Recently, a farmer on Weston Mountain called Nard Jones's son in Walla Walla and asked if he could still buy a copy of the novel. Also, a woman who'd spent her summers in Weston for forty years finally sought out a copy of the novel in 1982 and read it herself. Her conclusion: the book was tame. Finally, the novel is in demand. Umatilla County Library records show that, between 1937 and 1959, one of two main library copies circulated 22 times for 3 weeks each. Another Umatilla County Library copy circulated 29 times between 1966 and 1973, including three successful circulations to the Weston branch.[16] Most of the individuals interviewed during this research in 1981 wanted to know where they could find a copy of the novel, or if there was one in the Weston library. There wasn't at that time; only two noncirculating copies of *Oregon Detour* remained in the central Umatilla County Library in Pendleton, and both were in moderate demand even though they had to be read in the library. After this successful circulations to the Weston branch.168 Most of the individuals interviewed during this research in 1981 wanted to know where they could find a copy of the novel, or if there was one in the Weston library. There wasn't at that time; only two noncirculating copies of *Oregon Detour* remained in the central Umatilla County Library in Pendleton, and both were in moderate demand even though they had to be read in the library. After this research was completed in 1981, three copies of the novel became available in the

Weston Library. There seems to be a continuing if not increasing readership for *Oregon Detour*—the local classic, which competes with that other unknown northeast Oregon classic, *Beyond The Black Stump,* by the Australian novelist Nevil Shute.

IV

Why all this fear of a book? There are three factors at work here—all very concrete and powerful—which might serve to explain what happened. First, the events and characters in *Oregon Detour* were neither genteel nor romantic, and didn't fit with the formula romances and westerns that dominated popular reading tastes in Weston in 1930. Realistic treatment of local sexual adventures and authentic descriptions of wild, small town characters were unprecedented in Northwest fiction, which even caused the novel to be a best seller in Portland for more than two months.

Also, whatever he claimed, Nard Jones had actually changed these events and characters very little, and where he did alter events those alterations were not understood by his Weston audience. Adopting New Realism, Jones had written a contemporary pageant without the benefit of historical distance. The only place name Jones changed was Weston, which became "Creston." All other place names—Walla Walla, Pendleton, Portland—remained the same. No common landmarks in the community were renamed, local character names were only slightly altered, e.g., Clark Wood became Clark Tipp, and some local character names were not altered at all—as Jones acknowledged in *It's Only Fiction.* Local traditions and events—a flash flood,[17] the Pioneer Reunion,[18] and high school graduation,[19]—were all basically unaltered. In fact, they were hardly disguised. Where Jones needed plot material, he took it directly from community rumor, public event, or his own experience among his peers—including all sexual antics.[20] Thus, suspension of disbelief was impossible for the Weston audience. While Jones's close group may have hoped to see their collective portrait in the novelist's mirror, they didn't expect to see so much of that face—the shadow.

This fracturing of genteel literary expectations by *Oregon Detour* extended itself to become a second cause of uproar and popularity. The community's illusions about itself had been threatened by a New Realist novel—a common event in the decade. As Donald Meinig has noted in *The Great Columbia Plain,* the Weston-Walla Walla area "during the first decades of this century seemed to be overshadowed by the massive influences of a crass materialism, strident boosterism, and a frantic concern to be in the forefront of 'progress'."[21] Like other New Realists, Jones had stripped away Weston's white enamel of piety, progress, and propriety to show local individuals becoming the natural victims of their own ignorance, fear, violence, customs, and self-deceptions. The sons and daughters of the golden pioneers were not only masters of a beautiful landscape; they were also slaves to their inner landscape, especially their sexuality, loneliness, and insecurity.

Third, *Oregon Detour* also reversed community power structure and social privilege, a potent change which Jones himself might not have recognized would occur when he wrote the novel. Suddenly, an "outsider" had exposed the "natives" to the possibility of public censure. In many Northwestern towns, these two social classes are defined by the Oregon Trail experience. The ancestors of the "natives" came overland, homesteaded, founded the community, created its institutions, and commanded its wealth. According to Weston sources, the "natives" did not hold their members up to public censure. In contrast, the "newcomers" were those individuals whose families had settled in the community after 1900. More than likely, the "newcomers" bought land from one of the "natives," or carried on business, services, or other forms of labor. They would not be invited to join the Saturday Afternoon Club, but would form the Fun and Fiction Club. At the Pioneer Reunion, they would not be eligible to nominate the Pioneer Queen. When *Oregon Detour* appeared, the "newcomers" were not threatened, since Jones had taken his major characters largely from "native" wheat families whose lands surrounded "Creston." However, the life beyond reproach that the "natives" enjoyed had been redrawn by some newcomer who'd kept his eyes and ears open. Ironically, it is the outrage of the "natives" that has kept the novel alive in the community.

V

It is obvious that this microcosmic conflict and its causes are not unique. The information here invites the reminder that such conflicts are universal in literature—Flaubert, Steinbeck, Wolfe, and Malamud (after *A New Life*), to name a few. However, in the Northwest this is the first and oldest case of local censorship and of public furor between a novelist and members of his community—perhaps a sign that literary culture had begun to rise from those authentic sources called for by H. L. Davis and James Stevens in their 1927 Mencken-style polemic, *Status Rerum*.[22] With the single exception of Vardis Fisher's agrarian novel, *Toilers of the Hills* (1928), the modern Northwest novel did not begin to appear before *Oregon Detour* was published. In fact, Northwest novelists whose works are still reprinted and studied today all began to publish their major books after 1930: H.L. Davis, James Stevens, Darcy McNickle, Vardis Fisher, to name a few. Thus, it may be fair to conclude that *Oregon Detour* was the region's first modern novel, certainly the Northwest's first exercise in ''New Realism.''

Notes

1. A Nard Jones bibliography is provided following these notes, but many of these titles are out of print.

2. See the following for brief biographical or critical sources on Nard Jones:

Lancaster Pollard, "The Pacific Northwest: A Regional Study," *Oregon Historical Quarterly,* LII (September 1951):226.

Alfred Powers, *History of Oregon Literature* (Portland: Metropolitan Press, 1935), p. 638.

Harry R. Warfel, *American Novelists of Today* (New York: American Book Company, 1951), p. 232.

Who's Who in America (Chicago: Marquis Publishers, 1956), p. 1343.

Jean Cook, *Washington Authors* (Seattle: Washington State Library, 1936), p. 3.

3. See George S. Turnbull, *History of Oregon Newspapers* (Portland: Binfords and Mort, 1939), pp. 326-27, for a sketch of this unique and talented journalist.

4. Interviews with the Jones family confirmed that Jones's use of alcohol, which began at an early age, became a liability to him and his family throughout his career. The shots of whiskey, according to one source, increased to fifths during an evening's writing. Sources confirmed that, when drunk, Jones could become violent, poetic, or both. When he was sober, his sense of humor and compassion returned. His struggle with alcoholism reached its peak in New York in 1952, a fact which eventually caused his family to return to Seattle without him.

5. All biographical information in this and subsequent paragraphs has been gathered from Jones's unpublished papers, Whitman College archives, interviews with the Jones family, the *Weston Leader,* and sources listed in 2 and 4 above.

6. Letter from William Rose Benet, Assistant Editor of *Saturday Review* and Editorial Advisor to Payson and Clark to Nard Jones. New York, April 1, 1929.

7. Evidence in this and subsequent paragraphs was gathered from more than thirty interviews made by the author in the Weston-Walla Walla-Pendleton area between March and July 1981. Because of the controversial nature of this inquiry, all quotations and sources are presented anonymously.

8. Interview with Audrey Jones Baker, Walla Walla, June 3, 1981.

9. Letter from Clark Wood, Editor and Publisher of *Weston Leader*, to Nard Jones, April 16, 1930. Jones's original letter to Clark Wood has been lost, as have the Clark Wood papers.

10. Jones continued to write about Umatilla County people and events throughout his career. His description of the Pioneer Reunion from *Evergreen Land* was republished in *An Anthology of Northwest Writing*, Michael Strelow, ed. (Eugene: Northwest Review Books, 1979).

11. Interview with Audrey Jones Baker, Walla Walla, June 3, 1981.

12. *The Frontier*, 11 (November 1930), 101.

13. *Weston Leader*, November 21, 1930.

14. Unpublished circulation records, Umatilla County Library, Pendleton and Weston Branch Library, Weston, 1930-1959.

15. All informants were guaranteed anonymity.

16. This confirms the continuing absence of the novel in the Weston Branch.

17. A major flash flood swept through Weston on Sunday afternoon, July 1, 1927. It was carefully reported by Clark Wood in the *Weston Leader*'s next issue. Jones included the same flood in *Oregon Detour*, pp. 74-88, but made major changes. In the actual flood, Newt O'Harras's home was completely washed away, but no one was killed. In the novel, the flood kills an innocent woman, Lura Dyer, which causes one of the main characters, Etta Dant, to blaspheme.

18. Jones's description in *Oregon Detour* of the annual Pioneer Reunion was praised by the student writer referred to in the Introduction to this paper for its continuing accuracy. Others, including Clark Wood in the letter cited earlier, have also noted Jones's accuracy in detailing this event. He later included a similar description in his history of Washington, *Evergreen Land,* as noted in 10 above.

19. High school graduation, pp. 100-114 in *Oregon Detour*, was presented to the current high school student body in May 1983 as a brief reading. The nearly unanimous opinion of both students and faculty was that the same atmosphere—right down to expressions on faces—still prevailed, as did the aftermath of a night out in Pendleton.

20. The accuracy of Jones's transcription from his peers' experience was confirmed in numerous interviews. Many informants either knew or recalled without assistance the individuals in the community who had served Jones as models for Etta Dant, Florence Larson, Peg Nettleship, Swede Mongsen, and Charlie Fraser. Many interviews also confirmed that Jones made composite characters, concentrating separate historical events into one character's experience in the novel.

21. Donald Meinig, *The Great Columbia Plain* (Seattle, University of Washington Press, 1968), p. 511.

22. H. L. Davis and James Stevens, *Status Rerum: A Manifesto, Upon the Present Condition of Northwestern Literature* (The Dalles, Oregon: privately printed, 1927).

xxx

A Nard Jones Bibliography

Oregon Detour (realistic novel). New York: Payson and Clarke, 1930

The Petlands (realistic novel). New York: Brewer, Warren and Putnam, 1931

Wheat Women (realistic novel). New York: Duffield and Green, 1933

All Six Were Lovers (realistic novel). New York: Dodd, Mead & Co., 1934

West, Young Man (or *Young Pioneer*) (juvenile novel). Portland: Metropolitan Press, 1937

The Case of the Hanging Lady (mystery novel). New York: Dodd, Mead & Co., 1941

Swift Flows the River (historical novel). New York: Dodd, Mead & Co., 1941

Scarlet Petticoat (historical novel). New York: Dodd, Mead & Co., 1941

Still to the West (realistic novel). New York: Dodd, Mead & Co., 1946

Evergreen Land (state history of Washington). New York: Dodd, Mead & Co., 1947

The Island (realistic novel). New York: William Sloan Associate, 1948

I'll Take What's Mine (original paperback). New York: Gold Medal Originals, 1955

Ride The Dark Storm (original paperback). New York: Gold Medal Originals, 1955

Driver's Seat (biography of Dave Beck). New York: Doubleday, 1956

The Great Command (or *Marcus Whitman*) (Whitman mission history). Boston: Little, Brown, and Co., 1959

The Pacific Northwest (with Holbrook and Haig-Brown) (regional history). New York: Doubleday, 1963

Seattle (history/memoir of the city). New York: Doubleday, 1972

Oregon
Detour

NARD JONES

Oregon
Detour

PAYSON & CLARKE LTD
NEW YORK
1930

For
NELS & EDYTHE
who have not
always lived in
CRESTON

PART ONE: FALLOW GROUND

WITH a dubious expression Etta Dant regarded her new teacher, and she was not yet ready to pronounce Miss Larson either pretty or at all desirable as an instructor. Through her experience in the grades Etta had learned that all teachers are homely at first, but that by the end of the year they acquire, somewhere along the pedant's road, a fugitive beauty. Etta, from the secure wisdom which she had attained suddenly by being promoted to the first year of high school, had begun to suspect that this was only because one got used to them.

Slowly and deliberately she gazed at Miss Larson. She decided that she dressed very well. But Etta could not like her hair; it was not bobbed, and it was drawn back too smoothly to suit Etta, whose current taste in coiffure ran to the bob that was "fuzzed out" in prodigal confusion. Miss Larson's long smooth hair made her more alien than she need be, Etta thought. The girl resented that the teacher should display so patently the fact that she did not belong to Creston—or perhaps, what would be more alarming still, to any of Oregon.

Etta realized, she knew with that malicious insight of the quite young, that Miss Larson was conscious of the fact that she was being appraised, not only by Etta but by the twenty or so others of the freshman class at Creston High School. She was being more sweet than she would be on many subsequent occasions, and she was trying, without too much success, to impress upon them her well bred superiority. Her method of doing this was to move as gracefully as she could, and place her hands in the most attractive positions possible on the desks and on her blue dress with the glittering insignia which Etta did not know was a sorority pin.

Miss Larson had never seen young girls like these of Creston. Their type had developed while she had been cloistered in a small college town. Because her college had succeeded in absorbing them quickly she had never noticed the few who came there from various high schools in the state.

But this younger class did not frighten her as much as the others. The boys were respectful, even abashed before her. The girls were reasonably unpainted, reasonably dressed. Only four or five, Miss Larson noted, used powder, were too careful about their bobbed hair, and wore nearsilk stockings not quite touching their scant dresses.

Etta was one of these, and it was not difficult to see why she should be a little sorry for Miss Larson, whose skirts were an inch below her knees and who wore woolen hosiery. Etta had worn her present dress enough times now to have forgotten the arguments with her mother about it. But Mrs. Dant had finally conceded that a girl in high school was an almost unbridgable gap from a girl in the eighth grade. And she had weakened to Etta's point that her daughter shouldn't be dowdy when all the rest of the girls in Creston High School were up-to-date.

Etta felt very well satisfied with herself when she came to school that first day and found she was one of but four or five in her class who were dressed in the mode that Creston's girlhood had accepted as authentic from the photographic illustrations in "True Confessions" of broadminded young women of the larger centers, from exaggerated cartoons of gilded youth in the newspapers, or an occasional collegiate motion picture showing at the Memorial Hall.

Etta sat up in her school chair as straight as she could without looking awkward, and pushed out her inadequate bosom which she realized already was one of the charms of a young woman. She was a bit doubtful about her own, though she was willing to be patient in the matter because she had noticed that by the time a girl got to be a senior she was well enough blessed. Poor Miss Larson, Etta saw, wore a strap. Etta always felt sorry for girls who wore, obviously, a strap.

Peg Nettleship, who had strategically taken her place across the aisle from Etta and who was hoping that Miss Larson would not seat the class alphabetically, leaned over and whispered.

"I don't think she's goin' to be any fun, do you?"

"Maybe," Etta replied, purposely enigmatical. Peg evidently did not realize that in high school you didn't have as much fun as you'd had in the grades. That is, you weren't allowed games and you didn't get Friday afternoon off when the whole class had been neither tardy nor absent for a certain preceding period of time. Disregarding these drawbacks, Etta rather looked forward to high school. There was the girls' basket ball team on which she intended to play running center, and there was the high school privilege of wearing a bright two-colored fez at the boys' games. The high school had parties, too. Not dances, but almost as thrilling in anticipation. There would be a party for the freshmen soon

11

after the opening of school. It was called the Initiation Party, a title which didn't frighten Etta. After the initiation there were always games and ice cream and cakes.

Miss Larson began to talk and from the tone of her voice the class knew that it might be rather a long talk. So far she hadn't said very much except to enquire about names.

"All the freshmen are to meet in here every morning at eight so that I can take the roll. When the second bell rings you will go to your first class, which will be English One. After English there will be a study period in the library. The third period is for Algebra One and you will meet in here again for that . . ."

Etta listened attentively, fascinated by Miss Larson's careful syllables. She was lulled by the soft voice and was almost ready to admit that Miss Larson would be wholly satisfactory. Something prompted Etta to ask a question. She wasn't interested in her own query, but somehow she wanted to be the cause of starting Miss Larson's voice again.

"Do you teach Algebra One?"

Miss Larson smiled in such a way that Etta was now certain she would like her. "I think Mr. Henderson will teach that," Miss Larson said. "I am to teach Civics, English, and History. And I am to be the freshman advisor, too."

A tall boy who wore faded washed overalls and a heavy red sweater waved his arm frantically, snapping his hand so that his fingers cracked together.

"Yes?"

With Miss Larson's permission granted him, the boy seemed in imminent danger of forgetting what he had intended to say. Finally he burst out: "Can we pick our colours and motto?"

The rest of the students turned toward him with something akin to envy. Class colors had not occurred to them, and many were not at all certain as to what constituted a motto.

"If the class wishes to take the time," Miss Larson answered him, "we can choose them now. But it's the dismissal hour for the first day, you know."

They began to sense the approaching conflict of wills and were keen for the fray. Possible as well as impossible colour combinations popped into every young head.

"First are there any suggestions? I'll write them on the board and then we can vote by ballot."

It became suddenly evident that the tall boy had been pondering the matter deeply. He boomed out: "Purple and gold!"

The richness of this suggestion staggered his classmates for a brief second or two. Their own ideas were shaded by this royal combination. But Etta, for one, was not to be denied an opinion.

"Pink and white," she said, deliberately and coldly.

She was met with groans and whistles, mostly from the boys. They repeated her offering aloud and in various overtones of disgust and sarcasm.

The girls, noting at once that the battle was to be the old one of the sexes, took up Etta's standard with the zeal of a band of amazons. Their opponents rallied to the purple and gold.

"Let us have quiet, please," Miss Larson said.

But it became a fierce, bitter deadlock, the timid pink and white against the more vivid colours, and amid the pandemonium Miss Larson managed to suggest that

13

they put it to a vote. There were sighs and more groans from the boys. They were outnumbered and the ballot would be a matter of form. In a hopeless endeavour to win her over, each young male began to argue heatedly with the female nearest him.

The colours, according to the ballot Miss Larson counted, were to be pink and white.

The motto was not so easy a matter. It was eventually decided, after the tall boy's insistence in a loud voice on "Practice Makes Perfect," that it would be best to leave the motto to Miss Larson. She accepted the commission, relieved that there would be no more voting.

"I will choose something in French," she told them. "Something that won't mean anything to us and might mean something or other to everyone else."

Etta thought that there was irony in Miss Larson's tone. Irony was a word of Etta's that she had discovered in the dictionary that Summer. She was proud of it, and she was always detecting irony in people's voices, or trying to put it into her own.

When the class had gone outside, was collected in little groups on the steps of the building, the tall boy with the faded overalls and red sweater came near to Etta and gave her a shove.

"Pink and white!" he mimicked in a falsetto voice.

Etta wouldn't be outdone. "Pur*pul* and go-old!" she shot at him, and the last word was so low as to be guttural. Then to Peg Nettleship, in a voice not altogether conversational: "Some people never grow up, do they?" She threw a look of fine condescension toward Charlie Fraser.

Etta and Peg Nettleship decided that they would not

14

walk across the old school yard, which was now Creston's auto camp. That was the shortest way for them to reach their respective homes, but since Peg found that she would not, because school dismissed at nine-thirty, have to buy lunch at Cramer's they went toward town so that they could spend her twenty cents for ice cream or a large glass of orangeade.

Neither of them noticed what they passed. They had passed that way so many times. You went down the bright concrete steps of the new Creston High School (at least it was but three years old, and you had to contrast it with the one that had been torn down and had stood for almost fifteen years) and then you turned to walk down a graveled path that led to the Main Street. You began at the precise spot where the pavement stopped sharply and neatly—quite as if the council had decided there was no need of overdoing the improvement—and you passed the Memorial Hall, a fine building that had once been the opera house. Even people who lived in Creston did not speak of it now as the opera house. It had a stucco front and hollow wooden pillars with a frosted globe atop each one. At night there were two globes which still made connection with the central wiring system. Between each two pillars was a sagging chain; and there was a big double door to the building.

When you looked at it from the front the Memorial Hall seemed fitting enough for what it was intended; to keep alive the glory of Jans Gregson, Jimmy Blake, and Fred Huston, who had all been to Camp Lewis during the war—and of Sid Comings who had gotten over to France and been killed.

If Etta or Peg noticed the building as they passed

15

they would have remembered that brisk November morning when it was dedicated. The Reverend Alfred Horliss had given prayer for all the brave boys of Creston who had died for their country. He had been elected to the pastorate but shortly before and couldn't have been expected to know that Sid Comings was the only one of Creston who had died for his country. But all agreed that it was a good prayer, and it helped to catalogue the new minister in the minds of those townspeople who were interested in him. Charles Tipp, the editor of the *Creston Leader*, had given a moving talk in his deep rich voice that was much better for dedications than for choir work.

It had been the original intention to use the Memorial Hall for staid occasions like political meetings, town meetings, or exercises of the schools when the auditorium of the high school proved too small. But the board of directors of the Hall had made the mistake of waiting until the ardour of the benefactors—they were called subscribers—had cooled before they tried to collect the money to pay for the expense of converting it from an opera house. Lately there had been quite a number of motion picture performances in it, and one or two dances.

Peg and Etta walked swiftly by the Memorial Hall, not thinking of it. They passed the hotel, and the mercantile store, and crossed the street to the corner, where stood the Farmers' Bank of Creston. The bank had high curtains stretched almost to the top of the windows and they could not see that Johnnie Webb, the cashier, was tapping on the counter with a pencil and looking at the wall. They went on by the furniture store which, paradoxically, was a cheerful place in which to spend

16

an hour and was where they kept bodies until the undertaker arrived from Centerton to take care of them.

It wasn't Saturday afternoon and therefore it wasn't to be expected that they would think of the little library set back against the creek and snuggled against the barber shop. Its door was shut tightly for six days out of the week. But Etta and Peg did notice the barber shop; they looked to see who might be in the chairs. Both of the barbers were occupied and the wall was lined with those who waited their turn. The first day of school was always a good day for Clarence Needham, the owner of the shop, and for his helper, Craig Nettleship. Craig was Peg's brother and she told Etta that really he made more money now that the women and girls bobbed their hair.

Between the barber shop and the corner building where they were going to spend Peg's twenty cents, there were no structures. Once there had been three saloons there, built on stilts over the creek and unbothered by competition. That had been when Creston was a stage coach station and not just another town in a network of highways that meandered through the wheat.

It was at the corner where Peg and Etta turned into the Terminal Confectionery Store to get their orangeade, it was here that the old stage coach from Walla Walla had stopped on its way to Pendleton to allow its passengers to have dinner or a drink.

As they went into the Terminal Confectionery the orthophonic phonograph was playing and the place was full of other girls and boys who, like Etta and Peg, were spending lunch money. Etta felt the elation that any

17

young person will feel when there is a great deal of talking, some music, and a sense of freedom and camaraderie in the air.

She sat down at the fountain counter and peered around the huge porcelain-coated lemon with its faucets, and she saw herself in that part of the mirror which was not written on with soap to proclaim the "specials" for the day. Etta saw a thin faced girl who did not look as pretty as Etta always expected her to look when she gazed into a mirror. But she liked her hair because the light was at her back and where she had fluffed out her bob there was an amber aura. She stole a look at Peg and decided that she was very glad that she didn't have black hair like hers. She would have liked, though, to have Peg's black eyes instead of her own which were a faded blue. Peg's eyes made her look—made her look burning. That was as near as Etta could come to describing the effect of Peg's eyes upon her, and she had once known a heroine in a book whose eyes were burning, whose eyes inflamed the hero each time he saw them.

Fanny Brest waited on them. Fanny worked in the Terminal whenever there was a rush, or on Saturday, and Etta liked her. She liked her not in spite of what she had heard whispered, but because of it. Fanny had hair like Peg's, but her eyes were tired and brown. She wore shirtwaists that were loose at the throat and a tiny ribbon always peeked out. Sometimes it was white, but more often it was a blue ribbon and Etta wondered fantastically if Fanny's underclothes were shot through with a profusion of blue ribbons.

Fanny served them with tall glasses and poured the orange juice out of a pitcher held expertly in slender white hands. Peg and Etta stuck two straws into their glasses and drew deeply from them.

Etta watched the coloured fluid rise into the straw, rise and sink again like nervous yellowed mercury. The juice was cooling and her throat was grateful. She began to sip slowly, fearful that her first heedless gulp had made too great an inroad into her supply. She felt quite happy and at peace, and the noise of Peg's getting to the bottom of her drink irritated Etta so that she pretended not to hear.

11

George Dant did not remember having been called Mr. Dant for a very long time now. It was not since the new man had bought out Pope's Dry Goods Store and had called all his customers by their last names until he had seen them often enough to call them by their first. It had made George Dant half angry and he had looked up quickly to see if the new man had been joking. And once there had been an article in the *Creston Leader* after he had been run down by a speeding motorist in Walla Walla. After the first paragraph it had said that Mr. Dant was progressing favourably and would soon be on his feet again. His wife had read it to him from the side of the bed and she seemed rather proud, or so it occurred to him. But when she read "Mr. Dant will soon be on his feet" her husband felt ashamed, as if someone were poking fun at him for something he could not help.

He had worked hard since he was fourteen; he was now sixty-two and he had stopped active labor only recently. At harvest time, in the hot Summer weather,

19

he couldn't always be restrained from going out to the ranch which he had leased to Frank Dyer.

A man without convictions, without sorrow of any sort, George Dant did not, yet, give the impression of being exactly content. It may have been that his drooping mustaches aided a doleful expression, or his eyes that sagged down at the outer corners. When he laughed —and he frequently did—you knew it only by the sound of his laughter. The mustaches hid a mouth which must have curved in laughing, and his eyes never changed light.

He was wholly without memory. He did not remember Etta as a baby, or at least he never mentioned that he did. She existed as she was now. And he never fell to telling stories of what had happened to him in his youth. The past, for him, seemed not to extend beyond the days of the last week. And the future intruded itself even less upon his mental vision.

But George Dant was a tall man, and his shoulders were broad and hard and bony, so that he gave the impression of solidity. His skin was tanned and beaten to the colour of dusty ripe wheat. That was because he had come out of the soil of the wheat and had stood before the same winds and the same rains as the wheat.

His wife could not remember ever having any arguments with her husband. There had never been anything for them to argue about. She had only mildly insisted that he give up the ranch, lease it to Frank Dyer, and move into town. She had been only faintly insistent, but since she had never before been insistent at all George Dant readily conceded her this whim. Etta had persuaded him, too, by saying that she was getting too big to ride astride a horse into town every morning to school, and then back again in the evening. Etta had not asked for the car because she knew her father distrusted it too much himself to allow anyone else to drive it. And even last year he had noticed that Etta really *was* too big to be riding to school. Her dresses came up over her knees and showed her bare legs where her stockings ended. He had noticed it and had been too embarrassed to speak to either her or her mother about it.

Mrs. Dant would have received such information, had he given it, with seriousness. "Your father says that you must keep your dresses down, Etta, when you ride." But she hadn't needed to say that; they moved into town the Fall that Etta began high school.

Etta's mother was short, and bursting from whatever clothes she happened to be wearing. Her thick spectacles gave her a detached air, and people felt safe from her even when she looked at them directly. At church cooked-food sales she contributed not only cakes and cookies but always sold them at the booth. She also made dresses for the holiday entertainments that the Sunday School children held. Mrs. Dant was a worker, and dependable. But she had a temper in her head, as they were fond of saying, when she cared to use it. It was true that nobody remembered when she had ever cared to use it, but they remembered the rumour and did not push her too far.

She saw nothing wrong with Etta's going to the high school initiation party. It was true that it was Etta's first party at which she would be away at night. Yet it was to give Etta a chance at wider social circles that her mother had wanted to move into Creston.

21

George Dant was more doubtful about the advisability of letting her go.

"Initiation party?" he asked. "What do they do?" He belonged to the Knights of Pythias and the Masons and the Odd Fellows.

"Oh, crazy stuff," Etta said. "Just a lot of crazy stuff." She did not know for certain. She would have liked to have had some idea about it herself.

"Will the teachers be there?"

"Miss Larson'll be there. She's our class advisor. And Mr. Henderson."

Mr. Henderson was the principal of Creston's schools, and a Knight. George Dant went on smoking his pipe and reading the Pendleton *East Oregonian* which came down at six o'clock on the auto stage. Etta knew that she could go to the party.

III

Laurence Henderson did not approve of high school parties. That is, he was afraid of what might happen sometime at one of them. He went on allowing them because that had been the precedent at every school at which he had taught. Creston was his first principalship and he had originally intended to put into practice all those drastic measures which had occurred to him while he had been an underling at other country schools. But when he assumed the head chair of the little Creston high school he found that its system, like many another, was operated largely upon precedent.

On the first day a gangling Senior with red hair and a bulbous shining nose had come to Mr. Henderson and handed him a typewritten sheet.

22

"These're the parties we always have," the red haired youth had informed him. "What they're given for is down there, too. The principal always puts in the dates we can have 'em on and then tells the janitor so's he can have the building warm and the lights on."

Mr. Henderson had meekly taken the paper; he had scattered the dates judiciously so that none would fall upon the eve of a school day. Respectfully, almost, he handed the sheet again to the red haired youth who, as he was to discover, was the President of the Student Body.

He found other things handled in a similar fashion. Older teachers, in point of experience and in years, were forever showing him patiently how things had been done in the past. His little scepter was guided continually in his own hands.

But the townspeople called him "professor" and he was given the chance that first year to make several addresses. The women of the Saturday Afternoon Club often brought perplexing questions to him for answer, queries appertaining to geography or the lives of writers.

Tonight he had intended to be the first in the building, but he noticed as he climbed the steps that there was already a light in the basement, in the furnace room, and he concluded that the janitor was inside— or that he had forgotten to turn off the light when he had stoked the fire in the late afternoon. Mr. Henderson told himself that he must caution the janitor about that. He was disappointed when he tried the door and found it opened readily to his touch. The janitor was already in the building. He had not left the furnace room light burning. The principal was disappointed because he had wanted to speak to the janitor about leaving on the light. The old man had been attending the building a good deal longer than Mr. Henderson had been its head, and the status of each of them was not quite clear. If the old man had left the light on, if Mr. Henderson could have the chance to caution him against such waste, it would give the principal a nice opportunity to define their positions at the very beginning of the school year.

Mr. Henderson went through the door and into the wide downstairs hall. The party would be held on the second floor, in the auditorium. Mr. Henderson went about with his keys and locked the doors of all the rooms downstairs. He remembered that at the last school in which he had taught there had been a tendency on the part of certain amorous couples to sneak down from the party in progress and moon about in the darknesses of the various rooms below.

When he had finished the locking of the doors he started up the stairs and just at the turn of the landing he was startled to discover the janitor padding softly in the dark, his rubber-soled shoes making no noise on the steps. Henderson jumped to the wall.

He had been frightened and his voice was unnatural: "Good evening, Mr. Strong."

"Evenin', perfessor. Didn't know you was in the buildin'."

They went on silently together, up the stairway to the second floor, through the wide doorway of the auditorium. Strong's more experienced hands found the switchbox first and he bathed the big room in a glare of light as his skinny, nimble fingers played dangerously with wobbly switch-handles.

On the uncurtained stage of the auditorium the machines for the coming initiation had been arranged. They were not complicated, and yet Mr. Henderson wondered, with some discomfort, what they might be for. There were paper sacks filled with doughnuts; a box of pellets with the label of the Creston drug store; a jug of vile looking and vile smelling liquid which he suspected the upperclassmen would force the freshmen to drink. All this was on a table. On the floor of the stage was a chair beneath which were wires that led to an old storage battery.

He was gazing at these relics of inquisition—with a feeling that their operation should perhaps be stopped— when the red haired President of the Student Body came onto the platform and said good evening in a discreet and slightly worried voice.

"Tell me what all these things are for, will you, Lucas?"

Patiently Lucas explained to Mr. Henderson. His tone held both weariness and lightness. As much as possible he discounted the discomfort the new class might suffer.

"There's nothing gonna be done that will hurt 'em," he finally said. "Nothing that will do more'n scare 'em a little, maybe."

Mr. Henderson picked up the box of pellets with the drug store label. "What's this?"

"Oh, them. . . ." Lucas came as near a blush as his floridness would permit the change. "Them're pills. Test pills."

"*Test* pills?"

"Test pills," Lucas repeated. "They won't hurt you any. They're test pills for—for ven-e-re-al disease . . ." Lucas laughed disparagingly. "If you haven't got anything they make you—they make you . . ." He floundered hopelessly, but the principal's blank face gave him no encouragement. " 'Course, none of the fellows'll have it, and the next morning it will scare 'em half to death." And then hastily, "We only work that on the boys."

Mr. Henderson seemed to think it best not to go into the matter further. He had no idea what Lucas was talking about. He would speak to the druggist tomorrow and enlighten himself. Nervously he looked at his watch, cutting Lucas off from further elucidation.

"It appears to me that the party should begin," he said. "We have to be out of the building by ten, you know."

IV

Etta, her face coloured with green ink which would not entirely disappear for a day or two, and wearing a ludicrous hat at the request of the upperclass officers, was entirely happy. She had been initiated. The whole ceremony was over, and Mr. Henderson, standing in the corner and fingering his watch chain, was relieved. No one had been hurt. He expressed his approval to Miss Larson.

"I believe that we have a group this year that is essentially wholesome, and essentially a good one."

Miss Larson smiled. But she was irritated behind her smile. She wondered why any group would be *essentially* a good one. She had no dislike for her peer, yet she did not respect him. He struck her as—as essentially futile. She smiled again at her own contradiction, and the professor thought she was very amiable indeed and that he was fortunate to have her on his staff of teachers.

Young, perhaps, and a little too good looking for her work, but quite probably sincere.

The students were playing the game called "Farmer in the Dell." They held hands and walked around a girl in the center of the endless chain they made. The girl in the center pantomimed in time to the words of the chant . . . *farmer in the dell, the farmer's in the dell, heigho! the merrio, the farmer's in the dell . . . the farmer choose a wife* (the girl pointed shyly to the red headed Lucas and the circle broke into giggles and guffaws) . . . *the wife choose a cow, the wife choose a cow* (the red headed Lucas pointed with a burlesque, judicious gesture at Etta) . . .

Etta came into the circle promptly, proud at being the center of attraction, glad for the jeers and the laughs which were a part of the inverted game.

"Heigho, the merrio! The farmer's in the dell . . ."

They had found that by transposing the words the game had been made much funnier: the farmer, by being made a girl, could choose a boy for a wife, and when he chose a cow it would be a girl again—a vain and slender creature for a cow. It struck their vicious sense as hilarious, and they were not sure why. Mr. Henderson wondered if it were in quite good taste, but he was ashamed of his thought. He kept wondering if it mightn't hint of—of perversion. But, with a sidelong glance at Miss Larson, he decided that the children were essentially wholesome.

The older boys and girls played these games with an air of boredom, not altogether feigned. They had been to dances, would go to a dance tomorrow night, no doubt, and they were above these games in which they took part with broad and patronizing movements of

27

the hands and feet and mouth. They played them defiantly, as if they might force the school board—by appearing as silly as they could in puerile didoes—to allow the student body to hold dances in the school.

But Etta was enjoying herself and so were most of the rest of the boys and girls of her class. By the next year, or the next after that, they might look upon this as entirely an adolescent form of entertainment. But now they did not recognize that the juniors and the seniors were "entertaining" the freshmen with a serene indifference.

As the circle broke and another game was begun, Peg Nettleship rushed to Etta excitedly to whisper that Charlie Fraser was taking her home.

"Honest?" said Etta. She knew it was the first time that any boy had ever taken Peg home. Now Etta would have to go home alone, or with some other girl. Peg had rushed away again before Etta got a chance to scorn the announcement. She looked about her with sudden panic. Somehow she felt alone. There must have been real fear upon her face, for when she looked into the eyes of Lucas, by accident, he gazed back at her with interest.

Ten o'clock was approaching and some of the students, anxious to curry favour with Mr. Henderson, had already gone for hats and coats, saying good night in loud voices. Etta followed their suit. She put on her coat, wondering if she might arrange to walk home with Miss Larson. She hated being seen going down the steps alone, but she did not think of any boy taking her home. The hope to accompany the teacher was dashed when she saw Swede Mongsen waiting in the hallway.

Swede Mongsen had graduated from the old Creston

High School four years ago, but he had been attentive to every pretty teacher who had been hired since by the school board. He had gone to the Oregon Agricultural College for a year, had pledged a fraternity, and then come home on a footing which enabled him to talk with ease to the purveyors of education who enrolled with the faculty of Creston High School.

Her head down, for some reason feeling utterly forlorn, Etta made for the door. She found it opened for her by Lucas, felt that he was walking down the steps by her side. The silence was threatening them both and at length she came out with: "I had a good time, didn't you?"

They passed Peg and Charlie Fraser and Etta could not help going a little beyond the necessities of speech to call out good night to her friend. She was flattered by the astonishment that crept into Peg's answer.

Lucas turned out to be one of those tall, insufferable egotists who sometimes crop out in a red headed race. No amount of adversity would be able ever to put down his prodigious respect for himself. He swung easily above Etta, conscious of the fact that he was doing her a favour by passing Peg and Charlie in her company.

He talked about football with the ease of a young man who has made a study of it and who realizes that his brain and brawn are an undisputed asset to his team. He impressed upon Etta that Creston would be in a bad way, athletically speaking, when he graduated from high school at the end of the year. They reached Etta's home before he had quite finished his monologue, and he broke off abruptly to say good night.

Etta answered him and went into the house. Already,

with that swiftness of mind which is a gift to all harm-less liars, she had begun a fictitious dialogue between them which she could recount to Peg, word for word, at the earliest opportunity.

As she shut the front door she heard her father speak her name as a question. She replied to it, and went softly up the stairs. She felt redly guilty for no reason and she hoped that she would be able to stay in bed Saturday morning until her father had gone out of the house.

It was the first time that she had ever come into the house after her mother and father were in bed and she undressed quickly without turning on the light. She tried not to make the springs of the bed squeak as she climbed upon them, and she lay quietly in an uncom-fortable position until she fell asleep.

v

Like most of the young teachers who came to Cres-ton, Florence Larson found that she was not going to enjoy it. She resolved upon her very first day in town that she would not like it; and she held to that resolve. From the first day of school the teacher and the towns-people were natural enemies. The instructor to Creston's youth stood always at bay in her classroom corner. For one thing, she was new, alien, unknowing of the town's traditions, its prejudices; what was worse, she neither cared for them nor wanted to learn them for the sake of peace.

Secondly, the new teacher had knowledge. That was, at least, a supposition in his or her favour. Creston did not always care too much for people with knowledge.

It wasn't that it didn't respect knowledge, didn't want it for its children, but it was only that the town saw that people with knowledge are likely to be superior. Above all things, Creston could not stand superiority. Not from anyone but God.

Florence Larson, like most of them, had not wanted to be a teacher. The profession, in the small town, had somehow become a catch-all for college graduates. The women taught to pass the time until they should be married. The men taught to pay their college debts. Beyond it was what they wanted to do. It was the only profession which required neither skill, intelligence, nor experience.

At college Florence Larson had been a good student. She had been popular, too, within a circle that prided itself upon the books it had read, the plays it had seen, and its disdainful attitude toward anything which it designated as common or cheap or popular. Into Creston the Larson girl brought this same critical attitude. It was not a snobbish attitude, it wasn't without mercy. Yet Creston did not like it.

There was something about the way Miss Larson said good evening to the people she had met; something about the way her hair was so serenely smoothed over her ears; something about her easy, languid gaze, that they did not like. None could define that something in any case, none knew why, precisely, they did not like her—and because of that their dislike was all the more secure. Not one realized that if he approached Miss Larson evenly, that if he would talk to her in his own guise instead of raising himself on the heels of a pose, she would have proved animated and entirely human.

It was Swede Mongsen who had discovered that; and it was not exactly in the nature of a disclosure since he had learned it long ago from other teachers who had come into Creston without friends. He had been to college, and even though he had stayed but a year he knew that Miss Larson was one with the comradely girls he had known there, girls who had grown up gradually, graduated, and come into Creston to teach. The young man Mongsen was the only one in town to whom Florence Larson could show her real self, and she was thankful for his companionship. She enjoyed it just as others had enjoyed it during the four years that Swede had acted as a sort of gay Lothario to all the passing teachers who had no visible sweethearts or husbands. Swede knew that she was glad for his attentions, and he wondered just in what degree she would be glad. One or two experiences with lonely and fretted souls had, in the past, keened his anticipations. He had congratulated himself on the day he had seen Florence Larson, suitcase and patent leather hat bag in hand, step from the auto stage.

Whatever Swede's given name had been, almost everyone had forgotten it. Huge, goodnatured, and with a heavy head of straw coloured hair, he was doomed to be called Swede. But the fact that he came from good, solid, Germanic stock, stock which never failed—no matter with whom it crossed—to produce at least one honest worker, was shown again in Swede. His father and mother were dead; it had been upon the latter's death that he had given up his feeble effort to learn farming scientifically at the Agricultural school. His ranching did not suffer because of this. The Mongsens had been good farmers always. They were big and strong and not too lazy. They produced wheat out of the soil with the season's regularity.

That night after the Initiation Party these two walked—Florence Larson and Swede Mongsen—down through the path that led into the old school grounds. In Summer it would have been shadowed with the looming outlines of three or four tents of itinerant motorists. Now, in the first chill of September nights, it was barren, silvered with the moon.

Swede walked by her side, consciously apart from her, consciously keeping a distance between them. She was talking and he let her talk. He knew that the greater part of his rôle consisted of letting her talk, of listening to her, or occasionally helping her to pin an enemy or an aversion. He had a certain rough gift of words that pleased her. He said, and seemed to think, too, the same things as she. He merely said them and thought them in a different sort of way.

"Did you see old Henderson eye me tonight? He don't like to have roughnecks hang around waiting to take the knowledge-dispensers home. He always looks at me like a guy that's blowing up a balloon and expects somebody to stick a pin into it."

She laughed appreciatively. Now that he had said it, she was sure that Laurence Henderson did look like that.

"I don't believe that he quite approves of me, do you?" She seemed to hope that he did not. Mongsen did not disappoint her: "Probably not," he said.

He lit a cigarette and she watched the glow in the darkness, fascinated by it as if it were a weird single eye. "You'll find a lot of them," he went on, "who don't approve in this burg . . ." He started to put the cigarettes away and then casually, so very casually: "Gosh, I never thought! D'you use 'em?" He dragged them from his pocket again and offered her the pack.

She was amused at his effort to comply with one of the rules of metropolitanism as he conceived it; she knew that he was being worldly, that smoking in Eastern Oregon would be worldly.

But she hadn't smoked, although she had encountered it at school among the first Western revolutionists in the co-ed groups. She had refrained not because it shocked her—which it did—but because she believed it might be bad for her health. Now she sensed that here in Creston it was black evil for any woman to smoke, and for a teacher . . . She found it impossible to refuse his naïve gesture.

"Occasionally," she said. "But I wouldn't like them to think me—shall I use that lovely word?—fast."

"Oh, have one," he urged. "Two cigarette-ends in the dark might be Pat and Mike for all anybody'd know."

She took one, and with her palms she shielded her face as well as the lighted match he offered. Carefully she drew in the burning smoke of a brand of tobacco that was not too mild. It was cooling, after a while, and pleasant to her tongue.

Somehow she felt oddly wicked, irresponsible, dangerous. The curling smoke within her mouth seemed to be a potion that turned her sensual. "Good Lord," she thought with a movement of her lips that framed the words. "Out . . . behind the barn . . ."

Florence Larson wondered how she could be found walking a dirt path with a country lout, smoking bad cigarettes to defy something that did not need defying. Why, the man wore heavy, short boots and into them were shoved reclaimed army trousers! His unmatched gray coat smelled unmistakably of the stables! His hands were red and dry and cracked open, and the cracks were seamed with dirt!

Slowly she built up hate with which to defend herself against him. After tonight she must discourage him. A good book would be better for the lonelier hours in Creston.

She might have known—since she pretended to always want the truth—that there would come a night when Swede Mongsen would be as beautiful as any man. A night when his hands would be as caressing and as soft as the next. She might have known that there would come a night when she would go almost readily into his arms, and feel his harsh full lips against her cheek and throat. She might have known that she would experience this, knowing, too, at that moment, that she would never love him.

Or it may have been that she did know, and that was why she was telling herself how hateful, how uncouth he was.

They walked on together. Her cigarette seared pitilessly the black flesh of Creston's night.

CHAPTER TWO

I

SHE stood in the open doorway of the house in which she was attending her first dance. The room was small and stuffy and the dozen or so moist dancers within it were not adding to Etta's comfort. She leaned against the door which was pushed back against the wall, and the breeze that came in through the opening revived her a little. She had found, a moment before, that she was possessed of a desire to be home in the cool sheets of her upstairs bed. She was finding it, as so many people have found it, to be rather difficult—this feeling romantic and sinful where there is music and laughter and whatever may pass in the community for wine. This discovery on Etta's part was astonishing when she remembered how she fought with her father to get permission to come. As she had stood there in the front room of the Dant house it had seemed to her that nothing would ever matter unless George Dant allowed her to stay the night with Peg so that she might sneak into Swede Mongsen's country dance.

It was called a housewarming party. But the old house had long since seen that affair, and the well-worn smoothness of the fir floors gave evidence that it had been the scene of many such dances as the one tonight. It was the old Blodgett place, the north forty acres adjacent to the Mongsen ranch. The week before, from his careful savings, Swede had acquired the acreage and the house. So the old house which had more than once changed its tenants saw again a celebration in honour of a new régime.

Swede had issued invitations with pride. Such invitations called attention to his opulence among the environs of Creston, and they ended with, invariably, "tell anybody you happen to see. Everybody's welcome." The news had spread swiftly. As Etta stood by the door there were many more seated outside in cars, or lolling against the porch, or walking up and down the wet road, than could possibly get into the confines of the old house itself. She knew that Peg, for one, was outside. She was with Charlie Fraser in his old car, and Etta wished she could enter into the spirit of the evening as easily as Peg seemed to do.

She breathed deeply from the clean smelling breeze that veered in spasmodically through the opening. In the gusts that brushed her face was the odour of wet clods. In them was the vigorous smell of rain on old straw.

She became conscious of Swede Mongsen beside her. He stood looking at her silently, a meaningless grin on his broad face.

"Want to have the honour of dancing with the genial host?"

It was actually an honour to Etta, and she blushed, feeling a sudden warmth at being taken in by the crowd he represented—the "older crowd."

"I . . . I don't dance very good," she apologized. "I can't do any new steps."

"Thank God!" Swede breathed it honestly. "I can't either."

To the rhythmic sawing of Val Bark's bow on his ancient fiddle, and the thudding sound of piano keys as

37

Fanny Brest pressed them down resolutely, Swede and Etta stepped out together into the middle of the floor. It was one of those moments when most of the crowd had sought the outdoors—and Swede was at his unhampered best. He lumbered, half lifting Etta.

"Say," he finally broke into the silence they had been keeping, "can you hang onto a secret?"

"Surely can." She was proud in anticipation of sharing a secret with Swede, who was at least twenty-three. Twenty-three if a day.

"Well—Miss Larson sort of wanted to come tonight. I didn't bring her because I wanted to see first if there'd be anybody here who might care. You and Peg and the Fraser kid are the only high school kids here and I don't think you'd say anything . . ."

He paused, but Etta was too blank at visualizing Miss Larson there. She couldn't answer at once.

"Would you?"

"Of course not."

"Not that there's anything out of the way about it . . ." Mongsen's voice was large with lightness. "But you know how some people are."

"Mhm . . . I know."

Etta felt proud at being a party to Miss Larson's conspiracy and it didn't occur to her, to spoil the complacency of her mood, that this was why Swede had asked her to dance with him.

"She gets kinda lonely," Swede enlarged, "and of course she can't go to the public dances in Athena. About the only chances she gets to dance are at these country hops . . ." Fanny Brest lifted her hands abruptly from the piano and Bark brought his fiddle down to his knees. "Thanks for the dance," Swede said.

"I'll run to town in the car and get her. You tell Peg and the Fraser kid, won't you? An' for God's sake don't tell it around town."

As Etta went out the door to find Peg and Charlie Fraser she was preceded by Fanny Brest. Over Fanny's shoulder Etta caught the fumes of white liquor; they were mixed with the reek of not too faint perfume. Etta was sorry she hadn't looked for the blue ribbon peeping from Fanny's dress collar. Why were people always talking about her and men when you hardly ever saw her with a man? She waved at men when she said hello. Etta didn't see anything wrong with that. She thought it was rather nice. Men, older men especially, seemed sort of shut up within themselves, and they didn't seem to be having much fun.

When she got to Charlie Fraser's car she found that he and Peg had watched her coming. Their faces shone out at her like white discs in the half light. Etta saw that Peg was hunched over against Charlie and that her knees showed. She eyed them with a disdain she hoped Peg would not fail to catch.

"Miss Larson's going to be here," Etta told them directly, and watched to see the effect.

"Larson! Is Larson comin' here?" Charlie was obviously distressed. But presently logic asserted itself. "Well, she can't say no more'n I can, can she?"

"Is she honestly coming?" Peg seemed thrilled. "No foolin'? . . . Maybe her and Swede'll get married. I'll bet they do before the year's out." Peg allowed her romanticism to run forward of the present.

Charlie grinned. "This baby'll keep as quiet as an oyster—but boy, if she ever tries to pull anything over on *me*."

"Oh, *Char*-lie—don't be silly!" Peg slapped his shoulder like a fawning tigress cub.

Etta, thoroughly disgusted, turned on her heel and went back into the house . . .

II

Having lived all of her life upon a farm, Etta could not have been expected to be unversed in the varied, yet essentially alike, methods of procreation as applied to ranch animals. Rather earlier than may have been good for her she had observed that the birth of a calf followed upon the strange practice of one of the hired hands taking the cow to pen with the bull. She further noticed that the calf in question belonged always to that particular cow which the man took, with mysterious preparation, "to the bull."

The rabbit warren, the corral behind the stable, and overheard statements of hardened farm hands (statements which Etta had pieced together with a child's aptitude for puzzles) all gave her an insight into the subject which she sensed rather than knew was closed to her. By the time she was twelve or thirteen she had known enough not to press her mother about the question. But she remembered a time at a slightly earlier age when she had enquired about a baby which had come to the Schwabacher house half a mile away. She had connected this miraculous arrival with her own baby pictures and had put to Mrs. Dant that straightforward question which has ambushed so many mothers.

Mrs. Dant, who should have been prepared, found that she was not, and she gave an old answer: "Under a cabbage head, dear . . . Run out and play."

The odd part was that Etta half believed her. Like all people who persist, and will always persist at least half heartedly, in alienating the human animal from other and more dumb species, she held tenaciously to the hope that somehow, some way, the additions to man's family were engendered in a manner less mechanical and shameless. It was all very well for cows and rabbits and mares . . .

So Etta came into Creston High School with her mind still vague about it; and since she was not a morbid child she did not linger often in the bypaths of thought. She was, though, a curious child, and it could not be held against her that she listened with some interest to sketchy conversations of girls sometimes, though not always, older than herself. She wanted to forget about the time Edna Peabody had told of stumbling into the gymnasium on a Wednesday night when she thought it was a Tuesday night and found Lester Adams taking a shower. Edna spoke of oddities which made it impossible for Etta to look at Lester without lowering her eyes.

Then, too, there had been the virgin birth of Christ about which Mrs. Webster, Fanny Brest's married sister, had talked a great deal in Etta's Sunday School class. Etta, who had a passion for the dictionary, had looked up *virgin* and the definition had somewhat mixed her conception of this important Biblical event. When she found that the adjective might also mean a musical instrument of the sixteenth century she gave up the whole matter in disgust. As her chaotic information took some form, however, this paradox of the birth of Christ was often to recur in memory and trouble her.

But on the whole, Etta suffered no great adolescent thirst for forbidden knowledge. Like most Creston girls, she found herself too busy. Like most of them she found, too, that this knowledge was finally thrust upon her.

III

. . . It was two in the morning and Etta was becoming very sleepy in spite of Fanny Brest's insistent fingers on the piano keys and the rasping sound of Val Bark's bow on his fiddle. Beneath the current of their seesaw rhythm could be heard the endless shuffle of feet on the floor of the old Blodgett house. The couples seemed to increase their speed with each new dance: the younger were waking into their second wind; the older were hectic with an active weariness. It was never until three or four that a country dance ended, and sometimes they waited until late morning so that "they could see to drive home." Swede's guests seemed to realize this tradition, and be determined to carry through the celebration of which they were a part. Tomorrow—or today— was Sunday, and they could sleep.

Some of the younger men had taken too much moonshine whiskey and had become sick. They slept like dead, or were uncovered and shivering in their sleep, in the cars that were parked along the road in front of the house. Or they leaned against the outside of the house gazing sleepily into the night and wishing they could vomit.

The fittest survived—and again Etta watched them from the doorway where she might catch an occasional breath of wind. She felt the pity of a child for the older women who danced dance after dance, a little short of breath, sticking too far out in the rear to be quite graceful. She saw their faces resolutely set in smiles, moulded lips below eyes that were tired and red.

Her gaze fell upon Peg Nettleship. Peg in a new and pretty black dress with short sleeves was dancing once more with Charlie Fraser. Etta found admiration for Peg mixed with the thought that she had the next dance with Charlie.

"When are we going home?" she asked Peg when Charlie had brought her friend to the wall. "This is mine with Charlie, and then you and him dance one more?"

"Home?" Peg discouraged the idea with a scornful word.

"Well . . . I don't care. Whenever you say."

Etta found herself more fatigued than she had imagined, and she could think of nothing to say to Charlie when they began their dance.

"You're sort of quiet, ain't you?" he demanded.

"Oh . . . I don't know. Why?"

"Well, I thought you were—well, kind of quiet, you know."

"Maybe I am, sort of."

Her inability to talk when she wanted especially to talk had not occurred to Etta as a possible part to be fitted into a personality she was trying to build. For the remainder of the dance she concentrated on trying to make her eyes look deep. She decided that Peg was the bubbling, effusive kind, and that she herself was quiet—and deep.

She noticed that Charlie held her more closely than he held Peg and she wondered whether it was because he liked her better or cared more for Peg.

43

When the dance had ended she told Peg: "I'm going up to get my coat. I'll be out in the car when you get ready to go home."

"Stick around, why don't you?" Charlie wanted to know. "Can't tell what might happen."

It struck her suddenly that, in the face of Peg's enthusiasm, boredom might not be a bad pose: "I've been here all night and nothing's happened yet."

"Maybe," Peg told her with a worldliness that surprised them both, "you haven't kept your eyes open."

Etta shrugged and turned to the stairway. As she climbed the bare steps she heard the beginning of another monotonous duo by Fanny and Val. She caught Fanny's eye as she went up the stairway and the woman at the piano smiled. From where she stood on the stair, Etta saw the blue ribbon from the neck of Fanny's dress.

Upstairs it was dark, darker than the night outside. She did not try to find the light button because she knew that the old Blodgett place wouldn't be wired upstairs. She could find her coat among the array of them on the two beds in the south room. She would feel the fur collar and the big round buttons on the front.

Once inside the room she was frightened. She stopped to listen for the helpful noises downstairs. It had begun to rain again and the patter on the roof drowned out the music; she could hear nothing but the rain and the endless shuffle of the dance downstairs. With a hurried movement she pawed over the clothes on the bed. They were damp and smelly. She could not find her own, and she could no longer stand there with her back to that square pale light of the window behind her.

She decided that she must find a lamp, or go down

44

and borrow some matches from Charlie. But she forced herself to walk from the room slowly, and to stop a moment by the stair landing in the hall. She mustn't be afraid like that, because it was foolish.

She would then have gone downstairs had not her heart stood so still because of a sound at her back. Silent and white she turned upon it, irresolute of movement as a startled cat, and her fear gave way to interest as she recognized the dim forms of Swede Mongsen and Florence Larson.

She remembered now that they had gone out, that Swede supposedly was taking Miss Larson home. They must have come in by the back door, up the narrow stair at the rear. Etta put herself softly against the railing, watching them with a frankness hidden by the dark. She was grateful to be not alone there, too.

Swede's husky whisper floated to her, words that he was saying to Etta's teacher. And the girl heard Miss Larson's soft voice, so different that she would not have believed it Miss Larson's had not she seen her there.

She saw the two forms merge in the darkness. One bulky shadow taking the shape of an animal that Etta might have read of yet not seen. The shadow of an animal in the dark, a huge heavy monster with two heads and four entangling arms. In that awful moment before they walked into the room where Etta had searched for her coat she knew that what she had heard whispered was true. Without anyone telling her, now, she knew that Swede Mongsen and Florence Larson, that her own mother and father, were one with the animals she knew about.

Not realizing it, she did not class herself with them. As Etta stumbled vaguely down the stairs to look into

Fanny's vapid eyes she felt serene and contemptuous and alone.

"I couldn't find my coat," she told Peg. "Charlie can get it for me . . . No—not now. I'll wait until you two are ready to go."

I V

The Reverend Alfred Horliss was a small man with a perpetual smile. Sometimes it broadened, but never lessened, from its natural state. The Horliss smile was present at weddings, funerals, church socials, and during sermons in the pulpit. His wife, who had insomnia and missed whole nights of rest, often noticed that Alfred smiled even in his sleep. When a very young man in theological school it had been impressed upon him that a pleasing personality was a necessity in the work he was to do. He had therefore begun the smile early, and it would be present, some time hence, when a straggling line passed by to peer into his coffin.

Alfred Horliss was an earnest little man who, had he not been sent to the seminary by his parents, would have been one of those indispensable office individuals who carries pencils in his outside coat pocket and knows all the facts and figures of the firm. He would have always been assured of forty dollars a week, or perhaps fifty, and he would have taken out enough insurance to care for any emergency. As it was, he received fifteen hundred a year, not all of it in cash, and he was shifted about frequently from small town to small town by the bishops of the church.

He wanted, some time, to write a book for high school students on the life of Jesus. He believed that if

46

there were such a book it would be incorporated into the curriculum of the high schools of many states. He was not certain of the advisability of this ambition. The life of Jesus was already beautifully written and he knew that no man could improve upon that account. But people, especially young people, did not seem to want to read the Bible.

He had hoped sometime to come into a town where he would be master of his own church, but Creston was not one of these. Just as Laurence Henderson found his school overridden with precedent, so Alfred Horliss found the petty affairs of his church. It was Clarissa Hempel who was the thorn in the minister's side. For fifteen years she had dictated the policies of the local church, set the dates for the socials, doled out the pastor's salary, and even parceled out his groceries when money was scarce.

She had succeeded in subjugating her husband two short years after they were married and since that time she had preferred to test her metal on the itinerant and always meek preachers of the South Methodist Church.

Her latest suggestion for the good of Creston was that a visiting evangelist, who happened to be including nearby towns in his route, be invited to aid Alfred Horliss in a revival. Revivals were not a novelty in Creston, but it had been two years or more since it had experienced one. The last saver of souls beneath a tent had been a wild, shouting individual who styled himself "Four-fingered Pete," a name he had gained while engaged in his old profession of safe-cracking. He had, of course, reformed, and he coloured his sermons with tales of his past iniquity. Creston had opened its collective hearts to him, and not a few of its purses. When

"Four-fingered Pete" had gone the town felt purged and new. But scarcely a week later came the news that he had been arrested on what the dailies charitably described as "a statutory charge" in connection with a young girl of his junior classes. "Four-fingered Pete" now languished in the penitentiary which he had somehow escaped in his first era, and Creston still held a hurt feeling with regard to tent evangelists.

But the town, after two years, was ripe, and Mrs. Hempel knew it. She suggested her idea to the Reverend Alfred Horliss.

"But—ah—don't you think, Mrs. Hempel, that it would take money from the church which might well be expended on—ah—say, the mission work?"

Mrs. Hempel only enquired acidly if money were a question when souls were to be saved and good work was to be done.

"These travelling ministers work hard," she said. "They are able to do a lot more than someone who's been here all the time. We can't begrudge a few dollars when it will do so much good."

"No," said Alfred Horliss. "No . . ."

Sadly he visioned the little white envelopes that would be passed among the congregation seated under the big white tent. Envelopes that were too small for a quarter, and were made to hold a bill, folded four times and doubled. He foresaw himself seated on the platform in the shadow of a huge bulk of a man with a stentorian voice. It would be the Reverend Horliss's duty to lead the invocation and the benediction, to repeat "amen" endlessly after particularly brilliant observations of the' revival leader.

He consoled himself with the thought that it would,

48

Mrs. Hempel had said, do Creston some good. He admitted that he seemed unable to increase the roll of the church, or even to keep the old members in their seats of a Sunday with any regularity. He should be unselfish in this; he should welcome another brother who could stand with him shoulder to shoulder in the fight for God.

That night, as he climbed into bed, Alfred Horliss managed to fancy that he would be thankful for the newcomer.

He told his wife: "I told Mrs. Hempel today that I thought that a revival might invigorate the local condition."

Mrs. Horliss, wide-eyed beside him, turned over restlessly. "An evangelist, you mean?"

"Yes. Someone dependable, of course. Someone recommended by the bishop . . ."

"Will any commission apply on your salary, Alfred?"

"I don't know. We hadn't gone into it that far."

"It seems to me," his wife went on, "that you should be paid what back salary is due you before any outsider is brought in. I don't see how they can expect——"

"You never seem to understand that a minister must always do more than he needs to . . ."

"You mean he must always earn more than he gets."

"Now, Mary." Alfred Horliss put reproach into his voice.

"Well, just the same I should think you would mention it. There's no sense in needing things around the house as we do when the church members owe us money and can pay it if they weren't so selfishly buying cars . . ."

49

"Now, Mary. We shall get along."

Mrs. Horliss bit her thin lips. She turned her back again, knowing that she would be awake, probably, half the night and would need to sleep tomorrow. But there was a meeting of the missionary society tomorrow at three. They were to get clothes ready for shipping to the headquarters. She wondered if anyone could possibly recognize the shirt which Alfred had been wearing and which she had saved from the last collection of clothes for the Near East. And Alfred—he would have died had he realized that the shirt he had worn was actually consigned by a farmer to clothe some native to whom the Christians had just taught the indecency of not wearing any shirt at all.

v

From copy which was given him by Clarissa Hempel, the editor of the *Creston Leader* set up in type and printed the advance notice of the coming of Jerry Fleeter. As an introduction to the program which Mrs. Hempel had presented for publication Charles Tipp allowed his florid prose full sway.

"Creston (the article began) is to have the privilege of hearing that well known evangelist, Mr. Jerry Fleeter, and his wife, Mrs. Jessie Fleeter, a pianist of the first class. In addition to being the most successful revivalist leader in the Northwest Mr. Fleeter is well respected in artistic circles for his beautiful crayon colour drawings, the production of which will be a feature of his meetings and which he gives away after each night's meeting. Our city may count itself fortunate to be allowed to hear Jerry and Mrs. Fleeter and it is only through the efforts of the South Methodist Church that it is made possible. Mrs. Clarissa Hempel is the chairman of the Revival Committee for the local church, and the Reverend Alfred Horliss will introduce Mr. Fleeter.

"The program is as follows: Monday night: Crayon demonstration by Mr. Fleeter; piano solo by Mrs. Fleeter; lecture by Mr. Fleeter, Who Pays the Price? Tuesday afternoon lecture by Mr. Fleeter, God or Gorilla? Tuesday night: piano solo by Mrs. Fleeter; violin solo by Val Bark; lecture by Mr. Fleeter, Is Your Son or Daughter Bound for Hell? Wednesday afternoon and night: Biblical Pageant produced by Mrs. Fleeter and Creston's young folk. Thursday afternoon: lecture for women by Mr. Fleeter. Thursday night: lecture for men by Mr. Fleeter. Friday afternoon: religious clinic by Mr. and Mrs. Fleeter—bring your troubles through them to God. Friday night: lecture by Mr. Fleeter, The Second Coming. Saturday afternoon: rest. Saturday night: lecture by Mr. Fleeter, Are You Waiting Too Long to Come to Jesus?"

When Charles Tipp had used the type for the article in the *Leader*, he lifted the form from the press to his job-printing machine, turned out five hundred circulars to be distributed throughout the town, and billed them to the South Methodist Church.

VI

Jerry Fleeter, besides being a "well known evangelist" could, in the words of Clarissa Hempel, sketch beautifully. His drawings were multicoloured affairs with flaming sunsets and broad expanses of deep blue water. Sometimes, with an awesome and lightning movement, he placed a sail on the distant horizon, or drew in a gull winging below a buxom white cloud. On the platform, when the masterpiece was finished, Jerry Fleeter would tear it from the drawing board and hand it with a magnificent gesture to some gaping youngster in the front row.

Most of his first night congregations—they were actually audiences—were made up of the curious who came to see him make crayon drawings and to hear Mrs. Fleeter play the piano. But once Fleeter had gotten his following, once they had fallen under the spell of his tongue, he held them genuinely. He held them not because of his voice, his mentality, or his simple sincerity, for he had none of these. He held them because his speeches were lurid and sensational and full of blasphemous similes. People were drawn to him for the same reason that a certain public is drawn to buy a certain kind of daily. They listened to his talk in the same frame of mind as they opened the rotogravure section or one of the cheaper magazines. Had Jerry Fleeter not been admittedly a man of God they would have entered his tent as furtively as though he had been a fortune teller or a coochie dancer.

His methods were simple and direct. He opened his Monday night session with a few compliments to the town and its people. In three nights he would be calling the pool hall a den of iniquity, the high school parties breeders of vice, and every woman who wore short skirts a harlot to be damned to hell. But on Monday nights he always extolled.

He dazzled them on his Monday night introduction, by the careful pronunciation and the basso profundo voice of the professional zealot. He impressed upon them that he was cultured by the use of his coloured crayons. His wife—a sallow woman whose black dress hung from bony shoulders—furthered the illusion by playing hymnals with discreet variations.

His first lecture really contained no subject. It was a rambling teaser, filled with sentences which ended: ". . . but I shall speak of that, my friends, in one of my subsequent sermons" or " . . . In my lecture 'God or Gorilla?' I shall point out how the Catholic Church of Rome aids in the distribution of evolution literature while professing to be against it."

For an entire week this heavy set, deep-eyed preacher ran his frenzied gamut and bellowed over the heads of people seated in a tent. For an entire week he ripped the town into factions, uncovered old wounds, stirred old women and young girls and spoiled the complacency of the middle-aged. For an entire week he related in detail the sins of history, of the present, and the future. He drew no idea of God, outlined no life of Christ. He raved and ranted and cursed God to strike him dead if he were not telling the truth. He lived, and Creston believed him implicitly.

Etta did not miss a single night's meeting, and she attended as many of the afternoon sessions as was possible with her hours at school. The Thursday afternoon meeting for women she was not permitted to attend, but as she came home from school she listened outside the tent. Fleeter's crashing voice carried to her easily, but she was disappointed to find that he was talking about a woman's place in the church with regard to her husband and her children.

She wondered why she was allowed to go to the meetings at all. She was often shocked by Fleeter's words from the platform. There was something most terribly wrong about the thought of sitting there by the side of her mother, about Alfred Horliss on the platform saying "amen, amen," while Fleeter lectured about things Etta had known as tabus.

She remembered almost word for word a story of Fleeter's which had been the subject of much discussion between her and some of the girls at school. He had been talking on the evils of the dance . . . "I am going to tell you a story, my friends, of what happened to one boy and one girl who danced just once too often. May God strike me dead here before you if it isn't true, every word of it! The boy and the girl were brother and sister and in vain the mother pleaded with them to refrain from attending the dance halls of the town. She knew that no man can hold a woman in his arms and go through sensual movements in time to music without unclean thoughts. And she knew that unclean thoughts lead to hell. But they would not listen, my friends. They shut their ears. And then one night the boy went to a masked ball. While there he danced with a beautiful girl dressed as a gypsy, her face masked with a domino. They danced dance after dance until they were overcome with passion, my friends. They went into the garden. (A long, deep impressive pause.) Afterwards, the boy snatched away the mask and saw—his own sister. His own sister, my friends . . ."

Then Etta felt very ashamed, very uncomfortable, there by the side of her mother. But she could not help thinking that the brother and sister couldn't have seen each other often. And since she had no brother of her own, Etta was relieved to realize that she could attend masked balls with impunity so far as any happening of that sort was concerned.

Etta and Peg went to most of the meetings; they went through all the clever psychological preliminaries to the final lecture at which Fleeter could gather his harvest of converts. As yet not many had come to the platform to kneel before Jerry Fleeter as the nearest and most tangible representative of God. Jans Gregson was one of the most important of the earlier converts. Since coming back from Camp Lewis at the end of the war he had been drinking rather steadily. Hope for him was renewed when he began to attend the Fleeter meetings, choosing a seat on the aisle against the time when the black haired evangelist should start up the canvas carpet to tap the nearest prospects on the shoulder and ask them to kneel and be forgiven.

But when the moment came Fleeter had somehow approached Gregson before he had time to flee. He felt the evangelist's hand on his arm and the eyes of almost all Creston upon him.

"Brother, are you going to get right with God at last?"

Jans felt the men and women he knew boring their eyes into him. He experienced a sudden warmth at being the center of that entire group. Not since he had returned in uniform and been marched up the street with shouts and handclapping had he felt so important.

"Brother, are you coming with me to the platform and tell these people that you are going to fight for God?" The sharp black eyes of Fleeter had caught the Legion badge on Gregson's coat lapel. "Brother, when your country called you answered it, didn't you?"

Jans, defiantly, proudly: "Yes."

"Well, then, God is calling you now. He needs a fighter like you. He needs them to combat forces far greater and more evil than the Hun. Are you going to fail Him, brother?"

Jans stiffened, his legs flexed to rise.

"Are you going to fail Him, brother?"

"No . . ." His voice sounded strange, unnatural, louder than he had meant it to be. He felt himself being helped by Fleeter to rise, felt himself being marched down the aisle, his face burning with the imprint of people staring.

An old lady cried: "Glory to God. We're glad, Jans. Glory to God!" A small boy who knew Gregson intimately yelled out half in awe and half uncontrolled humour: "Hooray for old Jans!"

Jans knelt on the platform. He wanted to talk and to shout and he knew that God was giving him power that he had never known before.

"Oh, God, forgive me my sins," he said. His eyes were shut tight as if in pain. His face was caricatured with ludicrous wrinkles. "Oh, God, forgive me! I'm all for You now. I'm all on Your side. Forgive me for not seeing before . . ."

While he talked on, his words louder and louder, Alfred Horliss dutifully repeated "amen, amen . . . hear the boy, oh, Lord, hear him!" And amid the small pandemonium Fleeter strode up and down the aisles pleading for someone to join Jans. But no one came that night, and Jans was alone on the platform in his particular capacity. At length he arose looking rather sheepish and sat down beside Alfred Horliss. He wished he hadn't come now. Yet he felt somehow glad, somehow new. He folded his arms and gazed at the top of

56

one of the tent-poles as if he were admiring the eventual environment to which he had, tonight, paved his way.

As the Saturday approached when Fleeter would hold his last meeting, Peg Nettleship became vaguely troubled.

"Are you goin' up?" she asked Etta.

"No," Etta said positively. "You aren't, are you?"

"I don't know. If you would, I would. I feel like I ought to, Etta. If you would, I would."

"Why does a person *have* to?" Etta said. "I belong to the church. I've never done nothing out of the way. Not awfully, I mean. Why," a sudden thought assailed her, "have you? What do *you* want to go up for?"

Vaguely: "I don't know. I think I ought to. I would, too, if you would, Etta. Mama wants me to."

"What've you done. What have you got to go up for?"

"I've—I've let Charlie kiss me. I've been to dances and I've lied."

"I have, too," Etta told her naïvely. "I mean I've been to dances and lied. I don't see anything wrong with letting a boy kiss you if he wants to. Everybody kisses before they're married, don't they?"

"I suppose. I've let Charlie kiss me and hug me when I knew I shouldn't. It ain't right and I know it. You'll know it, too, if it ever happens to you."

"Oh, who said it hadn't?"

"Well, then, we both ought to go up."

"You can if you want to."

"I won't unless you do, I told you."

The matter was left at that uncertain stage and it did not change until Saturday came and Jerry Fleeter girded for his last stand against the town's evil. The collection had not increased appreciably. It was true that the first envelopes to be passed around had been marked "to defray the expenses of their work, Mr. and Mrs. Fleeter ask your aid." A few stinging remarks scattered through his lectures had loosened the consciences of a few, but as yet the envelopes were certainly no record of Fleeter's spiritual progress against the devil.

At the conclusion of the Friday night lecture, Fleeter warned them.

"Tomorrow night, my friends, is the last time I shall speak to you here on this visit. I am not at all satisfied with the work I have been able to do. You have been asleep too long before God. You have not listened to Him in a long time. Tomorrow night I will need to make you listen. If necessary we will stay in this tent until midnight—yes, into the Sabbath morning, until I have scraped the barnacles of sin from your encrusted souls! I am going to drive the devil out of here. I am going to drive him back into Hell, my friends! Your good minister has brought me here to aid you and I will do that, so help me God. I will not leave my brother here without a hand. I want you to come tomorrow prepared to leave your sins in this tent. I want you to come prepared to lift up your voices and throw the dirt out of your minds and hearts.

"You are unclean and sinful and you sit there complacently and stare at me! Oh, I am not mincing words, and if there is any one of you who cannot stand the truth he had better not come tomorrow night." His voice suddenly lowered. "Let me tell you, friends, that Creston is by far the saddest case I have encountered in a long time. I shall put it to Mrs. Fleeter here, if this isn't true."

He turned to his wife who sat on the piano stool with her hands palms upward in her lap. "Jessie, is it not true that you and I have never had such a hard fight in all our years together in the Cause?"

Jessie, with no word, sadly bowed her head. Her husband gazed at her with compassion, as if he realized her position before all these people. He again turned to his flock.

"But we are not defeated. If we gave up now we would be cowards and unworthy of our mission, friends . . ."

Then the Reverend Alfred Horliss gave an anemic benediction over the heads of a chastened throng. But they filed out of the tent feeling gloriously sinful. Fleeter, in designating them as the hardest cases he had known, had paid them a compliment which gave them entity, identification, and they were somehow proud.

VII

Etta would not forget the sight of Peg Nettleship, on that hot Saturday night, half running up to Jerry Fleeter's platform. She would always be able to remember it in after years whenever she wanted to hate her, or whenever she wanted to feel sorry for her: Peg, her hair damp and tangled about her forehead, her face white and drawn, kneeling awkwardly on the platform with one trembling knee bent under her.

All through the loud meeting Peg had sat by Etta's side, more strange than usual, more silent. It was so crowded that they had not been able to sit with their mothers. They huddled precariously on a crowded bench over in one corner of the tent.

From the very first there had been something electric, impending, in the air. Alfred Horliss's opening prayer was stiff and high in tone. There was a moving quality to Mrs. Fleeter's selections that may have been inspired, or only something that she always saved for her husband's last efforts in a town. Fleeter's own manner was strained. He stood about the platform as a relative waits outside an operating room, with that same high-strung air of realizing something disastrous or inevitable.

His sermon was a study in ascending discords, and the heat of one of Creston's first spring nights crept into the tent and mingled with the odours of tobacco, and clothes, and bodies.

It was not all due to the artistry of Fleeter, though he had prepared them for the scene. It was something in the gathering itself. Collectively, the congregation was a huge giant with the ganglia of a dwarf. They sat nervously ready. And, relentless and steady, Fleeter's voice boomed down at them. Whatever years they had left to live in Creston seemed as minutes to them; they began to feel that fear of being snatched tomorrow into the lap of a deity about whose uncertain temperament they knew, after all, very little.

The spirit of the meeting rose until it attained a combination of a negro camp meeting and an ancient Orphic frenzy. Fleeter began his pleas and his threats. They drifted—these men and women who would, in two weeks, forget their firm resolves—up the aisleways in twos and threes, seeking the strength of numbers in their enterprise. First came the old women, and the older men. Jerry Fleeter did not know, though perhaps he guessed, that they had been figures at every revival

60

held in Creston for the past twenty years or so, who periodically "got religion." After them, as the excitement grew, children—frightened bewildered children came to the platform.

With her eyes wide and staring Etta watched the motley group of converts, people that she knew, with whom she had talked. Their faces were odd, distorted. Their voices were shaken as with great grief or unspeakable joy. They talked in groans, in rasping whispers, and repeated over and over the name of their Saviour.

Up and down among the fury Fleeter strode, lashing them to a higher pitch. Sweat streamed down his face. His eyes bulged, and great veins stood out upon his neck. Shot from his coat was a dirty cuff, damp with perspiration, a gold link hanging from it loosely. His voice was hoarse and fearful.

Etta saw him stop once by Fanny Brest and glare at her. He was about to speak to the woman, when she gazed up at him, looked so straightly into his bloodshot eyes that he seemed to falter for a moment. Then he passed on up the aisle with a new shout upon his wet lips.

Etta felt Peg stiffen beside her and turned to find her companion watching Fleeter with a sort of hypnotic stare. Peg's limp mouth sagged open, her breast was heaving with her short, quick breaths.

"I'm goin' up, Etta. I'm goin' up now."

Too startled to restrain her, Etta saw Peg rise and stumble from the bench. She half ran down the aisle near the side of the tent, crying at every step, Fleeter caught sight of her and rushed forward to meet her. He lifted her in strong arms to the platform.

"Get right with God," he shouted. "Get right with

Him, and then help me out tonight, sister. Help me make these others see."

Above all the others, Peg's voice came to Etta: "Oh, forgive me! I've been a sinner. I've done everything I shouldn't have. Oh, forgive me! God, forgive me!"

Etta saw Fanny Brest rise from her seat and walk up the aisle to leave. On her face was the look of a woman who has seen something repulsive to all womankind. Just as she reached Peg's mother she stopped. She stopped and looked at the woman watching her daughter from an aisle seat. It was just for the space of a second; and then she stalked out of the entrance way.

But Mrs. Nettleship was looking at Peg with moist eyes. Etta wondered how she could be so quiet, so apparently glad. She guessed that Mrs. Nettleship thought it better to sin and be forgiven than never to have sinned at all. Fleeter was leading Peg down by the hand now.

"If you won't listen to me, will you listen to this little sister who has been washed in the blood of God?"

Wildly Etta sprang from her bench, crept swiftly along the canvas to the entrance. None saw her. All were straining toward the front. Outside, in the dark, she bumped into Charlie Fraser.

"God, you scared me!" he whispered. "Was you in there?"

Etta nodded. "Yes. Was you?"

"God, yes. I beat it when Peg went nuts up there. In another minute she'd 'a' come after me. The darned little fool—we never did nothing like all these old hens'll think now."

Etta was so ashamed for Peg that she could say nothing. From the inside of the tent came the uproar of the meeting, crashing into the peace of the Spring night.

"Listen to 'em," Charlie invited. "I can't see nothing in that, at all." And then, patronizingly: "It's all right if they want to be religious, but my gosh . . ."

They wandered away from the tent.

"You goin' home, Etta?"

"I think so. I'll tell Mother I got sick."

"That's enough back there to make anybody sick. Care if I walk home with you?"

On the steps of the Dant house Charlie tried to kiss her but Etta wouldn't let him. She could see Peg up there sobbing and shouting, bending down on one knee so you could see where the silk left off on her stocking. She closed the door on Charlie and when she was in the house she turned on all the downstairs lights.

She wished a minute afterward that she had kissed Charlie. She was trembling with the excitement of the meeting. She repressed a desire to run out and call to Charlie and walk around with him some more.

CHAPTER THREE

I

HE slow Summer crept over the valleys of wheat, crept over them first as smoky haze that turned blue against the hills with nightfall. It was not unbeautiful in Creston around the first of June. The charitable veil of an early Spring dulled every harsh outline. Seen from a distance, the town nestled into its little hollow, quiet and apart, a pastoral idyl.

Above it, stretching almost to the Western horizon were the wheat fields. In the full Summer they would seem to pour a liquid gold down the gentle slopes and into the town. But now they were only alternate blocks of wet black loam and green wisps of early grain.

The whole scene was waking from a lethargy. Locked tightly in the grasp of Winter, it was emerging almost painfully, slowly, bewildered, as a man gains consciousness after an unnatural sleep.

In another month or two it would be ruthless in its fierce activity. The fields, every hillside that was so quiet now, would echo with the roar of pounding cylinders in the harvesting engines. Men who were red with the sun and wind would ride through Creston atop of wagons loaded with pregnant sacks. Their arms would be straining against the pulling lines and their legs stiff from bracing against wheel-brakes. At night they would go to bed half an hour after supper, utterly weary and somehow proud and glad for a day's work.

Soon, before the ceaseless and erratic blades of the

64

harvesting machines, the tall stalks would fall slowly with a sort of majestic grace onto the revolving drapers, be carried into the whirring cylinder. Separated from the straw and the chaff, the precious kernels would flow into the waiting sack with a soft humming sound—tiny grain against tiny grain, millions and millions against one another, making a soft humming sound.

Against the farthest hill one might see them: the long string of horses creeping slowly, looking almost like a brown worm against the yellow wheat. Or, more often now, the thresher would move rather faster, and before it there would be an awkward, lumbering tractor, bouncing down into gullies with odd jerky movements and pulling out again with a determined growl of noisy motors.

Every year and every year, over and over the same ground. It was as if these sweating men were determined that nothing should ever grow upon these slopes while Summer lasted. And yet, before the first chill winds of Autumn, these same men would be turning the heavy clods under the plow. Before they had forgotten this one harvest they would be watching anxiously the weather calendars. Carefully, evenly, this same ground one day would be sown again with wheat. Carefully it would be harvested.

All the while in the interim between harvests a part of the soil would be groomed. It would be harrowed and reharrowed. Because of it men would hope for snow that would blanket it, for rain to give it moisture, for sun that would give it germination. It needed such a strange combination of nature and man in order for it to produce.

When September came the warehouse would be

bursting with wheat, and then the men would argue on the street corners, in the Creston Drug Store, or wherever a knot of them happened to congregate. They would not like the price they were to get for their labours. They would not be sure whether to sell now or wait until wheat went up a cent or two. Sometimes they would say they should get together and refuse to raise wheat. That would bring these outsiders to the realization that the wheat grower was a factor in the economics of the country.

But eventually they would sell; at least a part of their crop. Then they would buy new cars, radios, improve their houses, and forget all that they had threatened about not raising wheat.

They never meant that threat. Most of them were as indigenous to the soil as the wheat itself. They would have been like George Dant if they had quit the growing of grain. George had to be at his ranch in the summer harvest, even though he had leased it to Frank Dyer. He couldn't even think of staying at home while that wheat was being threshed.

He had a different idea from most. "The War spoiled us," he was always saying. "The government made us believe we were pretty important. We belong, all right, but we ain't to be done without. Any time we get too highty-tighty to work at what we know about there's plenty of foreigners who'd be willing to do a dam' sight more'n we do for a lot less money."

Frank Dyer would say: "But it ain't altogether right. These fellows in Chicago and Portland tellin' what wheat ought to be a bushel." Price fixing was a mystery to Dyer. He was vague about the method whereby prices were given from the trading centers. There was something suspicious about it. He maintained that "the gover'ment ought to set a price."

"That'd be class legislation," was Dant's inevitable reply. "There'd be no end to it if they started that."

"All the same, there ought to be a set price," Frank would insist. "We ought to be protected the same as the country protects its manufacturers."

Dant's argument with Dyer was rather typical. They all talked a great deal, though none was certain as to what the core of the argument was. All had a dim realization in the back of their minds that they would go on raising wheat for the nation, and that their children would, too.

II

Etta followed her father through the field. The heavy heads of the wheat brushed her shoulders; and in the gullies, where the spring freshets had once soaked the ground, she found that she could scarcely see above the stalks. She liked to walk through the dry, acrid smelling field. She pretended, whenever her father looked around to see if she were coming, to walk carefully, not treading down the wheat. But when his back was turned again she could not help making a new path for herself, walking into the yellow wall which pressed against her body and swayed downward before her determined strike.

Frank Dyer was on ahead of them. Every once in a while he would snatch a wheat head from its stalk and roll it between his palms, blowing away the chaff to show the brown kernels to Dant. The two men would look at them critically, each holding some in his palm.

Then, throwing the kernels into their mouth to chew, they would go on with their inspection.

"She ought to do fifty," Etta heard her father say. She was glad the wheat would be good this year. That might mean her father would get a new car and she could drive it, maybe. She forgot the present in order to fancy herself driving a load of girls in a green sedan to a basketball game at Athena.

"This is goin' to do better than the north forty," she heard Dyer call back over his shoulder. "That dam' north forty gets all the hot winds."

"It's been hotter than the hinges of hell lately," Dant agreed. "And hot winds. But this'll do fifty—maybe fifty-five."

When they had returned to the old house Etta was quite tired. She could see no real reason why her father and Dyer had gone over almost the whole field—it seemed to her—when the wheat stalks were so alike. She was fatigued and with it was a dull resentment which she did not try to understand.

Mrs. Dyer was standing on the kitchen porch, and she held the screen door open for them, waving away flies with her apron. Coming into the kitchen Etta smelled fried chicken. She knew that Mrs. Dyer always had fried chicken when her father came to look over the place; she felt proud and pretended to look at the kitchen with a critical eye. Her mother had cooked here, her glance said, and she wasn't sure but that it had been better looking then.

But Etta really liked Mrs. Dyer, and the woman didn't notice the girl's gaze anyway. She flurried about the hot stove and talked in time to the noisy banging of kettles and pans. Etta stood in a corner while Frank and

George washed themselves in the basin on the porch bench. She wondered how they had ever managed, when she and her mother and father were here, with that lavatory makeshift. In their Creston house they had a wash basin and a hot water tank. When the two men had finished washing, she dipped her hands disdainfully into the newly filled basin and tried to find a clean place on the towel hanging from a nail on the wall.

"You folks sit right down," Mrs. Dyer said. "Lester'll be in here in just a minute now. I saw him takin' the horses down to the creek. You folks go on and eat, though."

Dyer and Etta's father needed no further invitation and she followed their suit. Through the window she saw Lester Adams coming up the yard to the house. Lester was a senior in high school and Etta always felt a little embarrassed before him; and she could not forget about Edna Peabody and the gymnasium episode. She heard Lester's heavy boots on the porch, and she remembered that next Fall she would be a sophomore and need not feel too inferior.

Having washed, and pasted back his thick hair with water and a wet comb, Lester came into the room and his first glance caught Etta.

"Well! 'Haven't seen you since school was out, I guess."

"I haven't tried to put myself where you could," Etta told him.

Mrs. Dyer said: "Guess *that'll* hold you, Lester!" She brought a steaming plate of chicken for the center of the table.

"Lester thinks he's quite a lady's man," she confided; "and he does need takin' down a notch."

"Oh, I don't know . . ." Lester attained a blasé attitude.

"He's been worryin' about whether that Miss Larson will teach him again next year," Dyer spoke with heavy slyness.

Etta saw a chance to cut Lester again. "Guess she will so long as Swede Mongsen's around." She felt an enmity toward this boy, and she did not know why. There were split seconds when she liked him, wanted to have him give her a glance of warmth.

"That snooty teacher don't worry me," Lester told them. "Guess maybe I could put her in her place if I wanted. She's not so high and mighty as she lets on. Charlie Fraser give me a tip about her."

Etta suffered a sudden panic. Mrs. Dyer, instantly curious, made a questioning sound within her throat. There was a terrible silence through which Etta hated Charlie for telling—she thought—about Florence Larson coming to Swede's dance.

"I'm not sayin'," Lester added finally. "I just know."

"You shouldn't," Dant told him judiciously, "say anything like that unless you're sure."

Frank Dyer broke into the trend by asking, prosaically, for the bread. Etta was grateful to him; she and Lester and Mrs. Dyer all reached for it at once. There was laughter as they jerked their hands away. The incident of Miss Larson had passed.

Riding with her father back to Creston, Etta began to feel lonely. Summer was always lonely in Creston for her. Most of her friends were at home on the ranches, and only a few beside herself, of her own age, were in town. She hadn't seen Peg for almost a week and a half now. Although their friendship was rather strained Etta wanted to see Peg.

Peg was growing beyond Etta's horizon. She had attended several dances in Athena, and once, when her father and mother had been away and she had stayed with Edna Peabody, she had gone to Pendleton with two Athena high school boys. Peg had begun to talk casually of "dates" and was often seen talking with older boys. Etta consoled herself that she could do the same thing if she chose. Charlie liked her and he no longer sought Peg—who told Etta that he was "too dumb."

But Etta knew that Charlie had been ashamed of being seen with Peg after her "confession" there on Jerry Fleeter's platform. Peg, along with most of the other converts, had quite recovered from the excitement of the revival.

Indeed, if the truth was to be known, Peg's performance in the sight of God had increased tremendously her popularity with Creston's self styled rakes. Her stuttering and erratic confessional which hinted at blackness created toward her a new curiosity on the part of some of the town's young men.

Nevertheless, toward the end of the school year, Etta had discovered that she, too, held charm for some of the boys. The thought appealed to her vanity, but beyond that she was not interested. She used powder, sometimes rouged her lips, and she was always ready to assume the sophisticated style of Creston's young girls. But she did it partly to satisfy herself and partly to trump Peg.

As she rode with her father she projected her thoughts into what the next school year might bring.

With September in the distance she began to anticipate the excitement of going back to school.

"If the wheat turns out good are you going to get another car?"

"Can't tell what I'll do. Nothing much wrong with this one, is there?"

"I like a closed-in one," Etta said. "I like that Buick like the Ives' have got."

"We'll see when the time comes. Can't tell about the crop yet." He drove awhile in silence. "It won't be ready to cut for three weeks or more—anyhow, two and a half. Might be a lot of things happen in two weeks"

"But if it's good will you get one?"

"Maybe . . ."

His tone did not carry conviction to Etta. He wanted to build a new house on the ranch. That would mean they'd have to go back to the ranch again.

"If we go to the ranch next year we'll have to have a new car," she said.

Dant peered at the sky to his right. "Looks like it might be rainin' up in the mountains." They were not mountains. They were rolling foothills.

"Will that hurt?"

"Not the mountain fellows. They're later than we are down here. They can stand some rain right now . . . Bet the creek'll be a whooping it up tonight."

The little cloud had been to them no larger than a hand. As Etta watched it she fancied that it did take the shape of a hand. Five fingers stretched from the body of it, longer and longer until they spiraled into nothingness just as they were about to grasp the peak of the distant hill.

Something mystic and ancient in Etta frightened her for a moment, but her reason crowded it out; she diverted her attention to watching the town below her. From the Dant ranch they had climbed steadily to the brow of one of its surrounding knolls, and now began the easy descent. Dant switched off the engine and applied the brakes carefully. He turned all his attention to the road before him. Etta wished someone else were driving, someone who would have let the car down the hill and brought it up suddenly with a screech of brakes.

But they got to the main street; it seemed ages. They stopped before the Farmer's Bank. Johnnie Webb stood out on the walk smoking a cigarette.

"Just been out lookin' at the wheat," Dant told him as the car rolled to the curb.

"Look pretty good?"

"Goin' to make around fifty. Maybe fifty-five. Hope to God we get a good price."

"Yeah." Webb crushed his cigarette under his heel. "I don't know, but I believe if I had any I'd sell most right away and then gamble on the rest."

Etta got out of the car. "I'm goin' down to the library a minute," she told her father.

When she returned, Johnnie Webb and her father were still talking. She climbed into the seat and began flipping the pages of the book she had taken out. Mrs. Cramer, the librarian, had chosen it for her, and Etta was sure she was not going to like it. But she read a few pages to be sure.

Then she remembered that Peg was going to let her read a book which Peg's mother didn't know her daughter had found. It was called "The Sheik" and Rudolph Valentino had played in it at the Memorial Hall.

III

It was only a little after nine and Etta had gone to bed early. She had not been asleep very long. Perhaps ten minutes, though she was not certain until she finally got downstairs.

All she knew was that she found herself with eyes wide open, looking toward the window. She knew what had awakened her. The telephone had buzzed, and below she could hear her father putting on his shoes. He always sat in that old rocker and when he bent over to lace his shoes the ancient chair squeaked in a way that Etta knew. There was her mother's voice, too, in a tense undertone.

She knew something was awfully wrong. From the window the sky was blacker than a night sky should have been. It was more than a night without a moon or any stars. A square of opaque blackness seemed pressed against the pane.

"Etta . . ." Her mother's voice, full of premonition.

Silent, Etta leaped from bed and came downstairs. Mrs. Dant, looking futile in her woolen nightdress, waited for her.

"There's been a cloudburst," she said. "Frank just called and said there were horses from the mountain running down the creek bed and he and his wife were leaving."

"Where's Papa going?"

"He's goin' out to the ranch. I told him it was fool-hardy."

Dant came in from the other room, drawing on a coat. "Where's my leather jacket, Etta? You wore it on a picnic."

Glad to be doing something, she ran into the kitchen where she had left her father's jacket behind a door. She came back with it and said: "I want to go too."

"Of course not . . . You folks better dress. I don't think it'll do much more'n swell the creek here, but it pays to watch. If anything starts to happen just start up the hill and keep goin'."

"I can't go a step, George!" Mrs. Dant was stricken with sudden panic. "You've got to stay here!"

"You'll be all right. There ain't no danger. I got to see what's happened. You ought to be thinkin' about Frank and Lura. That water'll be goin' like hell out there inside of ten minutes."

Etta rushed up the stair excitedly and put on a dress over her nightgown. She stuffed the long gown into her bloomers and, with stockings and shoes in hand, ran down the stairs once more.

Her father had already gone. Peering out of the window she could see the garage doors gaping open. She turned to find her mother almost fully dressed, her hair pinned to the back of her neck in an erratic knot.

It began to rain, to drizzle at first and then to strike the porch and windows with intermittent splashes. Then it started in earnest; the two of them stood still and listened to the dinning of it upon the roof.

"I'm goin' over to Morrison's," Mrs. Dant said. "We can't stay here."

Etta switched on the porch light as they left, each bundled in her heaviest coat and with a shawl over her head. The rain fell dully all about them. As they crossed

75

the yard beneath the old tree they were drenched with water that had collected in the branches and fallen at a gust of wind.

Mr. Morrison met them at the door. He was in stocking feet and had evidently been preparing for bed. In the background, peering over his shoulder was Mrs. Morrison.

"Well, well! What's the trouble, folks?"

His unperturbed attitude consoled Etta and her mother. But they came inside and Mrs. Dant breathlessly told about the telephone message from Frank Dyer.

Morrison looked troubled then. "I was just wonderin' to the missis if maybe some of them that was in the creek bed wasn't gettin' it bad."

"I tried to tell George not to go, but he wouldn't listen."

"There ain't no real danger. Don't ever recollect the water gettin' high enough to drown anybody."

Etta started. She had been intensely excited, but she had not had any thought about drowning. Water as a force, as an eternal relentless enemy, never had occurred to her, just as it never occurred to most inland people.

"I saw a funny lookin' cloud when Papa and I were comin' back from the ranch this afternoon. It was just before supper and it looked like a hand."

This information struck them silent. Mr. Morrison, contracting the gregariousness of fear, decided to call the telephone office. He turned the little crank three times with increasing impatience, and then, hanging the receiver thoughtfully, he repeated the signal.

"Hello," he said at length. "Have you heard from anybody on the mountain or in the hollow?"

76

There was that breathless pause which always comes when interested people listen for an answer they can hear only indirectly.

"Have you heard from Dyer's? . . . Will you see if you can get them?"

From where she sat Etta could hear the frantic buzzing of the telephone. Then it ceased abruptly, unnaturally. Mr. Morrison held the receiver to his ear in that awkward way which people have when they recognize there is no connection being made.

He hung the receiver with a final, sharp, metallic click and turned to them dramatically. "She says that the only 'phone they can get on the mountain is Mel Rose's, and there's a lot of people there who ran over from Horse Heaven Flat. Dyer's 'phone's just cut off." He began to look about for his shoes. "I'm goin' over town," he said.

As he left, Etta sprang up to accompany him and she forestalled her mother's objection with: "I'm goin' with him."

Half running in the rain to keep up with Morrison's long strides, she went with him down the walk to the corner pool hall where a group of men stood in the entrance way.

"Hello, Jim . . . Ain't she a dandy!"

Etta saw that the water was beginning to run in rivulets against the curbing; it somehow frightened her and she thought of her father out on the road toward Dyer's.

"Etta's Dad hiked it over to Dyer's," Morrison yelled at them. "Frank called him up and said he and the old lady were high-tailin' it out. He said horses was runnin' down the canyon."

"God, that means a water wall and some of the fellows along the creek will get old billy hell!"

Gradually the excitement of the situation crept over the town. Wild bits of stories leaped from man to man. At the telephone office Etta and Mr. Morrison found a score of men and women crowded against the counter. The pale globe over the switchboard outlined them eerily and the long stairway which led to the embalming room above was bathed in shadows that were black and foreboding to Etta's mind.

The men and women were frightened now, and they felt they had no reason to be. They laughed more than they would have under other circumstances, and made a lot of poor jokes about the rain.

Some disparaged fear. "This is nothing at all. I've seen water clean up to the windows on the drug store over there. She flooded the basements and left two foot of mud and hail. That was before the crik went under the street."

"You go down and watch the creek," another spoke up, "if you think she ain't a stem-winder up on the hills. There's young trees a-comin' far down as town, roots and all, and you'll be seein' chicken coops and flivvers comin' down, too."

"Say . . . how about the dam?"

The question was like a shot into the midst of them. A picture of the dam flashed into every mind there: five miles above town, cracked concrete, never free from defects since the day it was built.

"Avery went up this afternoon and opened the gate."

There was a distinct and collective sigh.

"How'd he know this was comin'?"

"He wasn't sure. I heard him say he saw a funny lookin' cloud up near Basket Mountain."

"I seen it when Papa and I were comin' back from the ranch. It looked like a hand and had fingers stretchin' out."

The woman at the switchboard was pushing and pulling plugs with what seemed to Etta to be an aimless routine. Etta did not know that the woman had often read of switchboard operators who, in crises like these, made heroines of themselves. But the woman was a trifle exasperated. There seemed nothing she could do. Most of the mountain lines were down—not an infrequent condition; and there was the possibility that the thing would not attain any serious proportions. Nevertheless she kept trying the various lines, ringing them with frenzied preoccupation, an anxious stare on her face for the benefit of her beholders.

Etta heard the sound of a motor outside; she was filled with intense relief as she recognized her father's car. She turned to see him already within the office, his hand holding open the door.

But he did not see her. He looked at the crowd and through it. He was more white than Etta would have believed possible with his tanned face.

"You men—" he said. "Come on out here."

But he still stood there blocking the doorway, his hand upon the knob. The cold, damp wind veered in around the crowd. Something imperative in Dant's tone drew them forward. He was covered with mud that had dried only upon his face, where it was white and caked. His drooping mustache was flecked with it, and there was a tiny dark globule of mud just at the corner of his eye that gave him an oddly feminine look.

Etta saw Frank Dyer beyond, holding to the side of her father's car. He was wet and dripping; he was hatless and his eyes were wild. He seemed poised to break into a run, but he kept looking up and down the street as if he did not know which way to go. As Etta watched, men came up to Dyer and asked him something, but he only stared at them. He stared at them without seeing them, without speaking.

George Dant's voice: "My place is washed out—the house went down the creek. Lura was in it."

From the sidewalk Dyer heard the name. He suddenly came into consciousness and rushed up beside Dant.

"Good God, we got to find her!" he kept saying. "God, we got to find her!" And then, as if to justify himself before the crowd: "When I saw the horses comin' down the canyon in the rain I knew what was up. I called George . . . then I tried to call again and couldn't . . . I grabbed her and kept trying to pull her up the hill, but she kept wantin' to come back and was cryin' . . . she was scared. Pretty soon she let out a yell and broke away and went runnin' down the hill and onto the porch. I don't know why I couldn't move. By God, I don't know why I didn't move! . . . It hit her just as she got in the doorway. There didn't seem to be hardly no noise—the house——" his voice was almost a whisper now. "It just sort of folded and went out of sight around the bend of the creek . . ."

No one spoke. The woman at the switchboard had stopped pulling plugs and had leaned over the counter.

"It was like a wall . . ." Dyer was saying, "and there was trees and brush and boards a-stickin' up every which way and thrashin' around. You could hear a low sound like maybe there was boulders rollin' along at the bottom of it . . ." His voice kept trailing off into a whisper, and then rising again. But at length he was silent.

The man who had seen the trees coming down the creek bawled out crassly into the silence. "By God, I told you so!"

"We'd better search along the creek," Dant spoke up quietly. "The water's goin' down already . . . Most likely . . ." he added it with no conviction ". . . she ain't hurt. The water wasn't awful high."

"That dam' wall was high," Dyer told him crazily. "That God dam' wall was high. You never seen it goin' down at her. It was just like a dam' woman to go a-runnin' down that hill . . ." He turned to the street and Etta thought he was going to cry or start hitting people. "The dam' fool," she heard him say. "The crazy dam' fool."

The little man who had seen the other flood spoke again. "Some of us better go down the creek, and some up. You better get him over to your house, George."

Dant nodded and the two men went out to comfort Dyer. Etta wondered why they were too dull to see that Dyer would have to hunt for Lura with them. He would have to keep on hunting and hunting until he was so tired he would have to stop. She was not surprised when Dyer shook off the two men and started into the night.

For the first time since he had come into the door her father saw Etta. "You better get home, Etta. You got no business out here."

She followed the group of men out into the rain. On the walk they were joined by others, running up from the pool hall, from the drug store. Running out of side streets, buttoning coat collars around their throats. The woman at the switchboard had busied herself again: she had told the town that Lura Dyer was missing. A few women trotted toward the telephone office, their faces gaping white with curiosity and dread.

Etta didn't want to go home. She huddled against the building while the men argued as to the course they should take. Mrs. Adams, her voice cracking within a fear-tightened throat, enquired for her son Lester.

"Lester—was Lester there?"

He hadn't been, someone said. He'd gone to the dance at Athena. The sight of Mrs. Adams' eyes as she heard of this deliverance made Etta want to cry. Her nose felt twitchy and her lashes were suddenly wet. She wanted to kiss Lester's mother.

The group enlarged, a dark ungainly mass in the rain. Men's faces shone like blurred discs in the night. Etta's father stood tall among most of them, but he seemed indefinite, lost. It was the little man who kept telling them of the bends in the creek, and sent two or three of the crowd after lanterns and flashlights.

"It's got to be tonight," he said. "The mud'll be settled by mornin'—there'll be three or four feet of it."

I V

When the two groups of men had gone, huddled together, mumbling, certain faces lit by dim lanterns, Etta had sneaked back into the telephone office to join the women who had grown strangely quiet now. She hadn't wanted to go through the dark street alone to Mr. Morrison's house, and she had been too curious to leave the scene that frightened and held her. So she had turned back into the office when her father had gone off with one of the groups, his huge hand on Frank Dyer's shoulder.

She had found the women quiet. They sought chairs, or places to lean against. They waited. They knew that their men had gone away with that hope which is a part of all men. But with the reality which is a part of all women, those who stayed behind knew that Lura Dyer was dead.

Etta called Morrison's and asked for her mother, and when Mrs. Morrison answered the telephone in a frightened voice: "I'm at the 'phone office. Papa and Frank just came back . . . Yes, he's all right. Our house was washed away . . ."

It was not until she had said it did Etta realize that the old house was gone. The old house. Now, where it stood, there would be nothing.

" . . . No, they've gone to hunt for her," she answered.

Then she waited. There were no more chairs available. The steps which led upstairs to the grim room where dead people were placed for a night or two— these were unoccupied. On another night than this someone would have been seated there. But not now; not tonight. Etta could not go over to them and sit down upon them, as she had done before.

One of the groups of men returned. There were more than a dozen of them, wet and heavy. You would not have dreamed that so many men could be so quiet. There was only the shuffling of feet—damp, soggy, muddy boots—along the floor.

Two of them carried what had been Lura Dyer. Two of them held gently and awkwardly between them what to all appearances was yet Lura Dyer. But in one swift terrible wave Etta knew that this thing they lifted from the car was different from the woman who had—was it that afternoon?—laughed, and insisted they keep on eating.

The arms hung more than limply. They were unshapen, broken. Mud was in the tangled mass of hair, wet black mud that encircled Lura's hair like an incongruous smart turban that a young girl might wear. No one looked at her face. No one could look at her face. She hung between the two men and dripped water like a sodden rag.

When they had brought her in and left her they kept looking apprehensively toward the door and out of it. They were afraid of that moment when Frank Dyer would return with the others.

Smothering for want of something which was not air, Etta ran to the door, out upon the walk. The sky had cleared; she was astonished to see that there were a few errant stars above her. It no longer rained, and a warm breeze had started up to dry the walks and the sides of the building.

Yes, it had stopped now. What more could it do? It was Etta's question to the night: What more could it do? She was somehow not afraid of the night now. As she went home alone she was not afraid of the night because she hated it so. She despised a night that would do this to Lura Dyer, and would let off Lester Adams because he had gone to a dance—which everyone knew was wrong.

She stopped suddenly. It wasn't the night. The night could do nothing, one way or another. Someone had made the night. Someone had made it and all that it contained. She stood still, overcome, beaten down by the thought. It was God who had done this thing.

She felt tears coming and she began to run. She ran onto the porch of her house where she had left the light burning. She remembered that her mother was across the street, at Morrison's. Bewildered and frantic she rushed down the steps and across the street.

Stiffly seated in their chairs, their faces pale from want of sleep, her mother and Mrs. Morrison were waiting.

"What's happened, Etta? Etta! What has *happened?*"

"Lura—Lura Dyer's dead . . ."

She broke at last, sinking down against the couch, shaken in a paroxysm of grief. Then she remembered again. Into the couch cover she shot the muffled, angry words: "Oh, why does God do things like that? Why does he treat good people like that?" She turned to face them, still on the floor, her arms widespread against the couch, a tragic, twisted figure. Her cheeks were stained with tears, her mouth ugly with a woman's tearing sorrow. "I hate God for that! I hate God for that!"

Her words crowded into the room and pushed out even the thought of Lura Dyer. The two women had forgotten what prompted Etta's words in the blasphemous ferocity of them. They regarded her strangely; fright went through them like a faint chill.

Etta's mother said: "Why, Etta, *Etta!*"

Mrs. Morrison said: "His ways are unknowable and strange."

V

The swollen stream that rushed along the creek bed had been freakish in its movements. At some points it had confined itself, torn swiftly through the deeper channels; and at others had seemed to gather in a sudden frenzy. At this spot it had torn out a whole embankment interwoven with the thick roots of a gnarled tree. At another it had been easily deflected by the merest obstacle.

Rushing down its gully and into the hollow where Dant had built his house, its waters had piled like windblown snow to splinter the frame structure and drown the spark in Lura Dyer's body. Then, not two hundred yards away, the water wall had collapsed and the stream, contrite, meandered toward its inevitable goal, the Columbia and the sea.

Half forgetting Lura Dyer and yet coming to the scene because of her, people crowded the site of Dant's house the next morning. They waded ankle deep in the sucking mud and gathered in little groups to talk quietly of her. They had that mien of humans who visit the setting of recent catastrophe: they tried to veil a vulgar curiosity with a look of haunting sadness for what had passed there.

Etta came too. She was with her father and mother, and she found the old yard strange. Even the little knolls were gone, for the ground was level with black mud that oozed water when she stepped into it. Level black mud upon which nothing stood. There was a new horizon—a horizon which she had never seen because the familiar old house had blotted it out.

But above the yard, aloof from the now quiescent creek, the rolling hill was filled with Dant's wheat. Etta looked at the field above her. She could see the path she had made yesterday through it, and she remembered coming back to the house, sitting at the table and seeing Lester walk into the kitchen.

Mrs. Dant was standing alone, her eyes dry and red and a handkerchief to her mouth. It was the old house for which she sorrowed, and the old boardwalk, broken, treacherous, that had led to it from the gate. Etta had been born in that little side room; she had played on the porch and under the shade of the locust tree that looked so short now with the mud covering its trunk. Before her eyes was the house as a phantom. She saw every outline, every detail of its imperfection. She knew just where the squareheaded nails had rusted in the rain and dripped a ragged brown streak down the gray paint of it. She would have much preferred the wheat to be taken out than her old home.

She felt that if she had stayed there, if she had never moved into Creston, this would not have happened. She felt as all humans really feel: that they are exempted somehow from disaster. She, for instance, would never have stood irresolute before that door to be crushed into it by the waters of the creek.

As she recollected Lura, all her sympathies went to Frank, all her sorrow was for his dead wife, and she forgot the place where she had lived as a young girl with George Dant, and where Etta had been born.

When she rode back into town with her husband and Etta she began to plan already for Lura's funeral. It would be at two the following day, and she would have to leave the dinner dishes so that she could be ready in time.

Etta was thinking of it, too. She dreaded returning from it to sit down at the supper table. Houses were so dark and damp after you'd been to a funeral, even

87

if the house wasn't concerned directly. The ashes of the fire were always cold, and the afternoon had always grown chill. And, at the table, there was always that dreadful reserve out of respect for the one who had been covered over so summarily from the sight of them, so shut off from laughing and talking and tasting food.

CHAPTER FOUR

I

ETTA came back to school that September with the sure manner of the sophomore. So did Peg Nettleship, and they scurried as of old to find seats together in their classrooms. They had not seen a great deal of each other during the Summer, but the common bond of school brought them to a warm friendship once more.

"Are you glad to see school start?" Etta asked.

"No—are you?"

"Gosh, no!"

But they were, both of them. While they pretended to be bored with books and the insistence of the teachers as to Latin verbs and the date of the battle of Hastings they were in reality thrilled by it. It was the core of their existence. Summer was only a time when they waited for school to open again.

Florence Larson had returned, too. She had tried without success to gain another position which would pay her as well as a second year at Creston. She felt that any other town would present as many difficulties, and so she had come back to keep her contract for another year. She hated to return; the ride to Creston on the grimy auto coach had been a torture because of the memory it held before her. Swede Mongsen would be at the station to meet her. There was no possible way to avoid that, and she did not want to see Mongsen. Not that first afternoon, anyway. Not ever, really.

But it was good to find his grinning face looking up

at her as she stood uncertainly upon the bus step. It was rather nice to feel the clumsy touch of his hand and hear his husky voice. At his back was the little town which might prove more cruel this year—and here was Swede, anxious to be a friend.

She found that by some metamorphosis which had taken place during the Summer the students who had not liked her before were ready to accept her now. Her year of probation, evidently, was over. Boys and girls greeted her on the street with real pleasure at her return. She wondered with some distaste if it could be because she had seemed to "fit in" by accepting Swede Mongsen.

The year changed her a little. It was an uneventful year, because she had become used to the routine, to the people, to what Laurence Henderson expected of his teachers. She learned how to do almost anything she cared to without incurring the enmity of the townspeople.

She began to like Creston, to defend it in letters to her friends who wondered how she managed to stay there. They suspected, they wrote, that she might be in love. She answered them defiantly that such a thing wasn't, after all, an impossibility.

The end of that school year found her signing a contract once more; a third year in Creston. After that, of course, she could leave. But they had offered her four hundred more, and given her work that she enjoyed: the music and the coaching of the school plays.

11

For Etta it was one of those years which people ofttimes elect to use as a marker. That year George Dant built a new house on the site of the one Frank Dyer had leased. It was a time of excitement for Etta. The place was not begun until she started to school, and the construction was slow. Materials had to be hauled over the muddy road from town, and the periods during which Dant could hire good carpenters were intermittent. The building of the house stretched, for Etta, delightfully throughout the school year. Once or twice a week, after school, she would get out to see the progress made. In being the daughter of a man who was building a new house there was something that gave you a subtle prestige.

Sometimes her father would drive her and her mother out to see it, to display proudly where the bathroom would be, or to ask advice about some mooted question of arrangement. Mrs. Dant and Etta never decided at once. They took the problem home with them, mulled over it like two kittens over a catnip ball. They wouldn't see the building of another house, probably, that would mean anything to them.

That time began to be referred to by them, as "the year we built our house." Things happened before or after that time. It was the Before Christ and the Anno Domini of the Dants.

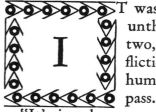T was, George Dant told his daughter, unthinkable. Besides, in a month or two, this childish affection—he said affliction, without being aware of any humour—for the Fraser boy would pass.

"It's just because you don't like him," Etta said.

He didn't like him. It was a fact of which he hadn't been sure until Etta stated it. And Dant did not know that a father cannot like any man who tries to take away a daughter before she is old enough to become a commonplace in the household.

But he said: "It ain't that. Jay Fraser's got a fine boy there." He stopped uncertainly. "A fine boy. But neither you nor him are old enough to be married."

"We're as old as you and mother were when you got married."

"Things was different. I'd been workin' a long time before I got married."

"Charlie's worked. He's going to rent a place. He's going to rent his father's place on Little Dry Creek."

The though seemed to strike Dant as funny. He maddened Etta by laughing. "Rent his father's place!"

Etta was not struck with the incongruity of it.

"You'll see!" she said.

Dant darkened. "I'll see nothing, young lady. As long as you're under this roof you'll respect your mother. I've done everything I could for you and this is the thanks I get."

It was an old trick. The sharper than a serpent's tooth trick, and it did not fail. A sudden surge of pity swept over Etta.

"It's not that I don't appreciate it. It's not that."

"I built this house for us. I got you the Ford to go back and forth to school."

It was all true. It was all so dishearteningly true to Etta. With no more words within her, she started to leave the room.

"I got to help Mam with the dishes."

Mrs. Dant had been listening carefully from the kitchen. The dishes were washed, stacked neatly on the drainboard for the hot water that Etta poured over them.

"You can dry them now. Don't forget to hang up the tea-towel." She wiped her hands on her apron, blowing a wisp of hair up from off her forehead. She placed the apron behind the door and as she went out she was careful that the door swung back, shut.

She found her husband behind his paper, unperturbed by the recent interview with Etta. Mrs. Dant held her hand tentatively over the hot-air register of the furnace.

"It's getting cold in here, don't you think?"

"I'll go down in a minute and look at the fire," George said. He turned the sheets of the paper with embarrassed care, sensing that his wife wanted to talk to him about Etta and Charlie. She stayed in the room, fussed with things in the room.

"I'll go down and see about the furnace," he said.

In a moment she was down the stairway behind him.

"This afternoon that light wouldn't go on. I couldn't find out what was the matter with it."

"It goes on all right now. Sometimes the lights're turned off in the afternoons. Sumphn wrong with the power plant at Walla Walla."

"I know . . . It's every time I want to iron."

He clanged the furnace door needlessly with the tip of the shovel.

"George, I don't think you ought to say anything to Etta about marrying Charlie Fraser."

"I don't talk to her. She talks to me. The sooner she forgets about it, the better."

"You asked her about it tonight."

"They were talkin' about it down to the pool hall. Gregson wanted to know when Etta was to be married. That dam' fool Charlie has been tellin' everybody he's goin' to marry Etta."

"Charlie's nice, though."

"I don't care whether he's nice or not. It's foolishness. She's a kid. She don't know what she wants. You got to expect things like this. You got to head 'em off."

"Just the same, I don't think you ought to be talkin' to her about it, do you?"

"I wasn't, I told you. The sooner she forgets about it, the better."

"I mean if you keep crossin' her you can't tell what she'll do. She might run off with him and get married."

"If she does that there's nothin' we can do anyhow. If she'd do anything like that I wouldn't have nothin' more to do with it."

"Charlie's nice in lots of ways. He's got nice manners. I think he's all right, don't you?"

"All right? . . ." Dant looked at her, and then turned his head. "Yeah, I guess he is. I guess he's all right."

94

"I don't see what's to prevent them plannin' on it . . ."

"Hell, do you *want* her to get married? What's the idea of rushin' the thing. She's only a kid."

"Of course I don't want her to. Not right now. But I don't know whether it's quite right to try and break them up. They might stop, anyhow. If they don't stop maybe we hadn't ought to try and break them up."

Dant examined the furnace gauge.

"This seems to be usin' a lot of coal for the time we use it."

"The days have been pretty cold, though. Lately it's been real cold and we've had a fire most all the time."

"Yeah. It's been colder. I guess it's all right. Beats a stove." He went over to the basement light. "You go on upstairs and I'll switch the light. Should 'a' had a button at the top of them stairs."

Etta, drying dishes in the kitchen, could hear their low mumbles below her. She knew that they were discussing her and it somehow made her sad. They seemed so futile, so pitiful, these two old persons down there worrying over her and Charlie. It was too bad that people worried over their children, that children meant so much to them. It made it hard for everyone, Etta saw clearly. She and Charlie would be all right; they would get along. It would be too bad to have to hurt them, but it was such a certainty that she and Charlie would be secure.

She heard them come up from their plotting, and when Mrs. Dant came into the kitchen her glance looked guilty as it met Etta's.

Without knowing why, in some quick move of com-

95

passion, Etta came to her and threw her arms around her.

"I love you, Mam, dear . . ." Tears stood in her eyes. She expected her mother to cry, too. But Mrs. Dant seemed oddly unmoved.

"I know you do, Etta. I know you do, child."

But the demonstration helped them both. Etta went into the room to heal what wounds she might have made on her father.

"Do you want your pipe, Dad?"

"Mhm . . . I might take it."

She crammed the moist tobacco into it, carefully trimmed away the shreds. As he held it in his teeth she applied the match while he drew the fire into the softly crinkling weed.

"Thanks, Etta."

She knew that he had accepted peace with as much demonstration as was ever his.

At that moment it seemed to Etta that these two meant so much more to her than this stranger whom she professed to love, with whom she had planned a meeting tonight. This house meant so much more to her than anything. Even the simple act of lighting her father's pipe was a gesture fraught with some meaning she didn't understand but which filled her, for the moment, wholly and completely.

The thought of Charlie Fraser waiting for her, Charlie with his hands thrust into his pockets, leaning against that tree, suddenly became repulsive to her. Charlie with his kisses, Charlie with his hands that were forever roaming about over her. She became swiftly ashamed, here under the roof of her father and mother.

Charlie, waiting out under the night for Etta who

was to have come down the road to see him for a little while, had no power to reach into that house, that room. There was something more there between him and Etta than a wall. As he stood there, not quite warm, it became obvious to him that she was not coming tonight. He kept assuring himself of the fact with something akin to pleasure. She wouldn't be here—and she had promised to be here. Tomorrow he would upbraid her for that. He would bring her to tears, because he had found that he could do that and it gave him an odd sense of power. She would be sorry she had not come; he would not believe the excuses she made. It would be true, what she told him. She wouldn't lie to him. But he would pretend not to believe it and he would make her faintly miserable.

His teeth clamped together in a sadistic joy. He was somehow more happy than if she had come. His desire for her had diverted itself into a cruel, martyr-like anger.

I I

Etta did not remember when she began to love Charlie Fraser. It seemed that she had always felt toward him just as she felt now. She did not remember that once she had not liked him at all, that he had seemed to her almost negative. Had she remembered this, she would not have known—or cared—that it might have been because of an adolescent hatred toward all boys who attracted her when she was afraid of being attracted. What she did remember was that once, after Jerry Fleeter's meeting when Peg had gone to the platform, Charlie had come home with her and tried to kiss her.

97

With that misty brush put into the hands of all women in love Etta had dimmed over the recollection of that first encounter into something wonderful and strange. She really believed that on that night she had first known the sweet power of Charlie toward her. She was not even certain, after a while, but that he had really kissed her there on the porch. Soon she was sure that he had, and that she had gone into the house transfigured into the being she now was.

There was another time that she remembered, one she wouldn't quite forget ever. The hot press of the dance hall at Athena. The rhythmic fox trot that beat into her body and raced her pulse with its own hectic time. Dancing with Charlie, dancing with someone else, dancing again with Charlie. Hot. The smells of her own body coming to her, making her afraid that someone else would detect them. Asking Charlie if he didn't want some fresh air. Walking along the board walk at the side of the dance hall, the little groups of men meaning nothing, the loud women meaning nothing. Red lips, parted like a bloody gash, meaning nothing. The music growing softer as they walked away from it; the board walk seeming to dissolve into a path with weeds that brushed her legs. Charlie's arm around her waist, low around her waist. Charlie's hand against her hip. Charlie holding her to him, different from what he had been before. She was different, too, somehow. The music further away and softer.

She remembered that. She remembered the silver thin serpent that had gone through her when Charlie kissed her that night. Something new. Something to live for, and anticipate. Something to dread growing old about.

It had been new for Charlie, too; it had been wonderful for him. They had stumbled, half-heartedly, onto a thing which is so secret and yet so common. It awed them. When they were alone they wondered about it. It seemed odd that the two of them had it within them to find more delight than an outside world could dream of.

They were afraid of it. Sometimes it seemed too big for them, too full of a meaning which they could translate into neither words nor actions. Yet, being young, they dared to play with it. They dared to taunt it.

Etta would think: "It cannot happen twice. When I kiss him now, when he holds me now, I will feel nothing but his lips, his arms around me."

But it would come again, sometimes with an added intensity that would surely, Etta thought, burn out and die forever.

Each knew to what it led. Each anticipated that time when it would overwhelm them both, take them into that inner shrine of Astarte and Aphrodite of which they had not heard except in terms quite far removed from any mythology. It was this that keened the edge of every new meeting. But time after time they parted again without knowing, unfulfilled and wanting each other beyond all things.

Presently there grew up around them a hallowed aura of safety. They began to think of marriage, of a distant horizon beyond which was the solution of the heartaches, the longings, that they felt. Something frugal in each of them made them want to save that moment until a later time. It was not morality. It was not religion. It was a combination of fear and sentiment which had been ingrained into them down through the years.

Charlie graduated that Spring. On a hot May night he sat on the platform of the high school auditorium; he felt very self conscious and very red. He was careful to maintain what he hoped was passing for an expression of utter boredom.

His shoes were painfully new, gloriously polished, and his dark suit, with that crease and shapeliness which only suits worn for the first time possess, had been bought at one of Mr. Penney's stores the day before. He felt that he was nicely turned out. He should have been: never at another time in his life had he been so careful about putting clothes upon himself.

All day long Etta had driven him around town in the old Ford her father had given her. She had conducted him personally to Athena, three miles away, where he had obtained the shoes which were that particular yellow tan he craved and were wide enough for the comfort he insisted should be an integral part of footwear. She had chosen the tie he wore. He was not taken with that tie, but he had consoled himself with the thought that women were supposed to have taste in such things.

As he sat there in the first row of the graduating class he felt that he was very complete, spiritually, mentally, materially. He was nineteen and not until he was twenty-five would he ever feel that old again. He had completed the four year course in three years by a special arrangement which an agriculturally inclined school board had provided for the sons of farmers who did not desire to linger too long in the paths of learning. He had had two or three "affairs" which had gone what he might have characterized as the limit, had been quite drunk on several auspicious occasions. Once, in Pendleton, he had, with two or three other drunken rowdies, prowled through an upstairs rooming house in search of women. Now Charlie was complete: he was in love and intending to be married.

He found it difficult to be sitting upon the platform. If you looked at your hands people might believe you to be embarrassed. If you looked at the rows of footlights you squinted. If you looked out into the auditorium you looked into a sea of vague faces, toward the back rows, which dissolved into blackness. But presently Charlie found that one might turn one's attention to the speaker. This, he discovered, gave a point of focus and a gaze of listening intelligence.

The speaker was a robust, white haired old man who had come down from Whitman College, in Walla Walla, to deliver a word of encouragement and praise for twenty-five dollars and his gasoline. Professor Enidcott found it profitable to supplement his last term teaching of Biblical Literature with a few high school graduation addresses. He discovered, because of his tendency to deliver "a wholesome message," that he was much in demand by the small preparatory schools of the towns clustered around Walla Walla.

Charlie fastened his gaze on Professor Enidcott and was soon fascinated by the profundity of the man's words, with the ease with which he poured them forth.

" . . . just as God, on the first day, divided the light from the darkness, so these young people here before you have taken as their first step the dividing of the light from the darkness. Knowledge is light. Ignorance is darkness . . ."

Laurence Henderson, the principal, beamed his approval of the learned professor's dictum. The ten boys and twelve girls, ranged in order behind the speaker, sat with their eyes in an hypnotic gaze, thinking of nothing.

Professor Enidcott was meandering a bit. He occasionally was called upon to fill a pulpit: "They have opened their minds to knowledge of literature, of science, but I hope, people of Creston, that they have not forgotten to open their hearts—to open their hearts to that Eternal Knowledge which is God. I am sure that Professor Henderson here has not left out of his admirable curriculum that most important part of education, the Holy Bible . . ."

Laurence Henderson felt vaguely uncomfortable. He mentally defied Professor Enidcott to find a place for Bible teaching in the schedule of English, Physics, Economics, Woodworking, and the countless other summarily taught subjects of the high school.

The time given to the main address was to have been an hour; but Professor Enidcott felt that it was better to speak a bit longer so that the school board would not think him too slight in his preparation. When he finally ended his twenty-five dollars worth of higher learning, with raised voice and uplifted hand, he had the audience completely beaten, tired and limp.

As he took his chair amid the applause which burst dutifully from the crowd, the twenty-two graduates sat straighter and looked with expectant eyes at Charles Tipp. Tipp, as editor of the *Leader*, had always been ideal to act as the distributor of the diplomas. He was pompous, had a deep-booming voice. He was proud of his profession, connected it with education in some

102

measure. The *Leader* made money: country people bought radios, cars, the newest canned edibles. Women wanted the new styles. The *Leader* now carried the advertisements of Henry Ford, General Electric, and Realsilk Hosiery, where once Tipp had oozed out more profit by printing butter wrappers. Tipp reflected his new glory—and he distributed diplomas as if they were largesse.

Charlie heard him but once, however. It was when he was awarded his own certificate of graduation. "And now I wish to present a special honor award, together with his diploma, to Charles MacMillan Fraser who has completed the course of Creston High School, with—ah—exceptional grades, in three years instead of the usual four."

When Charlie had taken the diploma with a moist hand, he heard Tipp's stereotyped: "I wish you success, young man."

The words meant nothing. No one even stopped to reflect whether they contained significance. What was the measure of success or failure in the business of tilling the soil? You went out and worked, and the sun and the rain and God Almighty made your work a success or a failure. This education, this graduation amid a blaze of auditorium lights, was a sort of youthful gesture, a concession to the platitude that "you never got anywhere nowadays unless you had some schooling." Every girl and boy there had heard from elders that, had schooling been possible, things would have been different. What did they mean by "different"? Was this to change them, this roll of heavy paper in their hands?

The twelve girls there, consciously or unconsciously, had marriage as their goal. If it were slow in coming, they would go to the Oregon Normal School, or to business college in Pendleton. Only one of the boys had college as his goal. To him, college seemed the password to the world, a bright secret word that beckoned him to something greater.

Lester Adams was one of the increasing number of young men who would go to college when they have no business going to college. He had once lived in Eugene, the locale of the University. He had gone to grammar school there, seen the huge buildings of the campus, watched the men and women who belonged there. He had walked alone at night down the dim street where the fraternities and sororities were built. He had seen cigarettes burning pinkly on the porches, heard the strange jargon, the carefree swearing. He had been stirred even then—not sexually, but with a sort of romantic, adventurous excitement—at the gaiety of the co-eds, at their fluttering about in bright coloured things.

With these images, strengthened later by stories of wild youth in the magazines, Lester Adams had moved away from Eugene into Creston. Eugene was west—near Oregon's metropolis of Portland. Creston was east, near no metropolis at all. Lester had carried with him into Creston an unpopular touch of urbanity.

He didn't forget the idea of going to college. He had decided firmly that he would not graduate from high school to work with the wheat, sweat with the lifting of sacks and be concerned with the health of mares. He would, he decided, be a pharmacist, own a drug store, and—finally—direct a chain of them in a dozen cities. He had startled Florence Larson by telling her of this ambition. She had been so astonished at this dream, intact and glittering within the environs of Creston, that she had pledged him to secrecy and promised that she would recommend him to what deans she knew at the University. She might, she said, give him a letter of introduction to an active Kappa Sigma whom she knew. She couldn't promise him that they would take him, of course, but no doubt there would be other fraternities interested, too.

Lester sat next to Charlie Fraser quite conscious of his superiority to him, to all of them. When he had taken his diploma from the hands of Tipp he leaned toward Charlie and whispered, "Well, what's the program for next year, old boy?"

"*Next* year?" There was tomorrow and tomorrow and tomorrow.

"Sure. I'm going to the 'U.' I'll work in the summers to carry me through. I'm goin' to pledge Kappa Sig."

Charlie was dimly aware of the University. He had not heard of Kappa Sig, but he was astute enough to gather that it must be a sort of lodge.

I V

They sped down the dark rutted road in Etta's decrepit machine, Charlie driving with a recklessness born of his graduation from the cares of high school. In the rear seat Peg Nettleship snuggled against Lester Adams who patted her shoulder with a combination of affection and patronage.

Etta turned in the seat. "I had an awful time getting Dad to let me stay all night at your place, Peg. Do you think he'd call up your house to see if we were in early?"

"I don't think he would . . . Do you think he would?"

"He never has. Maybe we ought to get in by twelve."

"Twelve!" Lester was gently contemptuous. "Twelve o'clock on a night like this? We've got to celebrate tonight, haven't we, Charlie?"

"Sure have." Charlie sidled the Ford into a convenient pair of ruts and let the wheel loose in his hands. The car swung along crazily, steering itself like a vehicle running on a track.

"Let's go to Pendleton. A bunch of the kids are goin' there to a dance tonight."

"Sure, let's go to Pendleton."

"It's after ten now."

"Aw . . . we can get there a little after eleven. That'll give us an hour to dance in."

Etta was doubtful. She sought Peg's advice. "Do you think we should?"

"Sure. Let's do. We'll come home right after the dance. We can get home by one o'clock, can't we, Charlie?"

Charlie, secure at the driver's position, was sure of it. He turned off the road, backed the car around with a buzzing sound of the reverse band, and headed again toward the highway.

"Pendleton or bust," he announced.

Resigned to their mission, the four of them caught up the spirit of the trip. Adventure beckoned, the only adventure that they knew. They had been to Pendleton many times, each of them, driven over the twenty or so miles more than once. But tonight they were going there when they had not intended to go there.

Peg was tense against the back cushion, against Lester Adams. "Gee! I do want to dance tonight! . . . *Oh, whaddleIdo on a doo-doo-dooey day. . . .*"

Lester pressed back her head with his lips; with his lips closed pressed against her mouth. When she was quiet in his arms he whispered to her: "I want to dance, too." Between them there was something quickly and intangibly potent.

Inadvertently Etta looked into the back of the car and saw the pantomime. She turned to Charlie with a giggle. "Guess I better keep my eyes on the road," she informed him loudly.

Charlie, associating ideas, drew Etta to him. She placed her head on his shoulders, was lulled almost to sleep by the monotony of the black asphalt, by the humming of the engine cylinders.

They fled from Creston, down the valley of wheat that took them into Athena at its end. The neighboring little town winked its lights wakefully, and a few rowdies on the corner yelled at the passing car.

The smooth road followed the old river bed, dived down breathlessly into hollows that were cool with the night wind. Etta shivered and involuntarily drew closer to Charlie. In the rear seat Peg and Lester were quiet, each surrendering to the peace of the moment. Through Acme—the Acme that had once been the scene of bad men's battles; men with two guns and nasty tongues. Men whose cattle had roamed the place where wheat grew now, and men who had stolen those cattle and been hanged for it. It was an oddly dilapidated little place. All the buildings on one side of the street had been razed or abandoned, and those on the other side were badly kept. There was a school, shining and new, and an old post office, hardware and grocery store.

"God, this place is dead," Charlie told them. "Gets worse every year."

"Creston'll be like it soon," Etta told him, not believing it.

Lester roused himself from amorous lethargy. "That's no foolin'," he said. "It won't be long now until there aren't any more small towns around here."

Peg was scornful. "Oh, chase yourself!"

"That's a fact," he persisted. "You'll see. These paved roads have spoiled the small town. People can get to Portland in a day. They can get to Walla Walla or Pendleton in an hour. It used to take 'em two days by hack to get all their shoppin' done and everything."

"Suppose they can," Peg shot out loyally. "Creston's been goin' longer than you have, Brightness. It'll be there a long while yet."

"Don't you think it. These bigger places will—they'll *absorb* the smaller ones. They'll absorb them. Some day Portland will take in all of them—or Seattle or Spokane. That's when the airplane gets perfected."

"Ain't he smart?" Peg wanted to know. "He's just graduated and he knows everything."

"Just the same, that's a fact. You'll see."

"It's just like fish," Charlie explained with an attempt at humour. "The big ones eat the little ones and then the bigger ones eat *them*."

Etta was complacent. "Oh, well. Creston'll be there long enough for me, anyway . . . Let's talk about something *in*teresting."   . . . .

Lester's try at prophecy seemed to depress them all

108

and they were silent for the remainder of the journey. Not until they crossed the railroad tracks which marked the north city limits of Pendleton did they brighten.

They passed the Catholic hospital where the Klan had made a forced search for arms, the huge woolen mill where the Pendleton blankets were made, and came eventually into the main street. It was fairly quiet. Two or three Saturday night · orchestras, playing in their respective upstairs halls, blared mingled jazz into the air. Respectable Pendleton had gotten in off the streets. Youth for miles around had come into the place to dance, to eat at the all night restaurants, to worry through the murky halls of dubious rooming houses, or stagger up and down the street with half pretended moonshine drunkenness.

Pendleton was open, a vestige of another day. There were no cowpunchers now. No soft shod Indians. The cool-eyed young man with the round sombrero and the hasty trigger-finger had been transformed, by the alchemy of progress, into the tight-coated clerk or farmer boy who raised hell with himself rather than with someone else.

Once a year, at Round-Up time, Pendleton dressed up for the effete East in the garb of yesterday. Bronchos were "busted," steers were bulldogged, and vain and harmless Indians went on parade in full regalia of war. The streets were crowded with citizens who wore (by order of the Chamber of Commerce) coloured shirts and wide ten-gallon hats. At night there was the celebration at Happy Canyon that differed from the old forty-nine dance-hall brawls only in point of date. Prostitutes oozed about with freedom, gay ladies from Seattle, Portland, Walla Walla, on their "vacations."

The Round-Up lasted four days a year and it placed Pendleton on the map. But the town was never able, throughout the remaining three hundred and sixty-one, to shake off the laxity of morals which those four days bred. In fact, people weren't unproud of their viewpoint. "Pendleton people are different from Walla Walla people," they would say. "They're more broadminded. They're a different sort altogether."

Walla Walla, Pendleton's rival over the line into Washington, admitted the difference. It had once been as wild as the Oregon town, but a college had sobered it. There grew up around the college and its faculty a set of intellectually élite. They formed clubs, read papers, brought in concerts, and critized books. Being a bit more prosperous than most of Pendleton, Walla Walla had sent some of its children away to gain a cultural sheen. Many of these had returned to spread it with broad and inaccurate brushes. Walla Walla was the West trying to behave itself and become cosmopolitan. It wore a Prince Albert and pinched shoes, but it still secreted a cud of tobacco in its cheek; the geographical Jiggs of the Northwest. Pendleton was the West with its coat off and its stockinged feet on the table. It still didn't give a damn. . . .

Charlie drove the car along the side of the curb near the entrance to one of the dance-halls. "They got the best music here. If it's too crowded we can try the Union."

As they climbed from the car he whispered to Etta: "As soon as they get to dancing let's us go for a ride."

Etta touched his hand in assent as they climbed the long narrow stairway to the dance floor above. Since they had fallen in love, they had stopped caring about dancing. Not being æsthetic, the rhythm, the joy of movement, meant little. It had been purely a sexual stimulation, and, when their emotions had finally been focused, they lost interest in dancing as a pleasurable pursuit.

Not glancing at the sign above them which warned against the entrance of minors, Etta and Peg, bravely rouged, sophisticate and smug, sauntered with the two boys into the crowded hall. Here and there Peg saw a face she knew, and she waved and smiled, tentative gestures that might bring her dances. But to Etta most of the people were wholly unfamiliar. She had been to a Pendleton dance but once and had not returned home until two in the morning. She would not forget George Dant's fierce anger, his hurt pride, as he was prevented from striking her by her mother.

She and Charlie danced once around the floor, lost Peg and Lester completely in the maze of dark suits and gaudy dresses. Etta—dizzy from an impression of gangling silken legs and flapping trousers over patent leather shoes—returned into the street with Charlie.

They got into the car with the breathlessness, the hush, that lately preceded all of their secret trysts. Over their recent meetings had been a portent of something insanely strange. They were both silent as the car was guided by Charlie down the street and out into the highway that led to Portland. He followed the macadam pavement for a distance and turned into a dirt road, less frequented.

"Why'd you turn?"

"You know why. I want to be alone with you."

"I like the paved road. It's nice, riding along with the moon."

111

Riding with the moon! Her ecstasy was taking her to heights that she didn't really know, bringing her to thoughts that were beyond her.

They encountered several cars, dejectedly parked by the roadside, cars which winked on their lights like lazy animals roused from sleep, to peer into the night. These cars embarrassed Etta and Charlie. They could only guess what went on in them. They were a burlesque, a profaning, of their own actions. Charlie increased the speed of the car, driving farther into solitude.

He switched off the lights and the bright clear rays of the moon bathed the road in such a silver that they could easily see around them. The bare hills—fallow ground in the night—that stretched out beyond the barbed wire fence on either side were tinted in the moonlight like the underside of a poplar's leaf.

The car stopped, jerked impotently without power against the wheels that Charlie had steered into the roadside. In one swift glance the two sought each other, locked themselves as if forever into a fierce embrace. They said nothing. They knew that everything they could say would sound crass and loud and unbeautiful. They knew that their voices would be too husky, that their lips would find no adequate words.

They became one with any pair of lovers ever in the world at any time. There was no one to say that Etta and Charlie, in their moment, were less crowned with glory than Adonis and Aphrodite, than Tammuz and Ishtar, than Isis and Osiris. Neither had heard of these, neither cared about them. But there was perfume in Etta's hair, there was a soft hurt to the roundness of her breasts; there were all these things that Charlie knew and did not know.

What they feared, what they had always dreaded and wanted and fought against, crashed down around them; and afterward they felt beaten and disappointed and sad. Etta could not remember it distinctly, though she tried. But they both felt cheated. They had been somehow fooled and they were vaguely piqued. Yet between them, even as they drove back to Lester and Peg that night, there was a new tenderness, a different love.

They found Adams and Peg standing on the curb impatiently. The dance-hall was dark. As Charlie drove to them he saw the members of the orchestra, in limp Tuxedos and soft shirts, emerging from the entrance way carrying their instruments.

"It's twelve-thirty," Peg said icily. "It's a wonder you wouldn't tell us you're leaving instead of sneaking off." She swung into the car with a flirt of skirts. "We been waiting half an hour."

Lester and Peg thoroughly disgruntled, Charlie and Etta awed with their own lives, the four headed for home. Peg and Lester sat sleepily against each other in the rear seat, and Etta—her throat beginning to get raw in the early morning air—huddled close beside Charlie.

As they came down the hill into Creston the town was wholly deserted, the score of street lights dimly displaying the buildings it had to offer. They went through it slowly, unconsciously fearful of disturbing the quiet, and then gathered speed as they took the road to the Nettleship farm.

"Stop the car a little ways from the house," Peg directed. "The folks won't wake up. They sleep on the other side of the house." By the light of a match she looked at her wrist watch. "God," she said impassionately. "It's one-thirty."

113

There were hurried kisses at the running board of Etta's car, and the two girls disappeared toward the house.

v

It was the next morning—or rather later that same morning—that fright suddenly took Charlie and Etta. He drove her Ford back to the Nettleship place to take her home after staying the night with Peg. There was something uncompromising about the morning; it seemed irresolute about Spring, half determined to turn back into the icy arms of Winter again.

Nothing had seemed real the night before, but it was all real now. They were frightened, and they knew that they must be careful, tread carefully, or they would begin to hate each other.

"We better get married," Charlie said. "We should 'a' got married before this, anyhow."

"I told you I couldn't. Dad won't stand for it until I get through school."

"Well, we'd better. We better not wait. If we get married now and something happens nobody'd think anything about it. You know how it would be if we waited and then got married."

"I don't like it, Charlie. I don't like gettin' married like that. Seems like we ought to wait either way."

"What are you going to *do*, then? Just sit around and wait?" He was irritated, nervous from want of sleep and from worry that had begun to work shortly after he and Lester Adams had left Peg's. "You can't sit around and wait."

Etta felt badgered, ready to cry, to scream, to kill

114

herself—to kill herself perhaps. She played with the melodramatic thought for a fantastic moment. "Oh—Charlie, I don't *know!* . . ."

They waited two terrible weeks and when nature had given them first warning they went miserably to Pendleton with Lester and Peg as witnesses, and were married. It was difficult to keep a brave front to Peg and Lester, to make those two believe that it was a lark to be running away and getting married just because you were in love.

They returned to Creston that same afternoon and went into the house for which Charlie had arranged, the old Hilliard place which belonged to his father.

"Tonight," Peg told them gleefully, "you'll have a shivaree."

Etta started. She didn't want any charivari. She'd seen them, been a party to them. A group of the boys and girls always waited until late, until the bride and groom had retired in sheer desperation. Then came the "shivaree"—a yelling bunch of hoodlums beating tin cans and stamping upon the porch. There was never anything to do but let them in. They sat around and made bad jokes about leaving the couple alone now. Finally the groom would pass cigars to help get rid of the crowd, and the bride would pass oranges and candy.

Etta had always thought that charivaris were fun, and she suddenly realized that they could be a horrid waking nightmare.

But that afternoon they were left to themselves. When Peg and Lester had departed, they were left alone in the old house. It seemed too big for them; it did not have quite enough furniture in it. There were empty rooms upstairs, rooms in which children had slept. Chil-

115

dren that had grown and been buried within recent years, been buried with long beards, with gray hair. There were too many empty rooms, even downstairs, so that the whole place seemed cold. It had a vague odour of other families, other years. You would have thought that it was morning, because the house had that hushed, finger-to-its-mouth air that houses have when people in it are asleep.

"I got to tell the folks," Etta kept saying. "I got to tell the folks, Charlie. I think if I could get that off my mind I'd be happy."

She wasn't happy and this fact startled her. After you married the man you loved you were supposed to be happy.

But Charlie had begun to feel lighter as soon as they had crossed the threshold into his new kingdom. "Call 'em up and tell them. I'll bet they won't be mad. Honest they won't. It's just sort of the *idea* of the thing that they don't like."

Urged by Charlie, and by an impulse to get it over with, she went to the telephone on the wall. "Is it two or three rings for central here?" There was an interminable wait. Her mother wasn't home. She began to hope that her mother wasn't home——

"Mother? . . . Mother, please don't be mad and please don't let Papa be mad. Charlie and I—we got married at Pendleton this morning."

Her husband stood by the telephone trying to read her face. He had a sudden fear that Mrs. Dant must be saying a great deal. After a long time Etta hung the receiver and sat down in the nearest rocker. Somehow he knew enough not to touch her, not to say anything to her. He wondered what Mrs. Dant had said.

She had said nothing for a moment; and then only this: "Oh, Etta—Etta, you child, you child . . ." Nothing more than that, except a faint sigh as Etta heard the receiver click distantly.

Etta sprang from the rocker and sank at Charlie's feet. "Oh, Charlie, please love me! Please keep me and love me always, Charlie. Now there ain't anyone but you. I've not anyone but you now, I know."

She clung desperately to his legs, pressed her cheeks against the hard cloth of his trousers, a gesture that was half within her, half learned from movies she had seen. He stood uncertainly above her, not knowing what to do. He had a desire to laugh at her and he was astonished to find his eyelids burning with quick tears.

V I

Florence Larson wrote friends that she was staying on in Creston for a week or two after the dismissal of school "to get things together." The vague phrase was ostensibly true, since she wasn't to come back there again. Yet there was a part of her that told her she need not stay that long. And there was a part of her that kept asking if it wouldn't be as well to sign a contract for another year under Laurence Henderson, now that she was acquainted and could get along. It would be much nicer, much easier than beginning in a new place.

At first she had thought to teach there a year, long enough to pay some of her college debts and get started in some undertaking of her own. She had thought of a small bookshop in Portland, or an antique store, or of going in for interior decorating. Anything that pretended to culture with no necessity of a background. At moments during her stay in Creston she had wondered what had swerved her from those paths so long. For three years now she had been teaching there; and she couldn't feel rightfully that she had done any good to anyone, least of all herself.

She hadn't, she felt with a tinge of conscience, been able to inspire any of her pupils. At first she had had an earnest desire to liberate some of the boys and girls from their surroundings, to make them yearn for dreams so that never again would they be satisfied with Creston—or happy in it. She had eventually abandoned this idea for two reasons: one was that she found it quite impossible; the other was that she decided it wasn't the right thing to do. She used the latter reason because it consoled her and made her feel somewhat omnipotent.

On the day that Etta and Charlie were married she met Swede Mongsen on the street. She hadn't seen him for a long time, had avoided him. She had often experienced periods when she would fight against seeing him. But loneliness and Swede's ingratiating good will always broke them down.

He always pretended to have forgotten the night of the country dance and Florence hated him for pretending that. She wanted him to presume upon her because of that occasion so that she could ignore him for it, tell him that it did not matter. That there was no reason he should feel too familiar toward her. Instead, though, Swede was damnably, studiously chivalrous and careful.

He met her on the street and told her of Etta and Charlie.

"They're at the old Hilliard house and a bunch are

goin' over tonight to shivaree 'em. Better come along."

"Those children!" she said. "Married?"

"It's a fact. They beat it off to Pendleton and did the deed. Don't it make you feel old and bent?"

Florence laughed. She felt anything but old at the news. She felt ageless and superior as she looked at Swede Mongsen.

"The poor kids," she said. "What will they ever do?"

"Do?" He looked at her aghast. "Why Charlie's got his old man's upper forty—the old Hilliard place. He's a good worker."

"And Etta—is Etta a good worker, too?"

Swede looked at her stupidly. She had not been like this since those first days in Creston.

"Why, I guess so—yes. I guess she is. What's a matter with the old spirit today, anyhow?"

"Nothing's the matter with it, Swede. It's—it's better than it's been for a long time."

"You'll hop over to the shivaree with me?"

"No. No, I'm leaving tonight for Portland."

"Why, I thought you were going to stay until the end of the week."

"I'm not, though. I have to leave tonight."

"If you got to go can I help or anything?"

"Everything's ready. I ought to say good-bye to you now because I mightn't see you again. And wish Charlie and Etta happiness for me, will you?"

"Why, sure—but . . ."

They shook hands wordlessly, and then Swede muttered the conventional farewells. He did not know this woman. This was a stranger to Swede Mongsen, this was an alien to Creston.

119

She walked on down the street to the Terminal Confectionery and from Fanny Brest bought a stage ticket to Pendleton.

That night at the Pendleton depot, while she waited for the Portland train, she wrote three or four hasty letters using her bag for a desk. One was to Swede Mongsen, and she did not mail it with the others. She took it to the Pullman with her and read it later as she lay in her berth. Then she tore it carefully and dropped it into the little hammock stretched across the windows. Parts of it sifted through like snow onto the covers.

Florence Larson cried herself to sleep that night, and her arms ached with loneliness. Yet she awakened the next morning, saw the shredded letter clinging to the hammock, and was not moved to anything but wonder that she could have written it. From the window she could see the green firs of Western Oregon, the sheer high rocks of the Columbia's channel. There was something different about the scenes flitting by that made her feel fit. There was something different about them from the dull rolling hills of wheat.

Creston's scenery is sterile, she thought. And then: it is like a lone naked woman, all desirous curves, lying in the sun.

As she stepped from the vestibule of the car to the boards of the track and heard Portland's dim rumblings coming down past the tower of the Union station she knew that never again would she be a part of Creston.

VII

When the last of the raucous crowd had gone, Etta and Charlie stood irresolutely behind the closed door,

120

listening to the faint sounds of the "shivaree's" departure.

Charlie seemed angry.

"What'd you get up and leave the room for? Leave them all sittin' in here?"

Etta, with Charlie's overcoat wrapped around her slight form, stood shivering in the night chill of the old house.

"I don't know—I—let's don't be mad at each other tonight."

He melted then, came toward her to take her into his arms, lead her back to their bed.

"It was nice of 'em to come when we didn't have any real wedding or anything, you know. You shouldn't have just up and left like that."

She struggled against telling him what he would know.

"I—Charlie, I couldn't help it. I came right back again when I got fixed up. We—I wasn't right about it."

"You weren't right about it?"

"No." She shook her head helplessly. "I mean—we didn't need to have run away like we did and get married. I guess that it was just that I was kind of upset that made me late, or something."

121

PART TWO: IN BETWEEN TIME IS DETOUR

I

OOKING out of the kitchen window, Etta saw the cook-house being drawn up the road by two black mares. Out of the stack on its roof there poured a gray smoke as if the vehicle were propelled, in addition to its horses, by steam.

It was nothing more than a tent with sideboards set upon a wagon-bed, and inside was a wood stove and a long table with benches on either side. Hanging to the door were three tin wash pans that jangled harshly as the wagon rumbled over the rutted road.

Etta could not see through the tiny round window in the cook-house door, but she knew by the smoke that Anna was inside, already preparing for the noon meal which would be served in the field where the men were threshing. As Etta let cold water run onto her hands and into the sink she idly wished that she had the stamina of Anna. The Norwegian was so huge that she had, on her very first day of employment at young Fraser's ranch, shoved her foot through the cook-house floor. She had scraped her ankle badly and Charlie had been afraid that she would quit. But the whole thing somehow struck her as humorous; she thought it funny that a cook-house should have such a toy floor. She repaired the break with her own hammer and nails and limped about the next day, happy at her job as cook for the Fraser crew.

Even though Etta had been raised on a farm, had

125

always been cognizant of the needs of the harvesters and seen those needs allayed, she could never prepare a meal for twelve or fifteen men day after day. It still was a mystery how Anna, with five kettles and a coffee pot on the diminutive cook-house stove, could fill the long table with so many foods. And, no matter how hot the weather was, the water was always cool and the butter wouldn't be soft until it had been on the table for a time.

Etta made pies and cakes at the house and took them up through the field to supplement Anna's staple fare. At first the big Norwegian was suspicious of such fancies, and once when Etta brought a bowl of combination salad she showed her disdain with a frankness altogether alarming in a hireling. But as soon as Anna observed that the men liked such additional dishes she was quick to encourage Etta to bring them.

She had one warning. "Don't put any lettuce in a-any of those sa-alads, Mrs. Fraser. It makes-s the men sleepy and they can't do no vo-ork when they is-s sleepy." Anna realized the part she played in the business of wheat, and she turned a deaf ear to Etta's argument that one couldn't make salad without lettuce. So Etta—though she was not certain that lettuce developed any marked degree of lassitude in the human system—was wise enough not to cross Anna's order on the matter.

The jangle of the wash pans grew fainter as the cook-house, with its load of Anna and the stove, was driven by one of Charlie's men into the east field.

Now there was no sound except for the continual droning of the flies about the screened kitchen door. Etta had cut strips of newspaper into fringes and tacked

126

them above the door so that when anyone came in the flies would be brushed back. This arrangement was only partly successful, and they were continually alighting on her moist forehead when her hands were too sticky with dough to brush them away. They seemed to know that she could only attack them ineffectually with the flesh of her arm.

While she busied herself about the kitchen she began to hear the whir of the engine at the horses brought the huge combine nearer to the house. The men would have time to make one more round before dinner, she decided, and that would give her a chance to clean up things before taking the pies to Anna.

The engine's whir became more insistent, as if the machine were bearing down upon the house like some iron monster; then finally the noise lessened in volume, grew indistinct as the thresher pulled over the hill.

This was Etta's second harvest since she had been married. The first had been a nightmare of days in which she had been hounded by fears for their welfare, and the seeming hatred of George Dant toward her had made matters worse. Her mother's attitude that first Summer and Winter had been one of pity. It seemed as if Mrs. Dant felt her daughter had been frightfully hurt somehow, and she had the sorrow of pity. It was as if she felt Etta had been marked forever.

The reconciliation—like all reconciliations—had come about suddenly. It had happened as suddenly, as surprisingly, to the Dants as to the Frasers. George Dant and his wife had been driving by the farm of their son-in-law; it was one of those Sunday drives of lonely people. They had both expected that they would, as they had so often done on other Sundays, drive by it silently. But that day Mrs. Dant could no longer drive by with no word, and as she spoke she put her hand upon her husband's arm—"Let's go in and see Etta, George."

Because he had been hoping that his wife would say that, because he was hurt inside with keeping his man's pose of being hard, George had stopped the car and the two of them had astonished Charlie and Etta by ringing the doorbell.

Charlie had been embarrassed and effusive and awfully glad. And the other three had been damp about the eyes and talked with voices that hungered to be heard by certain ears again.

The visit relieved Etta more than she at first realized. Charlie had been having a rather hard time of it and she could not feel so proud and aloof from her parents as if he had been doing well. Even the fact that Charlie's father had, generously, "rented" the Hilliard place to him did not help a great deal. Even the hiring of an extra man to plow cost more money than Charlie had; and then that had been the year there was reseeding to be done, and seed wheat had been unusually high. He had borrowed at the bank, really on his father's name, and had not yet been able to pay the note.

This year, Etta felt, would bring them out. Charlie had figured it out in the little black, greasy book that he kept. He was sure at least that he could pay the interest on the note and thereby obtain an extension. By keeping back the principal from the bank he could really pay his father some rent on the Hilliard place. This was a matter of pride. Old Fraser was inclined to smile indulgently whenever his son mentioned it. He liked to be helping Charlie, liked the good-natured tyranny of having him under his thumb. But his son wanted above all things to be considered "independent."

Etta did not, actually, like the farm, and she found this odd as the realization dawned upon her. She had always lived upon one; had always considered herself a part of one. She had helped her mother do just what she herself was doing now; hurrying about the kitchen at noontimes, and at dinner; scrubbing the uncarpeted kitchen floor whose old wood took water like a sponge; washing overalls and trying every new anti-grease preparation offered for the purpose . . .

But there was a difference in doing things as a woman and doing the same things as a child. It was as if, paradoxically, childhood was a time for working and womanhood a time for playing. Etta knew in her heart what, after all, is a truth that somehow has been twisted into a lie: that a little girl can afford to be very serious about living, but that a grown-up woman must play house.

She wondered vaguely why this should be, why these things she had always done now seemed drudgery at times. But beyond that dim feeling there was no thought of rebellion. It did not occur to her that she might do anything else except what she was doing now —being Charlie's wife, having children—sometime— for Charlie and for herself. She never found occasion to imagine Charlie at any other work than farming. In fact, she considered Johnnie Webb, the bank cashier, and Mr. Jackson at the hardware store, rather silly. They always wore coats, and white collars and looked as if they thought each day was Sunday. They were so eternally the same. But there was something nice about seeing Charlie emerge from the bathroom, his face pink with a clean shave and a scrubbing. She always felt a wave of pride when he put on his good suit and his gray cap. There was an element of surprise in this weekly sartorial change of his which was a foundation of marital happiness more important than Etta knew.

She had never wanted to go to another town than Creston. She hadn't been to Portland—the mecca of most east-Oregonians in quest of diversion. Sometime, Charlie had told her, they would go. But she had been to Walla Walla and Pendleton, and to the smaller towns near Creston. Other towns always struck Etta as stuffy and uninteresting. You saw people walking down the street and meeting each other and seeming to be happy and satisfied. As you sat in the car at the curb you wondered how they *could* be so satisfied.

Following an afternoon in Pendleton Etta always was glad to be coming back home. An afternoon away from Creston made her uncomfortable. She and Peg had sometimes gone with Etta's father to Pendleton and while he was busy shopping they would go into a motion picture theatre. It was never half so nice as watching a picture inside the Memorial Hall. There you felt warm and cosy and you had a certain seat in which you felt at home and into which you always managed to put yourself.

The farm people weren't like they had been. She and Charlie weren't like George Dant and her mother had been at that age. Nor were the Dants, now, like Etta's grandmother and grandfather had been. You couldn't make fun of a farmer any more, Etta knew, because they weren't poky and behind the times.

130

Etta could have hummed the latest tune of Jew composers in New York just as quickly as any city girl. She heard them every night over the radio. And, on the average, you wouldn't find as many big motor cars in the city as you would find in one-fourth of Umatilla County. Indians from the reservation drove Cadillacs and Lincolns—and they often drove them to swift ruin. There weren't many cheap cars in Creston. Fords were used as roustabouts. The wheat growers bought fine new cars with expensive upholsterings and brilliant finishes. They drove them as Jehu drove his chariot, and through dust and mud until they were not fine any more but only huge and powerful. Farmers didn't take care of their cars. A car didn't mean anything to a farmer.

Charlie was behind the times in using twenty-seven mares and geldings to pull his combine. Clause Price had bought a tractor, and someone said that Buzz Fisk, over in Athena, was getting one this year; and was buying three new gearshift Ford trucks in which to haul wheat to the warehouse. His harvest would be completed in four days—with half as many men. No more floaters and I. W. W.'s hanging around town looking for jobs.

Clause worked his tractor night and day. It had a big searchlight and Etta found it thrilling to sit on the porch at night and watch the shaft of light move erratically in the air. Price's farm was over the hill from them; you couldn't see the tractor. You could hear it, and when it went down into a gully and then pointed its nose upward to climb out the searchlight threw a white pillar against the murky night above.

All the people near Clause Price's farm would come out onto their porches at night and watch for it. They predicted that in some years the whole night sky would be split with these shafts of light, crossing one another until they were a geometric fantasy in the sky. The stillness of the evening would be broken with the roar of oiled cylinders pounding. This noise would kill the noise the crickets made, that soothing rhythmic noise that seemed woven somehow with the purple of a late sunset. They would drown that lazy sound which telephone wires made, wires that ran from house to house on poles that staggered down the road like a single file of drunken men.

That was what people predicted. They liked to hear themselves prophesying; it made them feel reckless and daring. But most of them, in their hearts, did not believe the time would ever come. They could not vision a country infested with tractors, a country without stables. Men couldn't, as yet, imagine coming into dinner from the field with no horses to take to water. They couldn't really imagine not getting out earlier to harness horses. They didn't want to fancy a place with no horses, no smell of horses, no sound of horses. Somehow they didn't like to think of their children not knowing a butt chain—just as an old seaman would hate to think of his children not knowing a halyard.

But they didn't care to be old-fashioned either. While they resented industrialists like Clause Price and Buzz Fisk, they didn't want to appear fogyish. Yet most of them were right in their hearts about believing it would never happen. Most of them were old people, and, for them, it wouldn't ever happen.

Bareheaded, her apron sleeves rolled almost to her shoulders, Etta drove their roustabout car into Creston's main street and up to the curb of Pope's grocery store. She crossed from the right to the left side of the street, secure in the thought that she wouldn't be hit broadside by another machine. The town was lazily inactive in the glare of the afternoon sun, though the curb was lined with cars of various sorts. Etta nosed the Ford expertly between two larger cars and jumped out of the seat and onto the walk with a single, vaulting movement.

Pope's was crowded and she had to await her turn. The three clerks were nervously busy with the Saturday rush of harvest orders. With frenzied haste they checked and rechecked what went into the big paperboard boxes which they carried, filled with harvest supplies, to the waiting automobiles outside. Etta looked out of the plate glass window and saw Peg Nettleship passing by and ran out of the store to hail her.

Peg hadn't changed. That was Etta's first thought each time she saw her, and she wondered if Peg thought that she had changed since her marriage to Charlie Fraser. Peg, unmarried, still was youth—that was how Etta really felt. A little outside, a little wistful, but not wanting to change positions.

"Well! What are *you* doing in town?" Peg wanted to know. They seemed to believe they hadn't seen one another only last Saturday, and the one before that, too.

"Oh, this eating business," Etta said. "I'll sure be glad when harvest is over." That was what all the women said about harvest. But, when it was over, they weren't glad. They actually found a zest in the activity of it after the winterlocked months of the rest of the year.

"I came into town with Mam," Peg informed Etta. "She won't really trust me buyin' the supplies. Guess you're pretty expert now, being a married lady and all."

"You better not talk. I've been hearing a lot about you and Swede lately."

They both giggled, and then Etta remembered that she would be losing her turn inside the store.

"Come inside with me while I get this stuff," she waved a piece of tablet paper with a list written on it. "Then we'll talk awhile."

A clerk was finally free, and Etta took the list she had gleaned from Anna that morning. She interspersed her order to the harried boy with snatches of conversation hurled at Peg.

"Bacon. I've got to have bacon . . . Charlie and I were over to Papa's last night to hear their radio. . . ."

"About how much bacon, Mrs. Fraser?"

"Oh, I don't know. A couple of pounds, I guess. Wouldn't you think a couple of pounds would be enough? We've got eleven men."

The boy grinned. "A couple of pounds ain't very much."

"Well, make it five pounds. I can't ever tell 'till I *see* it. . . . Have you folks got a radio?"

"No. Dad says he don't like them. He says they're not perfected or something. You know how much noise they always make."

"The one the folks have got is real nice. It came in

real nice last night. We got San Francisco and Los Angeles. They had some of the swellest orchestra music. You know, dancing at the Ambassador Hotel."

"That's six pounds, Mrs. Fraser."

Somehow the order was taken, and completed. The clerk, admirably hiding his exasperation at a woman who was not Cæsar and could not do two things at once, packed the order neatly into a cardboard box and carried it to the roustabout.

With that tirelessness of farm women, Etta and Peg stood on the sidewalk and talked for half an hour. Occasionally they were joined by others who contributed their share of personal harvest woes and then walked on. Saturday afternoon . . . shopping and visiting. And they all enjoyed it thoroughly.

Peg said that Lester Adams was in town for the summer.

"They said you ought to see him. Edna Peabody was saying she saw him in town."

"All dressed up, I'll bet. Like Frank Jeffrey was when he came back from the University of Washington that time."

"That's what Edna said. But he's goin' to work for Swede."

"Well, that's pretty nice. . . . Wouldn't imagine he would, not after going to college and all."

"Edna said he took Fanny Brest out riding."

"Fanny?"

Peg nodded and they grinned at each other.

Etta said: "You told me he was going to work for Swede. I see you've got Swede's harvest crew down pretty well. Maybe you're going to cook for him."

Peg reared her head disdainfully. "Say! You don't catch me cookin' for any harvest crew!"

"You can't tell what you'll do. Honest, though, I heard you and Swede were going to be married."

"Where'd you hear it?"

"Oh, I don't know. I heard, though."

"No chance," said Peg, trying to sound unconvincing. "He still likes Miss Larson."

"Any time! He's forgot all about her. Wonder if she's teaching yet, or what she's doing."

"I don't know. She never writes to anybody, I guess. Do you think she liked Swede very much?"

Etta remembered standing in a darkened hallway, standing at the stairway with the music of Val Bark and Fanny Brest below her. "I don't know," she said. "It's kind of hard to tell. She was funny, wasn't she?"

"She was—sort of," Peg agreed.

III

Each day of the midsummer brought down more wheat. It fell before the piston-like movement of the steel blades; its stalks and its chaff were blown to the wind behind the combine; its yellow kernels were poured into sacks or into bulk-wagons that were pulled alongside the combine. A steady stream of these wagons went down to the scales of the warehouses below town. The tracks, deserted in Winter except for an occasional coal or wood car, were crowded with freights. Puffing freight engines broke the stillness in the afternoon.

Sometimes, shrilling down the road, would come the solitary yowl of the man on the wheat wagon. *Yee-ow-ee!* Like a lone coyote. Something animalistic urging up inside of him, coming out his throat as sound. *Yee-ow-ee!* And the horses would prick up their ears and quicken their pace.

Farmers turned to the wheat market section of the evening papers and wondered whether to sell or to wait. Someone got hold of a report of the Federal Trade Commission and found that out of eight and one-half cents paid by the average American family for a pound of bread the farmer received but a trifle over one cent. The baker got five cents and even the grocer got more than the farmer. They all agreed that it wasn't right, and they were glad to find that the report was to be placed before the Senate. They were only vaguely aware of what this might entail in the matter of results. But as the days passed, the farmers quite evidently forgot about it; and the Senate, obviously, forgot about it too.

The ranchers argued that wheat prices should be higher, yet they objected strenuously to the cost of every sack of flour they bought. They thought the price of baker's bread was too high, they said. It was too high for what they got for the wheat. Some of the older people of Creston often remarked that more wives should bake bread. People didn't bake any more, or can their own vegetables. The old people felt that this was somehow a sign of degeneracy.

It was a good year. The wheat averaged from fifty to sixty bushels and the price wasn't bad at any time during the selling season. Many of the ranchers paid their notes at the bank or took up old past-due accounts for groceries and hardware and harness. Quite a number turned in their old cars, buying new ones. Some made improvements on their houses, and some built

137

new barns—much more pretentious and often much more costly than the houses.

Swede Mongsen, as foxy as his father and grandfather before him, sold enough wheat to pay his debts and gambled on the remainder. One morning in the barber shop he heard over the radio that an advance had been made. He walked across the street to Jim Price's wheat office and sold all that he had been holding. He was the only one who did not wait until the next day for an additional advance of a cent or two. When wheat dropped, Jim found his office crowded with disgruntled ranchers who felt cheated out of something which they failed to designate as good judgment.

Peg married Swede late that Summer. It was just as swift as most of the Creston marriages. People had scarcely been aware of any courtship. One day it was reported that they were married, and that night there was another charivari. A couple of the women's lodges of which Mrs. Nettleship was a member held some belated "showers" for Peg. And then Swede and his wife went to live in the old Blodgett place where Etta had been to her first dance.

That night when Swede extinguished the light of the upstairs room to begin their marriage eve he did not remember when that bed had been filled with the hats and coats of people he had invited to a dance below. He did not remember how Florence Larson had stood in outline against that square pane of glass where Peg stood trembling now. As he took this girl who by some odd legerdemain of clergy had become his wife he was not struck in memory by any similar gesture which had taken place in this very room. With a man's serene lack of recollection for such things he did not recognize that the very words he spoke to Peg were those he had used to Florence Larson.

Peg heard them, though. She heard them with her whole body that trembled so in the darkness. She grasped figuratively the paw of this changed animal, to be led into an adventure which she was to find was not an adventure at all but only a ludicrous incident that seemed not to be part of living and breathing.

They heard the door of Lester Adams' room open and shut, heard his booted feet go down the stairs.

Peg felt self-conscious, ashamed. "I wonder if we woke him up," she whispered.

The screen of the back porch swung open and Lester's boots resounded on the hard ground outside. There was the short sharp creak of the metal catch, and the hollow sounding slam of an outhouse door.

Peg hated Lester Adams: somehow he had spoiled forever the beauty of a night she had gropingly wanted to preserve.

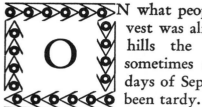N what people termed "the flat," harvest was almost over. Up in the foothills the threshing finished later, sometimes stretching into the earlier days of September if the Summer had been tardy. But in the valley, in the land surrounding Creston and Athena and the other small towns like a chain between Walla Walla and Pendleton, the few floaters who had been a part of some harvest crew went their various ways. Horses were put to Fall pasture; they were turned into fields of stubble where they straightway began to whinny and roll over and over in the warm dust as if realizing their work was finished until another harvest.

Town clubs began to hold post-harvest dances, lodges began again to conduct regular meetings, and Creston's periodic moving picture show revived itself. The weather was still open enough for people to "get around" and with a sort of carnival spirit they brought the camaraderie of harvest to a climax before they were forced to settle into the dull routine of winter.

Charlie and Etta were a part of the younger married crowd now, a circle to which they had once aspired when in the later months of their high school careers. This was the group that gave private dances or gathered together couples to drive to other towns to the dances there. The men experimented with homemade wine, each vying with the others to produce the strongest if not the best. Sometimes a quart of moonshine whiskey would put in its appearance,—a gala event.

The husbands quite often got maudlin drunk. They had neither the time, the instinct, the money, nor good enough whiskey to drink—as it is said—like gentlemen. Six days out of the week they didn't think of liquor. The seventh day they focused all their bacchanalian proclivities into one rousing spree.

The wives were tolerant. Very few of them drank anything. Etta never did, for one. She had tried it once and had become so deathly ill that she was discouraged from further trials. It was Peg who seemed to delight in taking more than any of them, and Etta was alarmed.

"I'd think Swede would stop her," Etta told Charlie. "She always did try to be smart. At that dance at their house she was disgusting. The way she carried on with Lester Adams didn't look very good to me. But I guess she'd just been drinking and that was all."

"If I were Swede," said Charlie dispassionately, "I'd knock the hell out of her once or twice and then she'd come to time."

Charlie's opinion didn't startle Etta. She agreed with him at once. "It wouldn't do her any harm. She was always crazy. That time she got up and confessed at Fleeter's meeting. . . ."

And then: "Charlie?"

"Yeah. . . ."

"Tell me, honest, was there anything—did you and her—"

"Of course not. . . ." For some reason the question embarrassed him. Although he was innocent of any charge, he felt somehow guilty. The mere thought of familiarity with anyone but his wife didn't appeal to

141

him now. "Peg is a fool and always was. I don't care
much about you goin' around with her, either."

"I can't help it some. We always went around together and I can't just not speak to her or anything."

"Yeah, I know. But I mean at these dances. I don't
like the way she monkeys with guys like Adams. She
wants to watch out. People'll get to talkin'. Another
thing is, you can't tell what Swede is thinking."

"Have you *heard* anything?" Etta knew that men
talked as much as women. If there were anything wrong
it would be pretty well known at the pool hall.

"What do you mean?"

"I mean—don't you think Peg is true to Swede?"

"True to him?" Charlie was not educated by means
of the magazines. "Oh—oh, I don't know. I don't think
there's anything off colour. Only Les better be careful.
He's too dam' smart." Fraser felt much older than
Lester Adams. The fact that he had married, was working out his own destiny as much as any man is allowed
to work it out, put him above this other youth who
had thrown himself into the protective arms of college.
He distrusted Lester. He felt that Lester put himself
above his surroundings, above men like Charlie Fraser.

"I don't think he means anything," Etta defended.
"Peg used to go with Lester long before she went with
Swede very much. Swede's a lot older than her."

But that Saturday night there were further demon-
strations of Peg's gaiety in the face of the marriage
bond. A crowd of them had driven to Athena to the
weekly dance. The old opera house which no longer
served its original purpose since the advent of the celluloid story was crowded with dancers as the Creston
adventurers arrived. There were three cars of them:

142

Etta and Charlie had taken Peg and Swede; Lester Adams came, too, in the little roadster he had rented for the occasion, and he brought Fanny Brest as a defiant gesture to a town he looked upon as unsophisticated; and in another car were Craig, Peg's brother, and his wife, and the Needhams.

They began dancing at once, nodding to those Athena people they knew, feeling the superiority of the small town visitor over rooted natives.

On the way over, Swede and Charlie had taken a couple of drinks from a little bottle of white whiskey that the former had bought from a Finlander on the mountain. Peg had taken a drink, too, against the mild protest of Mongsen. Etta could see that Peg's face was flushed already and that she seemed unnaturally gay. For a sudden inexplicable moment the whole thing appeared to Etta as pathetic: as if they were all trying to live up to something of which they were not sure. She was certain that Peg did not care for liquor; she felt that Charlie and Swede were not enthusiastic about it, nor about dancing. It was an imitation of something. Of the Sunday supplements, perhaps? Of those light-hearted adultresses, libertines, drug fiends, and drunkards, who strew themselves about the farm homes every Sabbath afternoon?

The five-piece orchestra stopped its number on a high, unexpected note that made the dancers laugh self-consciously as they found themselves taking further steps amid silence. A few kept on dancing even though there was no music; they slithered along noiselessly, pretending they did not know the orchestra had stopped, paying tribute to each other in a passionate vulgar embrace that excluded every onlooker from their secret of sex.

The Creston group changed partners. Charlie took Mrs. Nettleship, a frail washed-out blonde with perpetual dandruff on a perpetual dark suit; and Etta danced with Craig. She saw that Peg had gone into Lester Adams' arms, and that Swede was dancing sullenly with Fanny Brest. He handled her gingerly as if he were ashamed of touching her, and into Etta came that feeling of pity, of wonder at what Creston knew about her.

Etta had begun again to like to dance. She slid practiced feet over the smooth floor, not talking to Craig, and scarcely listening to his convivial gossip about Needham's barber shop where he worked and where he was able to digest a considerable portion of Creston's rumor.

Without losing step, Etta swung from Craig to Swede Mongsen. She passed Peg and Charlie, then, racing by them with increasing tempo. She saw Peg urge herself closer to Charlie, and she wondered if Charlie's hand, flat against Peg's back, had pulled her toward him. Peg's breasts seemed eager, high and promising, toward Charlie's vest. Etta mentally designated her as a little fool.

She was sorry she had asked the question almost as soon as it left her lips: "Is Lester going to stay at the ranch until he goes back to school?"

"I suppose so," Swede said. "He didn't say anything about goin' until September. I need a fellow around, anyhow."

They danced awhile in silence and then Swede said, "God, I'm gettin' thirsty!" He grinned at her slyly.

For no other reason but that she was suddenly jealous of Peg, she accepted the invitation. They became lost at the edge of the crowd, emerged into the cool night air. The car was parked around the corner, out of the glare of light that poured from the front of the opera house. Swede rummaged beneath the robe that lay in the tonneau and brought out the bottle.

"Have one?"

She took it recklessly, but she no more than wet her lips. Her mouth burned redly, and she handed the bottle back with a shudder.

"Wasn't much of a drink," Swede said.

"That's all I want."

He tipped the bottle upwards, and Etta watched the white bubbles in the moonlight as they fought against the upturned bottom.

They returned to the hall just as the music for that number had ended. People were letting go of one another, were gravitating toward the wall to find new partners.

Etta came toward Peg and Charlie with a defiant, careless air. She saw that both had noticed her disappearance with Swede. She put herself close to them, hoping they would smell the whiskey that was still moist on her lips.

"Good lord!" Swede remarked facetiously, "do I have to dance this one with my wife?"

For some reason—perhaps it was Etta's action; perhaps Swede's lightness in front of others—Peg flared. "You don't," she said. "I've promised it to Lester Adams. . . ."

Whether or not she had been lying, she was dancing with Lester in another moment. And with a feeling of something impending, Etta noticed that, half a minute later, they were not in the hall. . . .

As Lester walked along the side of the dance hall at Peg Mongsen's invitation he wondered what he should do, what was expected of him. He feared Swede Mongsen, and something deep inside him, too, made him respect his marriage to this slightly gaudy girl beside him. But there was no mistaking that she was throwing herself at him. A damned idiot, he thought. That was because he didn't like her; she had never struck him as worth while from any standpoint.

He knew why she picked him out. He knew that he was different in Creston, and he recognized this with no egotism. He had been to college, for one thing.

Something odd had happened to him at college. He had gone there with that dream of his to become a pharmacist, to own a chain of drug stores in a score of cities. He had pledged a fraternity in which there was a group of the younger literati who scorned the specialist, the technical expert. They had recited poetry in the night that stirred something deep within Lester, something he hadn't suspected. He was inveigled, not into the school of pharmacy, but into lecture courses of poetry and plays of the Reconstruction. He talked late into the night with these friends of his: they had decided that there was no intelligent God; they keened their sense of youth and beauty until a gorgeous lithe girl could cut into their hearts like a knife.

Lester had been drunk until his eyes were glazed and his heart was breaking with things he could think but could not say. He had uncovered beauty and filth and mixed them until his mind was torn with making eternal adjustments. He would never own a chain of drug

146

stores; he would never be able to come into Creston to stay. Just what he would be able to do he did not know. There were three years yet of school—and in the meantime half formed ambitions cluttered up his brain to fullness.

It struck him as amusing—principally because he had learned to have all things strike him as amusing—that he should be walking beside this girl who knew nothing. He wondered what she thought: probably only that she must eat, and sleep, and satisfy the longings of her body, whatever they were.

He struck a pose: "The night," he said, "is woven with the desires of women who want to be kissed."

It rang familiarly to him. But he could not remember whether he had said it before, or read it somewhere. He did know that it was no matter. Peg wouldn't know. There was a sickening second when he felt that she hadn't understood at all.

But she had understood. She was breathless with surprise. She looked at Lester as if he were an immortal who had come down to sear commonplace speech with golden phrases. With that inherent taste of those who are close to the soil, near to primal beauty, she had recognized the poetry of the words. Over her came swift desire to be embraced by this god, to give her lips to him, to hold him—if only for a moment—to her earthly flesh.

The god responded readily enough. The mere thought of being with Fanny Brest all evening had inflamed him, though he wouldn't have thought of making love to her. Peg was different. He had known Peg all his life.

He kissed her, and found that he didn't, after all,

dislike her. Her lips were wet and clinging, her cheek was soft against his own. Her excited breathing threw him into a small fervour.

"Let's go to the car, Peg. Let's take a ride in the car. . . ."

But when they had gone only a little distance their ardour cooled with the wind that brushed by them.

"We better go back," Peg said. "We hadn't ought to go off like this. We can meet sometime."

He kissed her perfunctorily. "All right, dear," he said. But each knew they wouldn't have the courage to meet again. This was the climax and the end.

He turned the car around and they were at the dance hall in another breath. There was a group of men standing in the entrance; but afterward they remembered only Swede there. He stood on the top step, looking at Lester's car, looking at Peg as she got out of it.

Lester was thinking fast as he bent down to take the key from the gearshift lock. And when he rose Swede Mongsen was standing on the curb. His thick hand was on the edge of the door. What was most alarming was the fact that he was not drunk. He was coldly sober. He was insanely cool.

Quickly Peg jumped out and stood beside him. But he did not look down at her. He kept on looking straight at the man in the car.

"What the hell's the idea, Les?"

"Why, nothing. . . . Peg and I just took a minute's ride."

There was no reply to that, and the fact seemed to infuriate Swede.

"It was a goddam long minute, and I don't know whether I like it or not."

148

"I can't help that. You're bein' a damned fool, Swede."

That would have worked with some, but not with Swede. He felt already wronged, already insulted. He would not be a damned fool on top of that.

"Get the hell out of that car," he said.

The professional promoters of amateur encounters were already active. They gathered around Swede to offer advice. . . . "You better get back in the alley, Swede. Old Linden'll spot you guys out here." "I'll drive my car around and switch on the lights if you guys think you gotta have it out." "Better get out of the city limits altogether."

Two or three men piled into Lester's car, others shoved Swede into a second machine. There was the sudden buzzing of starters, the roaring of quickly cranked Fords. Half the cars in front of the dance hall spurted out and down the road.

Peg, white and trembling, went back into the hall. She found Charlie and Etta just beginning the dance, unaware of what went on outside.

"Swede and Lester are goin' to fight."

Charlie shot her one swift look of accusation, and went toward the door.

"You women stay here," he threw back over his shoulder. But both of them were at his heels. Peg was twisting her handkerchief in her hands.

"I can't stay here. I got to go out there. . . ."

As Etta ran out the door to keep abreast of Charlie she wondered for whom Peg was concerned, or if she wanted only to watch the fight. . . .

About a hundred yards down a side road the promoters had improvised the gladiatorial field. A dozen

149

cars circled, their noses pointed at the road center, their headlights focusing, merging into a glare of light that bathed both Swede and Lester at the waist. They looked fantastically like headless men.

Swede had stripped off his coat and vest and his shirt hung down his back so that the sleeves dragged in the roadway. Lester's shirt was open only at the throat—beneath it his slight form was dark and hairy. Swede was like a giant baby—his skin was white, hairless, smooth.

Lester struck first. He did not want to strike. He did not want to fight. But there stood Swede in that glaring blaze of light. There stood a crowd of yelling men who did not want to fight.

Lester struck first. It resounded in the night. It sent Swede back so that his heels trod the sleeves of his hanging shirt, pulled it out of his trousers and left him more naked, more angry than before.

His hands shot out to the side—not straight at Lester. They shot out in great slow circles that ended with Lester's head, with his ear, his mouth. Just for an instant Lester bent his head under those reverberating blows that made flashes of silver against his eyelids. It was just for a moment, but it was too long. Accidentally, powerfully, cruelly, Swede's fist shot against the pit of Lester's stomach. It was an uncalculated blow. In his anger he was aiming only for that face he could not see but which he knew was just above the shoulders in the headlight glare. Lester sank down on his knees with a gasp. He slid forward on his face and his mouth bled into the road dust.

That was all. The crowd was a little disappointed, but they slapped Swede on the back and found his shirt for him. When Charlie got there with Peg and Etta they were standing around Swede cursing bravely. But someone had propped Lester against the wheel of a car, and a man was over him, wiping his mouth with a dirty handkerchief.

"You better get on home," Charlie told Swede.

"What'll I do with *him?* He's been stayin' at my place." Swede seemed dazed. He seemed to have forgotten what the fight had been for.

"I'll take him home with me and Etta. You go on."

"I came in your car. How'll I go home. I won't go in his."

"You take mine. I'll drive his."

Already the circle of cars had begun to disperse. The headlights crossed each other in the night. Men called out good-night to each other, or wildly pressed horn-buttons with the excitement of the occasion.

Etta and Charlie crowded into the Chevrolet with Lester between them. He was still groggy, and he sagged against Etta's shoulder, his mouth still bleeding. She took out her handkerchief and held it against his lips.

The three of them were silent. They were all embarrassed at what had happened. Each felt somehow ashamed, Lester perhaps least of all. He felt dreadfully ill and his head was bursting. Together with this was the bitterness of having been so unmercifully beaten. It was nice to be against Etta's shoulder . . . nice. His head touched her cheek and she felt sorry for him utterly. She began to hate Swede for what he had done, and to hate Peg more.

"Peg's always causin' trouble," she said to Charlie. "That's all she ever did do."

Charlie was noncommittal, his eyes on the road.

CHAPTER THREE

I

ESTER stayed with them until September. It was Charlie who had suggested it.

"Don't suppose you'll want to work for Swede now," he told Lester with a grin. "If you want, you can stay on here with us."

So Adams had stayed on at the Frasers', doing a little post-season wheat hauling, helping Charlie to repair the barn roof and stow away the machinery for the Winter. Swede owed him money, Lester said, but he wouldn't go after it. He was philosophical about the trouble he had had with Mongsen.

"I don't hold it against him," Lester told Etta. "I suppose it looked bad. Anyhow, that's all you could expect from fellows like him. That's all they know—possession or fight, raise wheat or starve."

He and Etta were sitting on the porch step. The fine, sifted dusk of Autumn was all about them like a mist. Etta was amused at the curl of Lester's lip, the scorn of his eyes. She remembered Lester in high school and she quickly flew to the side of the men like Swede —men like the man she'd married. Her men. The men she knew and understood. She felt that Lester was like them; that he wasn't different, as he pretended to be.

"Do you know what you're talking about, Lester?"

"Of course I do." He mentioned it casually, a statement of fact. "But I don't mean to say I know a whole lot. There's a whole lot I don't know. A whole lot I

152

never will know." In his young voice there was a throaty cynicism. He felt suddenly sad and impotent and futile. But his pose was lost on Etta.

"What did you mean—that Swede was all possession or fight?"

"Well . . . he gets sore at Peg for being out of his sight with me. It irked his sense of proprietorship. So he beat me up. . . . But he doesn't do anything to keep her."

Etta could not resist it. "He beat you up to keep her, didn't he?"

"Oh, that! That's just what I say."

"Well, what do you mean? How'll you keep *your* wife?" She felt years older than this boy who had gone away to school.

"Not like that, anyway. It's hard to tell you what I mean. It's hard to say what I really mean. I didn't realize a lot of things until I got down there to school. You can't stay here and realize it."

Etta was slowly growing curious and impatient. "You can't realize what, Lester? I wish you'd say. . . ."

He started to speak, and then arose and stood above her. "I don't know whether I can explain it or not. Anyhow, Charlie'll come back here in a minute. Come on and let's walk."

Flattered, she placed her husband outside the understanding circle in which she and Lester stood, and joined the boy. They walked down the road a way; the heavy dampness had settled the dry white dust.

Lester walked beside her, glad of the chance to say what he meant, as Etta put it. Not through the Summer had he ever really talked as he wanted to talk; as he had learned to talk at those midnight gatherings

153

in his room at the fraternity house, at tea room meetings with virgin co-eds sporting demi-virgin ideas.

"I don't know how to begin, Etta. There's so much, and it's all mixed up. . . . Do you ever think about God?"

"Think about Him?" There was astonishment in her voice. You couldn't, exactly, think about God. God *was*, that was all.

"Yeah. . . . Whether there is one—and if there is, what's he—or it—like?"

"Why, Lester!"

"You see? I told you. I can't even begin. You wouldn't get it. You can't stay around Creston and understand a damned thing but eating and sleeping."

"Oh—you *can't*? Maybe I have thought about God."

"When?"

"Once—that time we had the flood. Lura Dyer was drowned. I remember I kept wondering why it was. I knew how good she was, and how she never said a word, even, against anybody or anything. You went off to the dance. You weren't even there when it happened."

Lester was silent. He was chagrined to think she had hit his poor point so squarely. "That's more what I mean. . . . Well, what did you decide?"

"Decide? . . . Oh, nothing, I guess. I just sort of forgot it until now."

"You forgot about Lura Dyer and about all the other things you've seen this old boy do and you've sort of taken it for granted since that you were wrong and that there really is a good God to watch over us."

"Well, there must be, Lester." She looked about her

into the darkness. The sky was so black, so huge. "It would be so—so silly if there wasn't. Wouldn't it?"

"*Isn't* it silly? People lying and cheating and getting away with it. People being decent as they know how and living in hell on earth just the same. Peg going blindly on, not loving Swede—not loving anybody in particular. Not knowing what she wants. She'll go on and have Swede's kids and then some day she'll die."

"Some day you'll die. . . ."

"Sure. Sad but true. You, too, Etta. It's a lot of fun to think it over, isn't it? . . . You'll have Charlie's kids and then you'll die."

Etta shuddered. For a scant second she was without faith, without hope . . . without hope which makes life bearable at all. In that scant second she felt a living death. A spiritual pallidness. But it was only for a second.

"You make it so ugly, Lester. You just think you're smart. You'll see some day. I've had lots of fun and so have you. You can't deny it."

"I'm not. Just the same you got to admit we're all detouring on the way to death. We're born, and from that second we start out for death. What we do in between time is detour. Some kids die at birth. They take the straight road—all paved. It's shorter. You—"

"Oh, stop talking like that. It's—it's—sort of nasty, some way."

They walked along, and Lester felt infinitely better. These things he was telling Etta, without particular originality, were pleasing him. They hurt her, he knew. They sank deep into a soul that loved life fully. He knew, too, that tomorrow she would forget them; but for tonight they were making her utterly miserable.

"But this hasn't anything to do with marriage," she finally said.

"It has, in a way. You see, in the meantime you ought to live. You shouldn't miss anything. You and Swede and Peg and all the rest of them. I'm not trying to be high-hat. I don't think I'm better just because I went to college. Sometimes I wish to Christ I hadn't started."

He kicked into the roadway with his boot, sending up a fine cloud of white dust-mist. "There's so much you can do. Swede trying to keep Peg by beating me up —why don't he keep her because she wants to be kept? . . . Will you tell me something?"

"Why . . . yes."

"Did you and Charlie ever stand naked in the middle of a room and embrace each other?"

"Why, Lester! Of course we didn't!"

"I didn't think you had. I don't suppose Swede and Peg ever have."

"But what—why do you say that? What has that to do with it?"

"Oh . . . nothing, I guess. But if ever I get married I'm going to do it. I'm going to *dance* with my wife that way. Turn on the radio and pull down the shades and dance that way—" He broke off wildly, laughing at Etta, laughing into the night. Somehow his brief for paganism, for freedom in the wind of life had disintegrated before this girl. He felt frustrated, silly.

Instinctively Etta drew away from him. "You're crazy, Lester. I never heard anyone talk like that!"

The statement seemed to please him. "Maybe not," he said. "Come on, let's go back."

They walked back in silence, clear to the porch again

before they spoke a word. Lester was faintly angry, with himself and with Etta. What might have been beautiful had somehow crumbled into ugliness, into something perverted and shameful. Yet he felt that it was Etta's fault. What was, after all, a rather decent symbol had been to her . . . only two naked people.

The next day Lester left for school. Charlie drove him to the Adams ranch to say good-bye to his mother, and then to the train. When they left, Etta was upstairs and she called a farewell to him from the window, not wanting to come down and shake his hand.

I

THE flu came again that Winter. Not since it had first appeared—stealthily, guised with dignity as "Spanish influenza"—was it so prevalent or so intense as that Winter.

One Sunday Ned Cady sneezed in church. The next morning he was in bed with stomach pains and high fever. Then Mrs. Cady took it, and the three boys.

The news spread more quickly than the fever. The mountain was dotted with cases and the doctor's car was active. It was splattered with mud and rain, and the conglomerate mess of the roads froze to the front axle so that it was with difficulty that he steered his machine.

When people saw his car in front of the drug store they hurried over to question him. Who was sick now? How was Freddy Neil? The doctor would stand behind the prescription counter, filling his own orders, and tell them what he knew.

"Think it's as bad as the first year or two, Doc?"

"Well, some are pretty sick all right." The doctor was always—and wisely—noncommittal.

Incessantly the drug store telephone buzzed for new prescriptions or to call the doctor when he could not be found at his house. In a sudden panic, the board closed the schools and this added to the fright in the minds of the town. A "spell of sickness" was a terrible thing in Creston. Everyone knew personally those who were ill. They remembered the epidemic of the first two years when so many had died with what seemed innocently to be "a little grippe." At the first headache, men and women crawled into bed and the word went out that they were ill.

The crowd that usually gathered at the post office during the distribution of the mail diminished appreciably. Some were ill; others were avoiding crowds.

At Charlie Fraser's Etta kept a kettle full of water on the stove and into it she periodically poured a few drops of disinfectant. The house smelled to heaven, but a neighbour had told her that it was infallible as preventative. Etta was afraid, somehow. Over the whole country-side there was that air of moody desolation which is over a house when some occupant is deathly ill. People looked forward to a break just as they looked forward to Spring.

Among the first to take it was Etta's mother. She had suffered with it from the first year, and each subsequent Winter it had decreased in potency until she announced she was beginning to be immune. But Etta heard the news with alarm from her father when he telephoned her. He knew that people were having it worse this time, didn't he? And had she had the doctor?

She hadn't, Dant said, and furthermore she wouldn't. Etta promised to come at once. When Charlie had driven her to the Dant ranch she found her mother more ill than she would admit to either her husband or her daughter. She had always been one of those who ward off illness with a combination of physical and mental resistance. Nevertheless, Etta went out to the car where Charlie waited and told him that she'd better stay.

"You go along, and be sure to keep that kettle on, won't you?"

He promised, and Etta went back into the house full of her purpose. From long practice she knew what was best. She put Mrs. Dant through all the familiar paces. There was the physic, the hot water bottle, the mentholated salve, and the steaming lemonade. There was the dose of quinine tablets and the thin broth at intervals. Both of them enjoyed the process—the invalid almost as much as the nurse.

One morning the sun shone brightly by ten o'clock. It was not Spring—not near Spring either in fact or vision—but it was a precious break in the monotony of gray. Etta opened the doors and let in some badly needed air. Mrs. Dant was put by the kitchen stove. She sat in a rocker and ate two soft-boiled eggs and drank some coffee.

"You're pretty near well," Etta told her. "Now if *I* don't come down. Or Charlie. You're sure you feel well enough to be sitting there?"

"Lots better, Etta. I'll be fit as a fiddle in a day or two."

So that afternoon Etta telephoned Charlie to please come for her. He hadn't, he said, noticed anything wrong with himself. He'd thrown out the contents of that damned kettle that was smelling up the house. When he arrived for Etta he told her and Mrs. Dant, disparagingly, that it was mostly imagination, this flu.

"People get little colds," he said.

Riding home with Charlie, Etta told him: "Mamma's much better. I don't know what Papa would do if I

160

didn't come over when she gets those Winter spells of flu."

But that night Etta's mother died.

I I

The snow was gray and sprinkled with black dots where the rain drops had pierced the crust now melting with the first low temperature of the season. The chinook wind had come to the funeral, just as it seemed to delight in coming to all Winter funerals, howling among the sad-drooped trees—howling instead of moaning. An ill-mannered, devilish wind.

Most of the people who came to Mrs. Dant's funeral stayed in their cars. There was a roadway right into the cemetery and they could see all that went on without getting out into the weather. Not many cars were present. People were a little afraid, yet, of the weather and the influenza. Only Charlie and Etta, the minister and old Dant, were around the yawn of earth that would soon be a grave. The undertaker tried to keep in the shelter of the hearse, and the pall bearers had climbed back into their car until that point in the ceremony where they would be needed again.

The Reverend Alfred Horliss shielded his prayer book from the rain with his hat. Etta wondered whether it was to aid his sight, or to keep the pages from harm. If it were the latter, then she hated him. What was a book of prayers, now, in these last words to be said for her who could not hear them?

She saw the undertaker looking at her legs. . . . *Oh, God, doesn't anyone care but me?* . . . He glanced up and caught her gaze, resumed his concerned expression.

161

. . . I hate him, I hate him! I won't have him again—

Again? Who next, then? Yes, there would be another time. Her father, or Charlie, or herself. Nobody knew when, or who would be first. The minister's words slithered wetly through the rain. Eel-words. "Ashes to ashes. . . ." The undertaker from Pendleton stepped forward and was sprinkling something on the casket. Etta could not see with her blurred eyes. Was it rose leaves? They scattered in the wind. Not one fell upon her mother there. . . . *Oh, why shouldn't I step out and pick up one, just one, and put it there?*

But the machinery of it went on. The pall bearers, lowering the casket, were not quite adept. One end sank so low . . . *please be careful, won't you? Please.*

Under his breath in the cold wind the undertaker gave instructions to them. The crowd began to dismiss. It was over. All over. Some of the cars were already hurrying down the road, taking people on with the business of living. What a bitter thing was death. *Why can't we stay here, Charlie and me? Why can't we stay?* The undertaker's hand was on her shoulder. Did they wish to stay until the grave was filled, or did they want to come up afterward?

Afterward, Charlie said. Meekly Etta followed him to their machine. She saw her father going toward the car, his back showing how grief stricken he was, how at a loss he was to account for anything that had happened.

When they were seated in the car Alfred Horliss came up to them. His prayer book was not in his hands, Etta noted; it was safely in his pocket now. He put a curved hand out to each of them in turn.

162

"God bless you in your sorrow, brother. . . . God bless and keep you in your sorrow, sister. . . . God bless you, brother."

Charlie started the car forward. They were going now. Where?

"You'll come on home with us awhile?" Charlie said to Dant.

Stubbornly: "I'll go on home." Brokenly: "I'll just go on home."

What would he do at home, Etta wondered. He would make the fire that had gone out. He would boil some coffee. Would he try to read the Pendleton *Oregonian* that was left on the step each night and that he went out to get after dinner so religiously?

All that day she had not cried. All that day her eyes and throat had been strangely dry. Her eyes were blurred a little and her throat was hot and tight, but she did not cry. Her grief was too big to weep. In her heart there was an emptiness that seemed too big for her. She wondered how she could hold an emptiness so big inside her.

But the wells of her sorrow had overflown and emptied; they had given out, and in her smaller sadness she began to cry now. Charlie, anxious to comfort her, edged closer.

"Don't do that, Honey. It won't do any good. She's all right now. She's all right."

The words—she knew they were so futile—only brought her fresh impotency. There was nothing she could do. Nothing anyone could do. Nothing. Here was a thing without hope. No one had come back from death. Not one, ever . . . except Jesus. He had come back, for they had seen Him.

A dull resentment flared up inside her that He should be able to resurrect Himself, and that her mother could not. Charlie's silly words that she would be all right rang into her ears like the rhythm when an anesthetic is oozing into lungs.

But Charlie was near. He was alive and near. She clung to him with a sudden wild desperation, just as she had sought him that day they were married when she had lost her mother and father for a while.

"Charlie, she'll be so cold! She'll be so cold out there tonight!"

In mild astonishment he stole a sidelong glance at her; it was half fearful, half incredulous. She saw that glance. She knew that her words were crazy.

But she said them again because they escaped into her bleeding heart and hurt her. "Charlie, she'll be so cold . . . so cold. . . ." Her voice was muffled, lost into his overcoat.

They had forgotten old Dant behind them. He sat very straight, close to the edge of the cushion. He stared at the roadway, his eyes not captured by any object that flew by them on their way to town.

For the moment they had forgotten him, just as they would forget him at other moments—moments, when added, that would stretch into days. The one who did not forget him had gone now. He was aware of that. But he had a contempt for the grief of the two who sat in front of him. He had a disdain for Charlie's red eyes and Etta's inane moaning. He sat there, Olympian, sort of majestic in his grief, in spite of his hunched shoulders and his relaxed, open palms. He was closer to death than they. He could see it better. They had heard frightful stories of it, but he could see it now.

It was not half so terrible as they thought. It wasn't a monster, he saw, black and hooded.

He half turned in his seat to look behind him, to see again the hill they had just quitted. He had an earnest, honest longing to be with her who had been left behind.

III

It was three days before Etta came back to the cemetery. She was startled to see how the mound had fallen. Soon it would be sunk level with the rest. Why did they sink just to the level and never lower than that? Or would they, in years and years, when what was below had—had gone completely? As she placed the flowers she had brought she kept thinking of that question and not of her mother.

She was to know later what she did not know now. She was to notice later that in the actual act of tribute she would not be able to remember her. Yet in some small task at home, or at something wholly irrelevant that someone would say, Etta would have a vision of her mother that was startling in its reality. Charlie had told her she would forget, but he had lied. Sometimes, in a hundred little ways a day, Etta would remember her.

The Winter was hard. The snow threatened to drive her mad with its muffled quietness. It was the visits to her father that she hated most. He seemed to her lonelier than perhaps he really was. That big house— that house that she and her mother had planned, that house she had watched build. This kitchen they had planned with its utensils hanging just as always. She knew that some of them were never used by Dant. Some of them he didn't know how to use. They hung there on their brass hooks, just as his wife had left them.

She hated the visits to her father because they made her feel so miserable; and she felt certain that she was not helping him. But somehow she kept them up. Every Wednesday and every Sunday she went, alone or with Charlie. She dreaded the time he would ask them both to come there to stay. She knew that they dare not refuse—or thought that she knew. Etta wondered what went on in her father's mind, behind those eyes that were yet so sharp. It is not children who grow away from us, but old people. They draw into a world of their own and we cannot tell whether they love us or hate us.

One Sunday, when the first breath of March had revived them all a little, Dant brought the question to them.

"You kids might as well come here, hadn't you? It's a lot nicer and too blamed big for me. Charlie could farm both places mighty easy, I'd think."

Etta saw that all along Charlie had been coveting the invitation. He wanted to come, and she had not known it because they hadn't talked about it.

"Well, I suppose I'd have to take care of it some time, anyhow," he said. He was oblivious to what his words might mean. He had stated a patent fact. It was a thread of destiny that was obvious.

Old Dant smiled. "Sure. Might as well get the hang of it."

Etta relaxed for the first time in months. Only she, then, of the three, had been afraid to face it.

She laughed, genuinely happy. "You'll get some real cooking at last, Papa."

They looked forward eagerly to the bustle of a busy harvest.

ESTER ADAMS swung off the Eugene-Portland interurban, stood uncertainly in the street to let an auto pass, and started briskly toward the Multnomah Hotel.

He wondered why, of all places, Peg would choose the Multnomah at which to meet him. It was, he decided, the only hotel in Portland which she knew by name; he felt certain she wasn't stopping there. Her letter was in his pocket—and he would have read it again had not he remembered it so clearly. It had seemed adventurous to get that letter, addressed in Peg's scrawling hand to the Kappa Sigma house. One or two of the brothers had seen it on the table that morning, noted the postmark, and when he announced at luncheon that he was "running down to Portland" they made various semi-humorous comments.

If she'd written more, if she'd made herself clearer, he wouldn't have come. But the letter's very reticence (or Peg's lack of ability to express herself) piqued his curiosity. It told him nothing beyond the fact that she was coming to Portland that night, that she would be alone, and would like to see him. If he wanted, he could meet her at the Multnomah at seven-thirty.

A block from the hotel, Lester turned in at a garage and sought out the men's lavatory. Those damned interurbans were grimy. In the streaked glass of a medicine cabinet nailed to the wall he examined himself. He washed his hands, straightened his tie, and combed his hair with a pocket comb. When he emerged he felt better prepared to meet a girl in the lobby of the

Multnomah. Walking from the garage, he veered his course to avoid a huge blue sedan bouncing up the ramp. He was conscious of a woman's face behind the windshield, and it struck him as familiar.

He stared, and found Florence Larson's eyes looking into his own. She broke into a smile of recognition, and as the big car came to a halt she turned down the window and called Lester's name.

"Why . . . hello, Miss Larson!"

She held a gloved hand for him, and he saw beyond her, at the driver's seat, an elderly man.

"How *are* you, Lester? How's everything at school?" She seemed unnecessarily effusive, as though she were trying to impress upon him that she wouldn't ignore an old friend from Creston. "Lester, this is Mr. Hugon."

Mr. Hugon extended a flabby, fat hand across Miss Larson's chest and gripped Lester's palm.

"Pleased to know you," Mr. Hugon assured him, but there was no conviction in his tone. His eyes, cushioned in ringlets of flesh, seemed suspicious of Lester.

There was no further explanation of Mr. Hugon, and as Miss Larson ran on with forced gaiety, Lester watched him. He wore a green stiff collar, and a green shirt to match. His cuffs were shot out too far as if his coat were short in the sleeves. He appeared to Lester to be very impatient while Miss Larson talked on.

". . . and what are you doing in Portland, Lester?"

"Why, I'm meeting Peg. You remember Peg. She's here for a day or two."

"Peg Nettleship? I'd love to see her."

"She's right up here at the Multnomah. It's not Peg Nettleship now, though. She and Swede were married."

"Oh . . . oh, yes, I remember now. Someone told

me." But Lester could see that no one had told Miss Larson. He felt annoyed at himself, and he plunged into a question.

"You're teaching?"

"Oh, no. I've—I've a bookshop here in town." She plunged a hand swiftly into her bag and brought out a slender gray card, as though for proof to Lester.

"Here. . . . You must drop in on me." She laughed. "I'll sell you something at cost."

He took the card. Larson's Book Nook.

"Thanks. I'll make a point of it to see you. . . . Well, I'll have to be going. I'm awfully glad to have seen you."

"I'm glad to have seen *you*. Tell my friends hello for me, won't you?"

"Sure. . . . Hope I'll meet you again, Mr. Hugon."

Mr. Hugon thanked him without enthusiasm, and without recording the hope as mutual. Lester hurried on and out of the garage, somehow glad to be getting away. What in the devil had been different about Miss Larson? It was as if Hugon had been a poor relation of whom she was ashamed.

He kept thinking of her all the way to the hotel, and he was inside the big lobby before he was really aware of it. Then he saw Peg—almost at once, in a deep chair that stood against a pillar. She didn't look right in the Multnomah lobby. She wore a bright red hat that Lester was certain would be soiled where her fingers habitually pulled it onto her head. And before she rose to meet him he hadn't avoided seeing ribboned step-ins of an ungodly colour he couldn't name.

Already she'd attracted the notice of a group of men at the cigar counter. They were older men, lonely men, and suddenly Lester felt victorious as he confronted Peg. They would wonder what was in store for him; they would envy him. They would covet Peg because they didn't know, or care, how cheap she really was.

"Well—Lester!"

He wished she wouldn't say that, in such a tone. People would get the idea he was meeting a girl from the old home town. But no one except the cigar counter group seemed to be interested in them.

"Hello, Peg. What's the trouble?"

"Trouble? There's no trouble. I was just here and wanted to see somebody I knew."

He seemed disappointed. "Why are you in Portland?"

"My God . . ." she was faintly exasperated. "Can't anybody come to Portland if they want?"

Uneasily: "Have you had dinner?"

"I might eat a little something."

"All right. Let's go to Thiele's." There were secluded booths at Thiele's where Peg could talk all she pleased. "Are you staying here?"

"At the Multnomah? No, I haven't got a room anywhere yet. I just got in a couple of hours ago. I left my grip at the station, went to a movie, and here I am."

On the way to Thiele's they talked of the traffic, of Portland's lack of alleys for garbage pails, of the inconsistency of the crossing signals—whatever struck Peg's fancy and Lester could satisfactorily explain. At the restaurant they found a booth and conversation settled down once more.

"Did you and Swede have a battle?"

She shook her head. "No . . . I'm supposed to be at Seaside tonight. Mam's got an uncle there, and I got

171

staying-sickness from that darned old ranch. Swede didn't want me to come, but he finally gave in."

"Then they don't know you're here to-night?"

"I didn't say I wouldn't stop here. They might know anybody'd stop at Portland if they was going to Seaside, wouldn't they?"

He grinned at her evasions for her own peace of mind. "I guess they would."

"I sort of wanted to see you about—on account of that night at Athena when Swede got so mad."

"I'd forgotten it," he lied.

"Well, I haven't. I felt rotten over it. I meant to write you but I never did, and then when I knew I was coming down here I thought I'd tell you, and stop to see you . . . if you'd let me."

She looked at him appealingly. There was something fast and hard in her black eyes. The ends of her lashes were bright metallic beads. The unnatural rouge she wore gave her face the look of a pagan mask.

"I've let you," Lester said. Then he felt swiftly frightened. He added irrelevantly, "Guess who I saw tonight."

"I couldn't."

"Florence Larson."

Peg showed instant interest. "You did? What'd she look like? Is she married?"

"She looked different to me. Still, maybe she was just a little older. She's got a bookshop here now. She was with some fellow, an elderly bird."

"She was always sort of—well, funny. She didn't like anybody in Creston much, I guess."

"Sure she did. Nobody there knew her, that's all." He paused to light a cigarette. "You know, I think there's a connection between her and this old guy and the bookshop."

"Do you actually?" She would have carried it further, but food put in an appearance and she began attacking it seriously.

"What'll we do tonight, Peg?" Lester had mentally counted his money and decided it would be enough to show Peg quite a blowout.

"Oh, I don't care . . . go to the show, maybe." She picked up a butter knife. Her nails were too bright, too pink, too sharp. Her hands were tanned in contrast to her face and throat.

"Don't you want to go somewhere and dance?"

"Oh, I don't know. I don't care much about dancing where you don't know people. I think I'd rather go to the show."

"You don't like Portland, do you?"

"Well, I don't know. . . ."

They left Thiele's and walked down Washington Street so that Peg could window-shop. They turned south to get to the Broadway Theatre.

It was one of those motion picture palaces of the West Coast that attempt to vie with Roxy. In addition to the photoplay there was the glorified vaudeville act—a "New York revue" out of a San Francisco booking office, and like a New York revue in but one thing: the chorus came from Keokuk and Bend. The Sun Kissed Beauties did not dance, exactly, but performed acrobatic exercises to music. They wore high heeled slippers, tight and dangerous shorts, and bursting brassières. In the glare of the spotlight their flesh was cruelly like marble.

Lester, watching them, became more and more aware

173

of Peg beside him. Their knees, their shoulders, pressed. He kept remembering that night by the side of the Athena dance hall. He recognized, as they sat there watching young women throw their sex appeal at the mob, that there was a spell between himself and Peg that would be broken when they got outside again, had to walk down the street in the brisk, damp air. He wondered idly, then more acutely, what it would be worth to ask Peg to take a room with him. But he could think of no very smart way of putting it. It would be simpler if he knew just why she had written him.

Once out of the movie, they turned toward the river Peg said she wanted to see. The bridge showed its white round lights high above the water. Warehouse row, snug against the banks, was shut for the night and there were no grumbling trucks, no excitable Chinese, no hawk-eyed cosmopolites. An occasional cheap jewelry store, still open, threw into the night a gleam that was as false as its wares. In its window would be a pile of tawdry junk, each piece marked with an inked card.

On the bridge, they found the river silent beneath them . . . the Willamette, going toward the sea. One side of town was scarcely visible at all, but their side of the river showed proudly in a blaze of lights the concentrated business district of the Oregon metropolis.

Peg was silent, impressed. She liked the scene, yet felt strange toward it. The river fascinated her; it was so much larger than the creek of Creston. And she was going down to Seaside to glimpse an ocean she had never seen.

A tug glided under the bridge, sneaked under without a warning whistle. The lights of its single mast seemed near enough to touch.

"I wish we were in that boat," she told Lester, not wishing that they were at all.

They sauntered aimlessly down the length of the bridge and back again. Then they made a goal of the tall clock tower of the station. Lester got Peg's antiquated bag from the checking counter of the depot. As they came out of the swinging doors together they were hailed by a dozen taxi drivers, and accepted the first at hand.

"We should 'a' walked," Peg said. "It's longer that way."

"That bag's heavy," he informed her unromantically. But he kissed her there in the taxi, pressed her slenderness against him.

"Do you still like me?" she wanted to know.

He didn't answer, except to kiss her again—and she took this for reply.

At the hotel, chosen by Lester as less public than the Multnomah, he handed the bag—painfully aware of its scars—to the alert boy who met them at the curb. As he registered for Peg he felt himself flushing. The hotel pen scratched audibly on the card and failed halfway through her name. He finished it unsteadily after another dip into the corroded inkwell. He summoned ease enough to tell the boy that Mrs. Mongsen wouldn't go up as yet. And then he wondered why he hadn't had the courage to register them as man and wife. He'd heard classmates speak of it as too simple to be overlooked in the ceaseless quest for recreation. He wondered if Peg would think him a fool. Lester always dreaded what hard little women would think of him; and yet he had always been afraid to challenge them.

He was relieved an instant later by Peg's anxious question, "Lester, you aren't going up with me?"

He laughed. "I'm a man of honour, Mrs. Mongsen." He had a desire to strike her across that blood-like mouth. A cowardly teaser with no guts. At last he had hold of himself in front of the night clerk and the lobby loungers.

They talked for half an hour, finding it difficult to find words, and at length Lester got up.

"I'll have to go to make that last car," he said. "I've got an eight o'clock class in the morning and I might as well not miss it." The evening was deflating itself like a punctured balloon.

Peg looked down at her absurd shoes. She heard him say, "I'm glad you told me you'd be here."

"So'm I, Lester." She got up from the leather chair, stood near him. He sensed that she was suppliant now. But something of the brightness of the lobby edged in around her and she retreated within herself.

"Good-bye. . . ." They held hands for a moment, these two who wanted nothing of each other except the flesh. "Good-bye. . . ."

As he turned to go he was aware of her hard spiked heels clacking toward the desk to get her room key. Outside the hotel, his coat collar turned up against the breeze, he cursed himself. Before him loomed the long ride to Eugene in a musty car filled with the ghosts of dead cigars. . . .

Peg, from the window of her room, tried to catch sight of him. But on the walk below her none of the figures distinguished itself as Lester.

She knew that she couldn't sleep. The bed, the room, the whole city, were strange and she did not like them.

176

She wished she had let Lester stay. She stifled a desire to rush out and try to catch him, remembering that she didn't even know the direction of the interurban station.

She pulled her hat from her touseled black hair, and in one expert smear wiped off rouge and powder with a hotel towel. With the mask removed she looked pale and tired. Her feet were sore from the hard pavement to which she was not accustomed.

The unfamiliar noises of the street cars, newsboys and late pedestrians floated in upon her as she watched the ceiling from her bed. The sky outside was tinged with the reflections of electric signs. How did people ever sleep beneath such a sky as that?

In the next room she could hear a man and woman talking. Their voices seemed very clear, yet she could not distinguish words. It was funny, having strangers so near, loving, hating, maybe—and you not knowing their names.

The woman in the next room came into the bathroom to wash her teeth; Peg heard the brush clatter against the bowl as she dropped it. The man came in and kissed the woman. Their feet shuffled on the tile floor of the bathroom behind that thin wall. There was silence; and then the woman's laugh.

Peg sat up straight in bed. She climbed out quietly and came over to listen against the wall. She wanted to hear the woman talk again. The woman's voice sounded like a voice she knew. But the two next door went out of the bathroom and shut the door. Peg couldn't hear them any more.

Peg stood there a long time, aching with curiosity. Lester had seen Florence Larson in town. He had said he suspected something between her and a man. And you didn't hear a voice like Miss Larson's very often.

She walked to the window, assuring herself that it couldn't have been Miss Larson. Another laugh came up ten stories for Peg to hear. It was the laugh of a well dressed woman, bareheaded, getting into an automobile. The car drove off, looking odd from that height.

People going somewhere . . . people you didn't know.

A mile across the city was an electric sign—a huge star, and the words JESUS, THE LIGHT OF THE WORLD.

Peg crawled back into bed. She tried to sleep, and yet she kept listening for sounds outside, for sounds in the room next to hers.

The newsboy on the curb below startled her again: "Oregonian . . . late edition . . . Ore-gon-yan . . . man found dead in car!"

Peg wondered if there would be anyone who would care about what had happened to the man.

PART THREE: GOD GOT TIRED

I

CHARLIE lay half under the single rumpled sheet and half exposed to the thick air of the August night. He had been but partly asleep, going through one of those disconnected dreams that are a combination of day-thought and nightmare. He lay prone, exhausted. He had tried every method he knew to achieve coolness. He had changed the position of his pillow, searched it in vain for a spot that wasn't heated with his own head. He had thrown an arm loosely over his moist forehead, raised his knees to a height that might, on any other night than this, allow for some circulation of air.

Outside there was the dull droning as if the heat had attained some insistent rhythm of its own. It was a black night—a night the colour of Winter midnight and yet painfully August . . . stifling . . . sweating. . . . dry.

He sensed Etta getting out of bed beside him. He wondered feebly how she might have the energy to move, and her action irritated him. But he threw his arm across the unoccupied section of the bed, grateful for the new space. It was hot to his touch, hot where Etta had left it.

Her shadow, bulky these past months, loomed against the window. Poor kid, poor darlin' . . . She was fumbling for the light switch. God, why would she want to turn on the damned light on a night like this! It seemed that even the heat of the tenuous globe-wires would add to the inferno of the night.

In the glare of the light she was pale and drawn. She looked at him, and, blinking at the new light, he saw her set expression.

"Charlie," she said. "Get up . . ."

They were quiet words, but they jerked him forward from the bed as if she had cried out. He stood for a moment at a loss, looking foolish in the trunks of his underwear. He grabbed his shirt and swung into it with his long arms, leaped expertly into his trousers with two high and awkward steps.

"I'll call doc—I'll get Mrs. Morrison. . . ."

He went into the hall and turned the tiny crank of the telephone. As he listened for a response he heard only old Dant's heavy snoring from upstairs. Mustn't wake the old man, he thought. More bother. Can't do anything, anyhow.

Again he tried the signal. It must be later than he'd thought. It did seem as if he'd been in bed, trying to get to sleep, for hours. Mrs. Morrison should have stayed there all the time, like he'd wanted. But Etta wouldn't have it.

Once again he spun the crank. Three short rings and a long. He was vaguely frightened; he'd heard it was terribly painful for a woman to have a child. The most pain anyone could ever suffer, he'd heard.

Three short rings and a long . . . and at last a voice at the other end of the wire.

"Doc's house, please . . . Get me doc's house. Yes."

He wasn't there. At the pool hall, his wife said. Then it wasn't past ten o'clock, after all.

"Get the pool hall, then. The pool hall. She said he was at the pool hall."

Then there was the doctor's mild voice, a little fearful that he was going to be called from a game of "hog." But he'd be right out. Right out—Charlie mustn't get excited, that was all.

He rushed into the room again to tell Etta, and then remembered he hadn't got in touch with Mrs. Morrison. It seemed so inane, to be rushing around telephoning, not being able to do anything. He could hear Etta's low moaning and for a moment it frightened him into panic. Then he was certain that she, too, was scared, and that her moans weren't of pain.

"I'm gettin' ready now," Mrs. Morrison said over the telephone. "They just called me from the 'phone office."

He started for the bedroom again, calling Etta's name.

"Etta, Honey—Etta, they're comin'. They'll be here . . ."

He saw her by the bed. The sheet was pulled back over the foot and she was spreading newspapers over the mattress.

He turned away, went through the hall and out of the house. The road was dark. There were no headlights on it, no glare against the sky as there might be if a car were down the little hill to the Dant house. He stood on the porch and lit a cigarette. He drew the smoke of it deep into his lungs and felt nothing; the match burned down against his fingers and went out.

There was the humming of an engine, a muffled sound that mixed with the night droning. Dimly he saw a car up the road, coming slowly—so very slowly —with no lights. He ran to the front of the yard and yelled, waved his cigarette as if the pink glow of it were a lantern. But the doctor had already seen the lights of the house and had increased his speed.

183

"Dam' lights are on the blink," the physician said. "Meant to get 'em fixed today but never got to it."

"Hurry up, doc. She's in there."

"Of course she's in there. Didn't expect her to be runnin' around half nuts like you are. You stick around out here and I'll let you know when you're needed."

"Christ Almighty, doc . . . I ought to be shot, so help me, Jesus!"

But all he got was a pat on the shoulder. He stood uncertainly by the car and watched the door close behind the doctor. And when Morrison drove up with his wife Charlie was still standing there, looking at the front door through which the doctor had gone. As Mrs. Morrison got out of the car she nodded to him curtly. She accused him with a glance; she said plainly, with no words, that she had seen this sort of thing before and she knew very well how it came about.

Morrison spat viciously into the roadway.

"Perty excitin' times, these are, ain't they?"

Someone to talk to at last. "Think she'll be all right? Think she's got a good chance?"

"Likely got as good a chance as any," was Morrison's contribution to Charlie's peace. "Always seemed like a good healthy girl, Etta did. Depends a lot on whether they want to come through or not, my wife says. She ought to know. She's been to a lot of parties like this'n."

Depends a lot on whether they want to come through . . . That hadn't before occurred to Charlie. What if she didn't want to? How could you tell whether she really wanted to or not? All the things he might have done to make her happier—all that he might have done—and hadn't—flashed into his mind.

"I ought to go in there, hadn't I? I ought to, hadn't

184

I?" He was like a man suddenly aflame: a man who knows he shouldn't run but who runs so that he will be caught and thrown.

"You better stay right here, is my advice."

Charlie flopped down on the running board of Morrison's car. He tried another cigarette.

"Got another one, Fraser?"

Charlie offered him the pack and Morrison chose one, lighting it with a steady hand. The two of them sat there, wordless, and the gray smoke rose no higher than their heads. It seemed intent upon remaining near its source, floated on a thin plane in the darkness.

11

George Dant obtained a great deal of pleasure in telling how he had gone to bed, slept soundly through the night, and come downstairs the next morning to find himself a grandfather.

"Slept right through the whole shindig," he said. "Charlie, Etta, the doctor comin', and Mrs. Morrison—and the kid howling. 'Come down the next mornin' for wheat cakes and find nothin' in the kitchen but a tub."

Dant took more interest in Geraldine Fraser than he had taken in anything in his whole life. With the birth of Geraldine—an absurd name for a baby, and therefore duly shortened to Gerry—came the advent, too, of a new enthusiasm in Dant. But all of his enthusiasm was directed upon the baby. With that exasperating attitude of so many grandfathers, he ignored completely the father and mother. Charlie especially was counted, so far as Dant and Gerry were concerned, as a rank outsider. And Etta was tolerated only because she understood the mysteries of hoods, leggings, and diaper change.

Even when she was small, confining her conversation to bubbles, there was a camaraderie between Dant and her which couldn't be denied. She cried less with him than with Etta or Charlie. She would gaze at George Dant for hours with her wide blue eyes.

And as she grew older it became the usual thing to see her trotting beside him, holding to his legs in the drug store where he held conclave with others of his clan. Or she would be propped up against the cigar counter regarding him gravely while he recited a long monologue (he waxed voluble in her presence) for the benefit of their spectators.

Growing bigger, oriented to the niceties of grown-up standards, Gerry became more inseparable from him. She was never clean, but Etta kept for her a pair of passable coveralls always ready against the time when her grandfather would decide to "go to town" and Gerry would howl until she was taken with him.

Somewhere out of the past, and with astonishing memory, Dant dragged forgotten nursery limericks and taught them to Etta's child. Without embarrassment she learned to recite them before people. She was not yet at that age where recital is boresome to the hearers. She presented a quaint and delectable little tintype of her mother—standing on the floor of the drug store with her nervous little hands pressed tight, repeating the story of the jumping cow who one day surmounted the moon.

She was destined to be utterly and completely spoiled by George Dant. In a dismay that was half mocking and half in earnest, Etta and Charlie "gave her up."

186

Sometimes they felt that they should really take her in hand to keep Dant from spoiling her; but the companionship was somehow too precious a thing to mar.

"Who's girl are you?" people would ask her when she was out walking with old Dant.

"Gran'pa's girl an' next Mama's girl an' next Papa's girl," she would tell them in her faint treble.

Then he would take her to the Terminal Confectionery where she had already initiated him into the vices of ice cream sodas and cherry ices.

Sometimes he would try to get her to recite "a piece" in payment for such delicacies, but this never worked. Always she stubbornly refused to speak pieces in return for favours. Some odd quirk of stubbornness, or honour, or coquetry, in her diminutive head made her stand pat on this. Yet she would repeat them at other and less auspicious times for a casual stranger or some friend of Dant's.

She had, in fact, plenty of other ways to gain her ends. She knew, for instance, that if she could see Sim Barnes that gentleman could be depended upon to say to her: "Your Grandfather's no good, is he?"

And she would stamp her foot and deny the slander with all the strength of her baby voice. Grandfather would chuckle. He knew it was all in fun, but he liked it just the same. More than likely he would buy her something before the afternoon was out.

She became accustomed to men more than women. She trusted them more and liked to talk to them. She liked dogs, too, but once when she had tried to pet one it had snapped at her. She had cried and they had rushed her to the doctor's house when she had only a scratch on her hand.

That was very foolish, she knew. But she hadn't yet the words to tell them that it wasn't the snap that hurt. It was because she had wanted to be nice to the dog and he hadn't been nice to her at all.

III

There was to be a Christmas celebration at the church and Gerry was to take part in it. Etta spent more time than she could justly afford with the making of a white dress that stood out from Geraldine's chubby—and somewhat scarred—knees. Mrs. Webster, the Sunday School teacher, had assured Etta that Gerry was too cute for words and that she seemed to "catch on so."

But Gerry wouldn't sing her song at home. Not even the coaxing of her grandfather could get it out of her. They would hear it, she told them logically, at the church on Christmas evening. She told them shame-facedly that it was, though, a song about "Chrisin-themanger."

On Christmas eve there were people in the church who didn't usually come there. These were drawn for a variety of reasons. Some—the families of itinerant rail-road labourers who were parked for the week near the depot—came because of the candy and oranges, and because it is hard to catch the spirit of Christmas in a made-over freight car.

Others came because, on this night, they would find other people gathered there, and they did not want to be so alone on Christmas eve. These came because they could not bear to be alone on a night so full of the memory of Christ. It would be too fearful, and too utterly sad.

Etta, of course, would be there because of Gerry. She wanted to hear Gerry, to "see how she did." She wanted to watch Gerry's eyes as the grocer's boy, dressed as Santa Claus, handed out sacks of hard candy and bitter peanuts. She hadn't been to church for a long time, Etta hadn't, and she felt that she should go there more. Too busy, was her usual excuse; and it was half valid. It was really difficult to get into town of a Sunday morning—especially in the Winter time. Charlie wouldn't go because, he said, he didn't like Alfred Horliss.

"I'd go," he said, "if they'd get another preacher." But he knew that this would make no difference at all.

That night, before people began coming in, it was bitterly chill inside the church. But as the crowd gathered—composed of more people than would ever be there again until next Christmas eve—the poorly constructed building began to take on warmth. People came through the door, greeted the pastor, and hurried quickly toward the stove. The seats near the fire were taken first, late comers edging around the outside until the place was jammed to the walls and door.

The tree was gorgeous with popcorn balls, slightly dingy after several Christmas eves, three strings of electric lights, one of which still functioned, and gilded paper cornucopias. There were cardboard angels with gauzy wings and lithographed blonde hair. Atop the fir was the glory of the whole trimming: a spun-glass star which belonged personally to the Reverend Alfred Horliss. It had been carried from parish to parish in a pasteboard box padded with sawdust.

The first number of the entertainment was a pantomime with a reading. A girl from one of the upper

189

classes in the Sunday school read painfully and with no emotion about the three wise men. Her words were illustrated, were followed somewhat tardily, by the awkward gestures of three men—a trio of high school youths, minus camels, and dressed in long robes which were, on any other night, quite obviously couch covers.

They searched the smoked rafters for the fabled star, and at length the whole audience knew that it was found. All three pointed—each in a rather different direction—and hurried from the platform and out the door at the side. This was the end of the scene.

When the curtain had been pulled back it revealed what was to all intents a stable interior. There were piles of straw on the floor, and a manger was present. There was Joseph, callow and beardless, and, like the wise men, draped in a couch cover. There was Mary, a bundle of pillows in her arms, looking as ashamed as any girl would at having a child by the Holy Ghost, and at the age of thirteen.

In crashed the three wise men, hindered somewhat by their robes, and portraying mingled awe, admiration, reverence, and a deal of consternation.

The audience was phlegmatic. They had seen all this before. They were interested only in the personalities on the platform. It did strike them as humorous—John Buckles pretending he was Joseph; Mary Prendergast trying to be Mary. But nobody laughed. The pantomime was too sacred.

When Etta's Geraldine filed up to the platform with the others of her class there was a collective sound of approval. The little tots, all the women agreed, were so cute every year.

Charlie and Etta felt a wave of pride at seeing her

190

there, all the attention of Creston focused upon her. Etta looked anxiously at the white dress she had made, and decided that it compared favourably with any there. Her gaze swept the half dozen other children critically and then came back to Gerry.

Gerry was placid, serene. She gazed unflinching at the crowd below her. She had stood unabashed before too many drug store cronies—with her grandfather as her manager—to be frightened now. Charlie and Etta were a little disturbed at her fearlessness. She seemed so ready, so contemptuous of it all, and yet so very small.

Mrs. Webster sounded a note on the piano. Seven children set their faces and plunged relentlessly into the rote they knew . . . *In Bethlehem, in Bethlehem* . . .

Mrs. Webster softened her playing so as not to drown out the faltering voices. There was an anxious point at which all sank into silence but Gerry. Her treble sounded out, alone and unafraid: *Christ in the manger, sleeping softly, softly* . . . The others took heart then and joined in once more; but not before Etta had had time to enjoy a mother's pride in Gerry's astuteness.

Tears came into Etta's eyes. She didn't know why; she realized that Gerry scarcely knew what she sang. There was something, though, in Gerry's singing . . . "Christ in the manger, sleeping softly, softly."

There was something about it that tore into Etta's complacency. She became conscious of Charlie beside her, conscious of her love for him, of her love for everything that was a part of them, and Gerry, and her father.

The song ended, Gerry ran down the platform steps

191

and up the aisle, successfully avoiding outstretched arms of elders who would have talked with her on their knee. She climbed into her mother's lap, sat there very pleased with what she had just accomplished.

"How did I do, Mama?" She was sure of the answer as she looked up at Etta enquiringly.

"You were sweet," Etta said. "Wasn't she, Daddy?"

Charlie nodded, a little embarrassed, but quite proud. "You'll have to be quiet now," he told Gerry.

George Dant, for once where Etta's daughter was concerned, stood back against the wall. He was pleased with Gerry, though he felt a little resentful at her being taken away from his management. He kept looking about self consciously to see if any of them were noticing how well Gerry had done. He felt that he was wholly responsible for Gerry, for her talent, for her miniature beauty, for all of her.

"That was pretty cute," he said to the man next to him: "That Gerry's a corker."

"She sure is," the man obliged. "The rest of 'em forgot, but she kept right on goin'."

George Dant said: " 'Smart as a whip, believe me . . . She's just been dyin' to see Santa Claus. I'd like to see what she does. Wouldn't be a darned bit surprised if she didn't see right through the whole thing."

But if Gerry saw even through the precarious false whiskers of the grocer's boy, she gave no sign of it. She looked into his eyes and demanded an orange at once, and a Chinese doll whenever he found it convenient. So, next morning, when she found the Chinese doll under the Fraser tree, she was not even mildly surprised.

Driving home that night, after the entertainment, Etta said: "We all ought to go to church more."

Charlie laughed.

"Well, it wouldn't hurt us any," Etta told him. "We ought to, for Gerry's sake."

"I go to Sunday school," Gerry told them seriously. "I go to Sunday school whenever Papa brings me into town, don't I, Grandpa?" She sat in the back seat, close beside old Dant.

"Well, not unless it's Sunday," he said.

"But I go on Sundays . . ."

"Yeah. You give 'em a run for their money, too."

"I give 'em a run for their money, don't I?" She was pleased at herself, though she had no idea what he was talking about.

WHEN Gerry was a little older—yet still not old enough to understand completely all of what happened—there was a strange event took place at her house between Swede Mongsen and his wife, Peg.

Gerry had always been interested in Peg Mongsen— that is, from the time she was interested in anyone at all. And Gerry's mother and father were interested in her. She knew because they often talked of her. Their talk about Peg wasn't like their talk about other people. Peg was someone special. It was queer the way they mentioned her. They would talk quietly, and look at Gerry furtively as if she had something to do with Peg. They seemed not to want to say anything about Peg before Gerry; and she thought this rather humorous. Surely she had no especial love for this grown-up. Privately, Geraldine thought she was silly. Peg was too grown-up to giggle, and stand on one foot, and make faces. She persisted in acting as only little children, as Gerry knew very well, might act.

She never told her parents that they really didn't need to be afraid to talk about Peg. She could tell that they wanted to say something about her that they wouldn't say before their daughter. But instead of informing them, she kept that fine contemptuous reserve which children are so likely to bestow upon parents who, at times, seem frightfully stupid.

Whenever Peg came to the house (which wasn't so

often now, since Papa told Mama he didn't like to have her around) Gerry remembered odds and ends of conversation about her. It was a crazyquilt background that Geraldine had gathered for Peg Mongsen. Even when she looked at Peg she couldn't quite get it into a meaningful whole.

"Swede never lets on that there's anything wrong. Not since that time at Athena when he got mad at her and Lester." "Lester wrote somebody that she'd been down to Portland after him and he had an awful' time gettin' rid of her." "Clarissa Hempel said that when Swede was working at Athena and Mr. Hempel was sick and she was up most of the night she could see a car standing in front of Peg's house until four and five in the morning." Such was the crazyquilt of words that flashed into Gerry's mind whenever she saw Peg. It was all confusing.

But Peg didn't come to their house quite so frequently now. Gerry felt sure that Papa must have said something that made her stay away. She had heard Mama tell Mrs. Morrison that really Charlie was terrible to her when she came. Mama told Mrs. Morrison that she felt sorry for Peg in a way and that, after all, Mama was the only friend Peg had and she couldn't just keep her out of the house.

When Mother and Father went to dances and left her with Grandpa they sometimes talked about Peg when they returned and were getting ready for bed. Of course, Geraldine was supposed to be asleep; Grandpa had always seen to it that she was put to bed before they returned. But she always stayed awake until they were home. She didn't like it that they were out in the night; she was afraid of the night; and she could not rest until they had come in from it. She was not afraid for herself. Walls and windows were safe enough against it; and Grandpa always would begin to snore, and that was comforting. It was for Papa and Mama that she felt afraid.

She had learned, though, that if she kept her eyes tight shut she could hear a lot that wasn't intended for her. It was fun to hear Mama and Papa whisper. Sometimes it was hard to keep from laughing the way they tiptoed and whispered, or got cross with each other, or talked about Gerry—and all the time Gerry being awake and listening. Some day, when she grew up, she would tell them about it. It would be a splendid joke. But she felt it best not to say anything about it for the present.

She had an earnest desire to attend a dance and see Peg there. Peg seemed to be different at dances. And once—when Papa had had a drink (it was quite a while before Geraldine learned that when Mama said Papa had had a drink she didn't mean water) it seemed that he had liked Peg too much to suit Mama.

But she knew that Mama wasn't right about that. She knew—with an insight that wouldn't be hers always—that Papa loved her mother an awful lot. More than he could possibly love Peg. It was probably all because he had had a drink. That, she knew, made men different than they would be ordinarily. Not that Papa ever drank very much; he just took a drink sometimes when he went to places. It was only because people asked him to and he didn't want to be a dead head. She'd heard him impress that upon Mama more than once. But this was the first time that she'd ever heard Peg mentioned in connection with Papa.

He had said, taking off his collar (Geraldine could hear the rasping sound): "I'm going to quit goin' to these dances if that damned Peg doesn't quit fooling around with our crowd."

The collar slammed down on the bureau: "It's a wonder he don't kill her."

It was exciting to think of Swede killing Peg. But all Mama had said was: "You don't seem to mind. I notice you danced with her as much as anybody. You were drinking, too, and people smelled it on you. I don't see which is worse—you always taking a drink with that Swede Mongsen or my being friendly with Peg."

Gerry couldn't think of any answer for Papa, and evidently he couldn't think of one for himself. He had slammed the bathroom door and didn't come out until Mama was in bed.

It struck her that what Mama had asked wasn't very important. It didn't seem to make much difference. What mattered was that Peg seemed to be an important person. It was as if people revolved around her. Whatever she did seemed to make a difference to other people. Gerry hadn't known anyone like that—of course, there was God, and Santa Claus, and maybe Grandpa. But she hadn't seen God; and Santa Claus only occasionally. As for Grandpa, anyone could see that he wasn't interesting to anyone but herself.

Peg—there was a sort of blaze around Peg. Gerry couldn't tell what it was, couldn't define it. But when it happened, one night long after they had all gone to bed, she felt the climax of what had been a legend. As she saw Swede drag Peg through the open door of the Dant house and out into the yard, she knew that it

197

was sort of the end of things for Peg. Whatever Peg had done, this must surely be the height of it.

II

There is something frightful about a knocking on the door at night, late at night. Two, or maybe three of them, are knocks that you hear in your sleep. Noise against the soft darkness that closes you in and holds you. When you sit up in bed, listening for the sound again, you can tell what is wrong behind that door. Almost instantly you know that someone is ill, or that someone is dead—and there is always relief when you sense that it is only the timorous knock of someone who doesn't bring anything more than a feeble enquiry.

Peg's knock was different, too. Etta, who was awake first, knew that a woman was behind that door. She knew that the woman was frightened, that she was mad with fear. But not until she had leaped from bed and almost gained the hallway did it come over her that the scared girl on her porch was Peg Mongsen.

It was three in the morning—not quite light, not dark enough for midnight, and there was Peg, disheveled, a man's coat wrapped around her and her hair looking let down even though it was bobbed.

"Etta—please let me stay here, will you? I'm afraid to go home. I'm afraid Swede'll come there for me and there's nobody there!" She was wild, shaking, anxious to lie to Etta and yet wanting to tell her the truth, wanting to get it all out of her and be let off from it.

"Come on in the kitchen," Etta said. She didn't want

Charlie to wake. She wanted to hear Peg's story before Charlie came in to them.

She was startled at the girl's appearance when she switched on the kitchen light. At the lighting of the uncovered globe, swinging in an arc on its fly-specked cord, Peg seemed to recede within herself. She was white, oddly white, and her red lips stood out against her face like a gash under her nose. The man's coat was not Swede's coat. It was a belted whipcord, a slender man's coat. A coat that would belong to a hawkish, youngish man.

"You've been stepping out on Swede," Etta accused her. But somehow she felt inferior before Peg. She felt inadequate. A decent woman against a worldly one, it was. Armed against the unarmed. And yet Peg was strangely weak at that moment. Her eyes asked for forgiveness, and her hands trembled for the sleeve of Etta's night-dress.

"Oh, I know, Etta! I know I have. But I couldn't stay there. I couldn't let him beat me up like I know he will. I don't care what happens now. He's caught me—but it was the first time, Etta. Honest it was. It'd never been anything like that and I don't know who told him."

"Who's coat is that?"

"It's Frank's. Swede came busting up to the hotel and he was killing Frank and I ran out and got in his car."

Etta was sure that Swede was not killing Frank. She wished for a moment that she could be sure he was. "Who's Frank?"

"Frank Morris. He—oh, you don't know him, I guess. He works in Walla Walla."

"Were you at Walla Walla, then?"

199

Peg nodded silently. And then in a swift, new outburst. "I didn't dare go to the house. I drove like the devil to get here. I don't know why I came this way. The house was all the place I had to go, and then I knew I couldn't go there. He'll come there tonight sure . . . I wonder how he knew we were there?"

Something was creeping up into Etta's face, showing in her eyes.

"I suppose you hate whoever told him. I suppose you think they're stinking mean, don't you?"

But there was Charlie in the doorway. Charlie with his trousers and his union suit, and his socks showing beneath his trouser cuffs.

"What's the row?"

"Peg and Swede have had a run-in and he wants to beat her up."

He may have been too lethargic for expression; at least none passed over his features. They heard him open the front door and go out on the porch. They heard the sound of the car's engine, which Peg had not turned off. Then it died—Charlie had switched it off, and they heard him padding up on the porch in his stockinged feet.

"That's not your car," Charlie said, coming into the kitchen.

"No . . ." Peg groped for explanation, and then all sound choked within her.

"Swede'll be here in his own," Charlie mentioned, "and there'll be hell to pay if he's as roaring as I guess maybe he is."

Etta jumped. "He won't come here—why would he come here, Charlie?"

Charlie stood there rumpling his already tangled

hair. He looked like that smaller boy who had stood on the school steps years ago—or was it years ago?—and mocked at Etta and Peg because they were potential women and he a potential man.

"Sure he'll come here. He knows dam' well that a woman ain't goin' to her *mother's* when she's been caught in bed with another guy. And if he don't find her at home he knows he can find her here."

"Charlie! You haven't any right to insult her like that!"

"I'm not insulting anybody. I just mentioned the facts. This is none of my business, except that I don't care about having stuff like this goin' on in a house with Geraldine in it. That's all."

He turned and left the kitchen, left Etta torn with varied loyalties, hating Peg and loving her. She didn't know until a moment afterward that Charlie had gone out onto the porch to meet and ward off the Swede he knew would come. Presently she heard them talking out there. They were low-voiced, two men intense each with his own purpose. But at length the door scraped open and Swede was there. Swede was standing in the kitchen like the wrath of hell let loose.

She thought at first that he had been drinking, but she saw that his eyes were bleared by rage, not liquor. His spleen had shot through and through him.

Peg saw him there, as she stood against the wall with another man's coat around her. A corner of her brain told her of that coat, screamed of it. With another corner she was conscious of Etta standing there; she even had time to think that Etta was not too young with sleep around her eyes, with her shabby nightgown. And yet another corner told her that soon all corners

201

of all brains—hers and Swede's, too—would be stopped from telling anybody anything at all.

Charlie's arm seemed limp against Swede's chest. His words meant nothing. Peg couldn't even hear what the words were; and Swede seemed to walk through Charlie and not past him.

"Swede, for God's sake, let me alone! Let me alone—leave me. Do anything else you want, but let me alone!"

For a moment it seemed that she had won. He stood there looking at her, and both Etta and Charlie knew how much he loved her then. But he began to speak, and his words came out of his thick mouth in a stream that seemed to give him fresh physical impetus.

"You dam' little slut you!"

His fist shot down upon her shoulder, cruelly . . . there was a crack like a whip, but she did not scream.

"Mongsen, you can't do that in my house," Charlie said, and he gained the courage somehow to turn the man around to him. Swede glared down at him, blinking against the light, as if trying to weigh the import of Charlie's words.

Something like cunning broke into his blue eyes. "I can't, huh?" He laughed like the rasping of a wagon-brake. "If I can't do it here, I'll take her in the road, damn her!"

Nothing could stop him. Ten men would not have stopped him as he jerked that limp, sinful figure through the door to which she had come for protection.

"He'll kill her, Charlie," Etta said, and her husband followed them out, mumbling protestations that he knew would be of no use.

But if Swede contemplated any such move, he at least showed no intent of performing it there at once. He

202

half dragged and half carried his wayward woman to his car, forced her with contempt into the back seat, and drove fiercely away—as though he had loaded something foul and wanted to drive away at once to escape unpleasantness.

Charlie turned and came back into the house. "He won't kill her," he said. "He won't do nothing of the kind."

Still Etta was frightened; she wanted to call Peg's mother.

"You let them attend to this. If Swede don't take care of her she'll go to her mother, anyhow. If he does, then it'll all be jake."

Now, after it was over, it struck Etta that Charlie obtained from it a malicious satisfaction. It seemed almost to strike him as humorous, and she could clearly see his hate for Peg and what she had done. It bristled from him, as obvious as the hiked-up hairs of an angry tomcat.

Etta peered through the curtains of the front door. "That fellow's car's still out there."

"What fellow?"

"The one she was with. She took his car when Swede found them."

Charlie chuckled. "Maybe he won't come after it. He might not think it's healthy . . . I'll drive it out on the road tomorrow. It can rot to hell for all I care."

Etta turned out the kitchen light, and they started for their bedroom. There, on the steps up from the hall, was Geraldine. She stared at them with eyes that had not been closed for some time.

CHAPTER THREE

I

LINDBERGH had just slain distance with a gesture more heroic, more awesome, than David's toward Goliath. And in his wake there followed crashes —somehow less spectacular than victory—and a series of disappearances that filled the newspaper columns enough to set even Creston by its ears. Radio announcers, dropping their vaudeville jokes and their personality-plus voices, told of planes that had gone out into the horizon not to be heard from again. Sunday supplements spoke of a "Port of Missing Airmen" and reviewed the tragedies of the air. Giant aircraft whirred skyward day after day—and if they were lost it was astonishing how quickly people forgot them.

Air-minded, people were becoming. It was a phrase coined by development experts, progressive fanatics like Arthur Brisbane, and the promotors of dinky aircraft corporations. It was a pat, checked-suit phrase. But it was true. Even Creston became air-minded. The news was full of new records, of ovations to "Lindy" and then (as the Army became aware that somehow a hero had been born illegitimately, as it were, out of its ranks) to *Colonel* Charles Lindbergh.

The government instituted an air mail route from Portland to Pasco. The plane flew each day directly over Creston, zooming low on those times when the pilot felt playful. It made Crestonites feel important to have that plane overhead each day. They learned not to look up when they heard its engines. They soon began to be able to glance casually at their watches and say: "Well, it must be three-thirty. Yeah, right on the dot today." Or else: "He's a little late today accordin' to my time."

Once the plane suffered engine trouble and landed easily on Joe Key's land. In ten minutes cars from miles around had collected at the fence line. Men stood around the plane in a respectful circle. Small boys, less awed, ventured to climb on to the wings. The pilot went on repairing in a business-like manner. Finally he ordered them all out of the way, elected two proud youths to form a chain to help him spin the propeller, and went bouncing off down the field and into the air toward Pasco.

In taking off, he knocked down a good deal of wheat. Farmers often shot Chinese pheasants, against the law or not, because when they soared upward they shattered the wheat heads. But Joe Key didn't complain against the airman. He felt ever afterwards proud of that particular spot which had served the United States mail.

Because of all this sensitiveness to the air and its possibilities, Lester Adams created quite a sensation when he let it be known that he had joined the flying cadets at San Antonio. The *Creston Leader* went to the expense of the first halftone (not for election purposes) in years: a reproduction of a snapshot of Lester in a flying helmet.

When he passed his examinations, was one of the first to be allowed a solo flight in a heavy bombing plane, he began to take on the aura—locally at least—of Lindbergh and Byrd.

Lester, in Texas, couldn't be aware that he had somehow become a hero. He felt more like an outcast. Aviation had been, for him, what he called the last ditch. He'd gone to a movie—The Legion of the Condemned —in which several young men in one sort of trouble or another had joined an air force during the war and had vied for a chance at death.

This melodrama was what decided him. He had come almost directly from the theatre to a recruiting station. To his surprise he was accepted physically. There was a delay during which his professors at college were asked questions by letter, but even his recommendations came through in a manner that was, after he'd had time to think it over meanwhile, rather swift. Not a week later, in a Portland rooming house, he received word that he must report at San Antonio. Not knowing what else to do, he complied.

He hadn't graduated from college. There had been no trouble there, and his grades were not too bad. They had improved, at least, from the first and he was well liked by most of his instructors. But his interests had spread like a feather fan. He had no focus, no set idea as to where he might be going. Dissatisfaction settled down upon him like a fever. And then there was Rachel Smethurst—but that was later.

At high school there had been that vague but quite practical idea of starting a chain of drug stores. But once at the University, once pledged within a fraternity which happened to have a preponderance of literary members, he had fallen in with a clique that recited poetry all night and slept half the day. In another age they would have belonged to Wilde and his cohorts.

They talked philosophy—that is to say, they took God apart and reassembled Him, rather the worse for the experience at their hands. They ate and they were occasionally merry, certain that on some tomorrow they would die and at times feeling very sad about it. They drank, too, whenever they had the money to buy bootleg and it didn't gag them too much. They read Schopenhauer if they weren't in love; and even those who did read him managed to fall in love spasmodically.

They were all serious about it. Whatever they meant —whatever it was, was very important. And Lester was one of them, raw at first, countrified, but gradually blooming out into the glazed yellowish flower which might have personified them all. They majored, usually, in English, and managed to enroll in the majority of reading courses. Because of this, they made fair grades.

But they were not a crowd for a young man who had intended to own and manage a drug store chain. Nor a young man who might have to go back to Creston to raise wheat. Lester had floundered hopelessly toward the last year or two. As graduation loomed—a gaunt figure in a long black gown and foursquare cap —Lester realized that he was unarmed, naked to the world that was before him. Something practical in him, something that had oozed into him from out the prosaic soil of Oregon wheat, made him realize this when the rest of the crowd did not.

The quandary took the form of a question, and the question was "What will I do?" It referred to the time when he would be graduated. Before the question was ever answered he met Rachel Smethurst at the Junior Prom.

The men knew her as The Jewess. She'd been to three successive Junior Proms, looking no older at the third than at the first. That was astonishing when one stopped to think that at the first she was seventeen and at the third, quite naturally, twenty. Those three years would have brought change in most girls. But when Rachel Smethurst had first appeared, coming down to Eugene from Portland with Snobby Peters, she was just as glittering, as highly shellacked, as on the night when Lester noticed her for the first time.

Snobby Peters had brought her to all three of those Proms. It was a gesture of his to justify his name. He gloried so much in the name of Snobby, took it so calmly, that it had ceased to mean anything derogatory. He was aware of how it "burned up" the co-eds to have a fellow go up to Portland and bring in a rich little Jewess. Rachel, too, realized this. She knew that she was a barb in the side of every lithe figure there. So she pierced deeper whenever she got the chance.

She hadn't been to college, just to a fashionable preparatory school in California. She felt, she said, that college was too fearfully difficult and there was no need of appearing dull. Besides, everyone knew that her family could afford to send her to the most exclusive college in the country. So why bother to go?

Lester had come stag to the Prom. But Snobby Peters, dancing with Rachel, saw him standing by a pale blonde in a blue gown and he made the error of fancying that Lester was with her. The next moment he had confronted Lester, begun an introduction, when the pale blonde drifted away. Snobby had been chagrined, but he stuck it through. As the music began afresh Rachel was in Lester's arms and they danced away from Snobby.

She awakened him at once, brought him out of that lethargy which was the current collegiate mode, for the same reason that she affected others in an identical way. She was, in short, The Jewess.

He had the feeling that she was tense, compact, almost muscular. Her black hair was a sheen, a stygian cap over a well shaped head. Her features would have been too regular had it not been for the largeness of her eyes. She wore a dark dress of some material which Lester could not name. It had the cool feeling of unperturbed flesh and he could have sworn that she was aware of that. About her hung the wraith of perfume like the ghosts of romances of which she knew everything and he nothing.

Men had possessed her, Lester knew. Not boys, not anyone like himself or Snobby Peters, but older men. He was sure of it. It was a sign she wore that was oddly visible to men—and not to women.

He was painfully conscious of her beauty. It was a decadent, pagan beauty that went through him like a blade. He wondered how she would look at thirty. In Portland he had seen a great many Jewesses. The city was full of them, and almost all of them were pretty. Some, like Rachel here, were beautiful. People said that after thirty they became flabby, ugly. Lester looked down at Rachel and he was sure that it didn't matter. Thirty—she couldn't be thirty for ten years. Ten years with a Rachel such as he held in his arms . . .

She was rich, too. She boasted of it a little, not too cleverly, and Snobby Peters had said so. Snobby would know. It would be adventurous to marry Rachel—or someone like her. He hadn't yet become selective enough to focus on her. Rachel had only given him the idea. What would Creston think? He didn't care; he was merely curious, amused at the idea of it.

209

Rachel's father would be glad, probably, to have her marry a college student. He would be prodigal. He would be as prodigal as Jew fathers are supposed to be when they are rich and have beautiful daughters.

All during the first half of the dance they had spoken no word. Fused with the music's heat they glided over the polished floor, Rachel and Lester. The perfume of her hair and skin was full of portent for him. She was a woman who had skirted the edges of desire—like Peg Mongsen—and who had finally been drawn in. He had an unformed thought that her life was probably a continual sinning and penitence.

He spoke for the first time since the introduction.

"I've got to see you again," he told her. "It's got to be soon."

She was pleased and showed it just enough to gather him in. She promised, before they had got back to Peters, that she'd be glad to have him call at her home that next week-end.

And then she said, as if in afterthought: "Perhaps I'd better meet you at Mier and Frank's. At the tea room."

He agreed, and when he left her with Snobby he was genuinely torn with longing to keep her with him forever.

After the Prom he waited for Peters. It was five o'clock before Snobby returned to the room.

"You made a hell of a big hit with The Jewess, Les," he said.

"God, she's keen! I never saw anybody like her."

Peters chuckled. "There must be a thousand in Portland just exactly like her. Something pitiful about them

—they're so dam' beautiful, and some of them have everything, and yet——"

"You mean they're Jewesses? You're crazy. That doesn't make any difference to people."

"It does, though. That's why girls hate her so. They might not think it, but they hate her on that account. And because she's beautiful."

"A lot of girls here are Jewesses."

"Yeah . . . But they don't brag about it. Not that she does actually. But you know she is. She's proud of it. She's one of these proud Jewesses . . . Do you get the idea when you dance with her that she's old as—as sin?"

"As old as sin," Lester said, and he met Peters' grin soberly.

"Ancient and hard, that's what I mean. An eye for an eye—the Mosaic law, that's her."

"Does she neck, if you don't mind telling me? . . . It's five, you know."

"Hell, I've been over to the Sig house playing poker. I've never touched her. If you want to know the fact, she scares me to death. I wouldn't want to get her started."

Lester sat silently, staring at a cigarette's end.

"Are their old men pretty touchy about who the girl marries?"

"I hadn't studied them as a tribe," Peters said, and he turned to confront Lester with burlesque astonishment. "I knew you were progressing pretty firmly, but I'll be goddamed if I thought it had gone that far!"

"Oh, I don't mean her especially, Snobby . . . But by God, I got a notion to try and marry some rich woman. What the hell's the use of me graduating?

211

What'll I do? What is all this poetry and philosophy and life's-a-hell-of-a-mess business goin' to get me? I can't go out and get a job. Neither can you, only you've got money, damn you. I won't go back to Eastern Oregon and muck around in that damned wheat. I'd go nuts. I got a notion to chuck it all and get the hell out."

Snobby Peters carefully lit a cigarette and studied the snake-skin covered lighter in his palm. "It's not so easy to marry for money, old topper. You hear a hell of a lot about it, but it's not so easy. Besides—well, a guy that does that is—well, he's sort of a mucker, ain't he? Sort of be worse than tillin' the Oregon soil, if you see what I mean."

Lester got up out of his chair, began unloosening his tie.

"What the hell if I would be a mucker? I don't pretend to be any gentleman. I belong to farmer stock—Scotch-German-God knows what. I'm proud of the fact I've worked on a farm. There's nothing low about it. But every Summer I've gone back it's been harder. It's so—so damned empty. You don't realize it until you're away. Worst of all, they're happy. That's what scares a guy. You're afraid you'll get like that and won't know it, or give a damn. I can't go back there, Snobby. I'd go nuts."

Peters surveyed him with mock sadness.

"You won't have far to go, you egg . . . What we'd both better do right now is go to bed."

II

Rachel met him that week-end, as she'd promised, at Mier and Frank's. He hadn't found the tea room;

212

she caught him quite by accident near the elevators. He was looking bewildered, and then he was suddenly aware of white glistening teeth and a sense of fullness at seeing her.

"This is the damnedest place," he said.

She laughed, appreciating his failure to orient himself in a woman's realm.

"Let's don't go upstairs," she said, and she led him out of the maze of counters and crowded aisles.

He was surprised—though he thought afterward that he shouldn't have been—to have her guide him to a roadster, gaunt and sleek as a greyhound, at the curb.

"You drive," she offered him and he climbed willingly to the wheel of a car that cost more than he had spent at the University in three and a half years.

This Rachel was no different from the girl at the Prom. Even in the open, rushing along with the breeze, she was heavy with mystery and longing. Seated there beside her, he felt that he was actually living. The rhythm of life was going through him. He was conscious of functioning as a human organism.

They had met at three, and she suggested that he drive out the highway, along the Columbia to the Vista House. Soon it loomed before them, atop a spiral of asphalt, a small round building like a tower with a parapet. When they had climbed the spiral ribbon that led up to it they stopped and got out of the car. They went up the little stairway that led around the Vista House and up to its roof. They did this mainly because that was what everyone did who passed that way.

It was clear today, and they looked down the river to that misty point where it dissolved into the horizon; Below them were flat, sandy islands looking like spilled coffee on bright blue cloth. Over on the Washington side of the Columbia, the forests were a confusing green panorama.

But Rachel looked at it impassively.

"I always come up here and look," she said. "You see, I wasn't impressed the first time I came, and I've always thought perhaps it would *grow* on me." She sighed, and added: "It never has. A picture of it is always so much nicer."

She looked out of place, surely enough, there above the river. She looked odd in spite of her tan sport coat and her gay, flying scarf. Rachel belonged in a room; she was the kind of a woman who should have been set into a room forever.

Dusk fell as they started back for the town, and Lester suggested that they stop at one of the inns along the road. They were all called "inns," as if a country as young as the Pacific Coast could have an inn for at least another seventy-five years! What they really represented were buildings devoted to chicken dinners, third-rate orchestras, and booths for promiscuous couples who could not afford apartments and hotels. But at this hour they were almost respectable. At the Grayton, where Rachel and Lester stopped, they found they were the only patrons.

A waiter who plainly considered them a trifle early half-heartedly administered to their wants, leaving them mostly alone. Rachel was really hungry; she ate hurriedly, not speaking until she was quite satisfied. Lester was too nervous, too high strung over her presence to find appetite.

At length, frankly boorish, she stopped eating, sank back and stretched impolitely. Her eyes closed like a kitten's, her face was flushed with the effects of warm food and hot coffee.

"I want a cigarette," she said, and she used that as an excuse—so Lester thought—to come to his side of the booth to get a light. In the dull half light she was like a spell of evil beside him. As her cool fingers steadied his wrist while he held the lighter he was afraid that she would detect his swift pulse, his damp palms.

She seemed actually to be drawing out his energy, sapping him of strength. Into her fingertips he felt himself flooding . . . mercury . . . electrical current— the pictures flashed through his mind fantastically. She was, he thought, Delilah.

III

Both knew all along that there must be some sort of climax for them, though they may not have thought of that climax as marriage. But Lester, and Rachel, too, knew that they would carry the thing through. It was not to be any casual meeting of young man and personable young girl. They had not been aware of it at the Prom, but there in the booth of the Grayton they were both certain of it.

He promised not to wait until the next week-end to see her; he would come again to Portland on Wednesday night. Rachel told him she would meet him at the interurban station.

Useless for the remainder of the days until Wednesday, he moped around the fraternity house and attended classes only intermittently. He had lost his purpose completely. Rachel was the new goal. But he had not yet brought his words to Snobby Peters into an actual resolve. It didn't occur to him that he might marry Rachel and literally hold her, legally, for ransom. The ransom was to be a niche in the world. Some sort of niche—any sort except going back to Creston or owning a drug store chain. That part of the dilemna was up to Rachel's father, that legendary figure Lester hadn't even seen.

They were married regularly enough. The license he could pay for at once, but he found that if he were to make even a ghost of an attempt at a honeymoon he would have to buy the ring at an instalment jeweler's. Rachel seemed to enjoy this, and he had a swift thought that, after all, she was a good sport. She might actually love him. It was an angle that, as a matter of cold fact, hadn't entered into his mind.

The jeweler accepted Lester's five dollars down, his name and address and the recommendation, via telephone, of a Portland clothier where Lester had bought odds and ends.

It suddenly occurred to him that she might have religious preferences, but Rachel assured him that a justice of the peace would do as well as any particular clergyman.

Their honeymoon was a sticky, overplayed nightmare at the Portland Hotel. In the morning Lester went down to get shaved. He thought it over while prone in the barber chair; and Rachel stared at the ceiling, her mind equally occupied with their hasty action.

But, with the memory of the night, the half hour apart was torture enough. They met one another with fresh enthusiasm. Lester was delighted at being allowed to help Rachel dress. It was fascinating, crazily intriguing.

In a swift burst of words he drew her close to him: "Oh, Rachel, I've never been so damned happy!"

She was moved by his words, almost pitied him. She cooled swiftly in his embrace. His words, his actions, were almost womanish. She couldn't have done that, not even though she was a woman. He should have kissed her, caressed her, silently. She should have stood proud and unashamed while he worshipped her with human hands and idolatrous eyes.

Their breakfast was quiet. They had decided to inform Rachel's father. There was little else to do. Lester's allowance wouldn't come until the latter part of the month, and he would not listen to her suggestion that he go back to school and keep the marriage secret for a while. He had to stay with her, he told her. He did not say that she was his now, and that he would not trust her.

"What do you suppose he'll say?" Lester wanted to know.

"I've no idea. He's never been told before that I was married. I don't think it's come over him that I even might be thinking about it. It'll be quite as much of a surprise for me as for you, whatever he does."

Yet, Lester afterward remembered, Rachel did not seem to be astonished at what her father did. She took it resolutely, very calmly, and he knew that she was accustomed to bending before the patriarchal law of S. Smethurst. He became aware, as they had stood there together in the Smethurst home, that never once had she crossed her father's word.

He had expected—after Smethurst's smooth words which did not even faintly condone their actions—that

217

Rachel would renounce parental ties, that she would come to his arms defiantly beautiful.

He remembered how Smethurst (whose father's name was Solomon) stood stodgy and sleek to look over them both. He had known at once that here would be no prodigal Jew father, no forgiving character such as he had witnessed in movies and second-rate road companies. He would not grasp Lester's hand with a smooth flabby paw. He would not grin and pat him on the back. Lester realized slowly that he had done some terrible misjudging.

He who had been Solomon was large and dark; Lester thought that, underneath the expensive suiting, he would be glistening with body oil. There shot between the boy and the man at first glance an impenetrable wall. But that wall didn't prevent S. Smethurst from talking over it to Lester.

He said something for Rachel, too.

"I am hurt," he told her. "I am hurt that you think you could pull over a cheap trick on me. That you think you could do what all the boys and girls think is smart. And that I would let it go."

To Lester his voice was edged, but just as politely smooth.

"If you think you can make trouble you are wrong about the law. In Oregon a girl is not a woman until she is twenty-one."

"But we love each other, Mr. Smethurst. Can't you see that?" Lester felt lost and alone. He stood against Rachel and her father. He knew that she might as well not be in that room for all the assistance she was giving him.

S. Smethurst had smiled. He performed his idea of it

by drawing full lips back over teeth that were too white, too bright, for a man who smoked cigars all day.

"I see everything. I have not known you before." And then like a shot: "How long have you been going with Rachel—behind my back?"

The deception hadn't been long-lived, and Lester was forced to admit that.

Smethurst smiled again, that drawing back of lips— as if pulled by a hidden string.

"You love each other! Hah!"

All the time Rachel standing there, saying nothing. Rachel obviously repentant, obviously weakening. Rachel with her blood red lips and night black hair. Rachel with her long firm legs and eloquent thighs.

"I know what may happen to young people," S. Smethurst reported. "I know all about it. You will go on to school, as I say. You need not bother over anything. I will see to it that the marriage is annulled. You don't need to worry over nothing."

"But . . . Rachel, you're going to stick it out with me, aren't you?"

For the first time since he had known her he saw pity in her eyes. She was torn at least a little.

"How can I, Lester? I thought—somehow I thought it would be all right with Papa."

Lester had looked quickly at Smethurst and saw no pleasure on his face. The man hadn't been even pleasantly astonished that his daughter was to obey. He had expected it; he had always possessed that obeisance.

But he was soothed and he had walked toward Lester.

"You see, it don't always work. Rachel knows now that she has made a mistake. You should know it, too.

You go back to school as I said. Everything will be all right and I am only sorry."

"Rachel!" Lester said. One agonizing word to her, one last try at the ghastly thing. Yet it was not because he loved her, not because he wanted her. It was because there was in his head that middle-class sense of fitness. This woman should denounce her father, her home, for the man she had married.

But she didn't. She stood immobile. She stood aloof like the evil angel she was becoming in Lester's mind.

"Now, now, Mr. Adams. Let's not make it too drawn out." The lips drew back again, but they revealed fangs this time. "I will write you out a little check and you will say nothing about this unfortunate thing."

A swift wave of relief came over Lester Adams. Now the thing was swinging around to where he could deal with it. He knew now what he must do. He drew himself into a fine frenzy of rage, an excellent picture of outraged youth.

"To hell with your damned check! Do you think I'd blat it all over hell that I was fool enough to marry a girl like that! I'm damned glad you won't have it—do you get that? You needn't worry. I won't tell anybody. So far as anyone'll know from me, she's still marketable and you can both go to hell."

And even then he had expected Rachel to shrink beneath his vitriolic words, to sob on his shoulder perhaps. But she stood there contemptuously, watching her father as if she thought it odd that he didn't kill the boy.

"Get out," S. Smethurst said. "Get out, you cheap skirmisher!"

Lester got out, too. Sickened physically, he went out

220

of that massive door and down the massive steps. He passed the rose bushes—S. Smethurst would be so proud of rose bushes—went down the sleek walk and into the street.

"Christ . . ." he kept muttering as if trying to impress upon himself how utterly disgusted he really was.

But before he had gone far, he had taken another tack. Gradually he began to feel embittered, lonely, cheated. He misted Rachel with a fineness she didn't have. He convinced himself that he loved her with a keen, youthful love that would have mellowed into something wonderful and beautiful beyond all reality. But she had thrown all that over, he told himself, to please a lousy parent, a God damned Jew. She would go down to the Prom next year and no one would realize she was any the wiser from life.

He walked the streets of Portland, simmering these things in his mental pot. Down to the warehouses at Front Street, passing gibbering Chinamen, jostling with less fortunate counterparts of S. Smethurst, touching elbows with blade-like Italians and swaggering Greeks. Then up again, toward the shops of Washington Street.

He wished for Snobby Peters. He wanted to talk to Snobby about it. He wanted to talk to somebody about it. Then he remembered a slender gray card in his pocket. Larson's Book Nook.

He sought out Florence Larson, not so much because he wanted advice, but so that he might have audience for the forlorn and cheated figure he was presenting. He found her shop, a two-by-four little place with book-lined walls and gaudily painted monk's cloth hangings. He opened the door and went inside. The place was empty, it seemed; but presently Florence

Larson came out of a back room shielded by a curtained doorway. He wondered if she lived in there.

"Why, Lester! How are you?"

He told her. He told her the whole story, and not once was he interrupted by any customers for Larson's Book Nook.

When he had finished, Florence Larson looked at him oddly. What did he expect from her? What did he want to be told? She felt that helplessness she had known when first she taught at Creston.

"I'd go back down to school and forget about it, Lester. That's what I'd do if I were you."

He shook his head. "I'm through with school. I wish to God I'd never seen the damned place."

"Why, what's wrong? I thought you liked it."

"I did. But I've just lately found out that it's not going to help me much. I shouldn't have gone at all."

Florence Larson remembered that she had encouraged him to go. It had seemed so fine to find Lester Adams wanting to go on, to grow out of Creston. She wondered if Creston people shouldn't always stay there, if perhaps they weren't meant to stay there.

"Why don't you go down home for a while, Lester, until this thing gets off your mind?" Miss Larson's voice was a little bored. After all, strangers had no right to unload their problems on you.

"I can't go home, either. I'd go crazy. What is there to do down there unless I farm?"

"Well . . . nothing, I suppose."

"You never liked it," he accused her. "You never could find what you wanted down there."

Miss Larson looked frightened. He thought for a moment that she had seen an accident out of the window of the shop. And then she answered him quietly.

"No. It's pretty hard to find what you want, anywhere at all." Somehow she felt drawn toward this youth, now. She stretched forth a cool hand and touched his wrist. "Some people get hedged in, Lester. With some people it seems that no matter which way they turn they're hedged in by something."

He looked up at her, grateful for her acquiescence to his mood. He felt suddenly desirous of saying something that would compliment her.

"You didn't let Creston hedge you in. You jerked loose and got this shop, and now you're free. I guess I thought I was getting free by going to college, and then by marrying Rachel. It——"

He was interrupted by the parting of the curtains leading to the back room of Larson's Book Nook. Mr. Hugon was peering out inquisitively. He saw Lester Adams and a look of recognition flashed into his little round eyes. He still wore a green stiff collar and a green shirt.

Miss Larson jumped up from her stool.

"You remember Mr. Hugon, Lester . . ."

The two men did not shake hands, and Mr. Hugon held to his place in the doorway. Lester took up his hat.

"Well, it's been a help to talk to you, Miss Larson . . ."

"I wish I could help, Lester. But—but you can see that I'm not very qualified."

He wondered afterward if her words had meant more than the tone conveyed. Remembering Mr. Hugon, he had a swift repulsion for Florence Larson. Somehow Mr. Hugon reminded him of S. Smethurst.

223

He turned into a movie because there seemed nowhere else to go. The picture was The Legion of the Condemned. At first he didn't give it notice. The screen was filled with huge images of Rachel . . . Rachel nakedly wild, startlingly lovely. . . . Rachel standing in that room there with her father—with Mr. Hugon. . . . Thick lips, drawing back. . . . Somehow Mr. Hugon and S. Smethurst, Rachel and Florence Larson, became inextricably interwoven.

But presently he was aware of the story of the celluloid, the heroic antics of young men cheated or thwarted because of a woman. They were handsome, brave and reckless in their leather coats and fur-lined helmets. They climbed into wingéd coffins with a smile and a wave of the hand.

It was when Lester had come out of the movie house that he decided to join the ranks of the airmen. The idea, what with all that had happened to him, seemed not at all fantastic. Creston and its waving yellow grain, its placid yet seeking people, was a dream. He was ashamed, too, of what he had done. He couldn't go back to his mother, the woman from whom he'd grown all too far away. He couldn't face anybody; he felt unclean and unwanted. He felt the sordid touch of Rachel's body, of her father's body through her.

These serious-minded film clowns had decided for him. He could see no great difference between their various plights and his own. He would have to wing himself above the Rachels, the Pegs, the Miss Larsons, and their clumsy fingering with life. And, too, above a world which had no place for a boy who read poetry and philosophy and knew nothing else.

He would challenge swift death, and welcome it.

224

Yet a month later, in his first solo effort above the hangars of San Antonio, he was keeping every wit about him so that he might avoid crashing into an earth that was imminent and hard.

CHAPTER FOUR

I

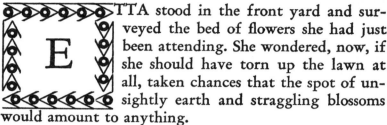

TTA stood in the front yard and surveyed the bed of flowers she had just been attending. She wondered, now, if she should have torn up the lawn at all, taken chances that the spot of unsightly earth and straggling blossoms would amount to anything.

She looked suspiciously at the plot, sighed, and went into the house. At least it was a try. Mrs. Morrison had had some awfully pretty tulips last year. Of course, some wretched youngsters had snapped them off—all of them—one night. But out here in the country they were perfectly safe. Provided, naturally, that they matured.

She put down the little hand trowel on the ledge of the kitchen window, removed her cotton gloves and washed her hands at the sink. For the first time she noticed how red they had become, how worn the nails. It was odd, she thought, that she hadn't noticed them before. It was certain they hadn't suddenly taken on that appearance. She remembered that her mother's hands had been like that. She had wondered why she didn't ever take more care of them.

Etta smiled to herself, ruefully. One didn't seem to have the time. Oh—as a matter of fact—one had the time. But you never got to it. There was something more important; that was it: always something more important.

Geraldine came in with the sober announcement that

one of the chickens was dead. She was not perturbed over the fact; she merely informed Etta as an underling informs an overlord of some condition of the manor.

"Are you sure?" Etta wanted to know. Geraldine often divided the condition into distinctions. "Is it quite dead?"

Gerry nodded. "There's flies all over it," she said, certain that this was definite proof.

"Well . . ." Etta said, and she went out into the back yard, Gerry at her heels.

"It's up by the barn," she directed her mother. "It's a hen, though."

Hens weren't as important as roosters, Gerry felt. Not even if they did lay eggs. There weren't so many roosters, and roosters crowed and were very certain about themselves.

Etta's prediction was a dire one: "One of our best layers, I'll bet."

"I s'pose . . ." Geraldine was willing to be agreeable. But she was already more interested in the fact that if you scooted your feet along the ground the dust oozed into your shoes and felt tickly and warm.

"*Ger*aldine!"

Geraldine stopped scooting her feet along the ground. She wondered how Mama noticed so much. She would be walking along and you wouldn't think she was watching anything and all of a sudden she would forbid you to do something. Grandpa wasn't like that. He never noticed things like that.

The deceased fowl gave evidence of its presence some time before they arrived on the scene of its demise.

"Heavens . . ." Etta made a face. But smells didn't

227

bother Geraldine in the least. Geraldine approved of smells; they twitched your nose.

A horde of angry, heavy black flies made a tentative rise into the air as the two approached. The flies kept their close formation and returned to the dead even while Etta grasped it gingerly by one leg.

"I wish Daddy was here . . . where on earth shall we put it?" She held it aloof by one leg, and looked about uncertainly.

Gerry's face lit with joy. She had a solution at once. "I know—let's bury it!"

Her mother had to admit the good judgment of this suggestion. She despatched Geraldine to the house to bring the coal shovel. The girl came back quickly, dragging the shovel behind her, and she began at once an ineffectual attack on the surface of the barn yard.

"Here, child—I've been digging in the ground all morning. I know how."

Reluctantly Gerry relinquished the tool. But she lost interest in the procedure shortly thereafter; while Etta dug a shallow hole Gerry watched the flies.

"Mama, are these blow flies?"

"What are blow flies?" she wanted to know, and then, before Etta could frame anything satisfactory: "What do they call them blow flies for?"

"Heavens! I don't know! Here . . ." Etta scraped the offensive bird into the hole she had scooped out. She threw on the dry dust, covering the drooped gray feathers. She patted down the mound with the shovel back.

Gerry was fascinated. She found herself wishing there were another hen to bury.

"It'd ought to have a cross on it, hadn't it, Mama? Can I put a cross on it?"

"Hush, dear. You mustn't think about things like that. Come on, we'll see if the paper's come."

"But why don't they put crosses on chickens' graves —and horses and animals?"

"Oh . . . there're too many of them. Besides—they aren't people."

The two of them walked briskly back to the house, both rather pleased at the thought of an unpleasant task over and done with.

"Wouldn't it be funny if the chickens put their own crosses on?" Gerry laughed at the picture, and it was so fantastic that her mother had to join her.

It was near to noon and Etta decided that Charlie was staying in town. He never called and she had to guess. But the *Oregonian* distributor had come by in his Ford and thrown a paper at the porch with a passable display of accuracy. Etta sat down on the steps with the paper and turned to the continued fiction story of marriage and divorce, money versus happiness.

"Mama, I bet you can't guess who's goin' to be our new Sunday school teacher."

Absently (It was just as she'd thought, and Ted Fanhurst *was* in love with the Meredith woman): "Isn't Mrs. Webster going to teach it any more?"

"She's taken an older class—the one Mrs. Henry had before she went to Athena to stay."

(The instalments were so short, but of course that was just so you'd get the paper every day. She resolved each time never to start a new one when they began. That was the trouble; once started, you had to finish them.)

229

"Guess who, Mama?"

"I can't imagine . . ."

"Mrs. Webster's sister."

Etta turned from the paper. "You mean Fanny?"

Gerry nodded. "Mhm . . . I bet she's a good teacher, too. I like her. She can make ice cream sodas better'n anybody at the Terminal."

Etta forgot the frenzied fragment of newspaper sentiment. The thought of Fanny Brest teaching Gerry at Sunday school had startled her. It was somehow upsetting. Of course, Fanny was older now—why, Fanny must be forty! No, she was about thirty-seven, maybe younger than that. Once she had seemed so old to Etta. And besides, nobody ever knew anything for certain about her.

"Do you have to be in her class?"

"Why? Why, Mama?"

"I just wondered."

"She's going to teach the class I'm in . . . Don't you like her? I do."

"Why of course I do, dear."

She would have to ask Charlie about it when he got home. Maybe it wouldn't be a good idea to let Gerry go on. There was still the Baptist—but she couldn't let her go there. It was silly, anyway, to even think about it. She wouldn't teach anything but what was in the Bible. It didn't make a particle of difference.

She decided not to say anything to Charlie about it. He might make a fuss and not let Gerry go. Like he had been over that party Peg had given for her little niece.

Certainly she didn't know anything about Fanny;

230

and it was not like it would be if Gerry were old
enough to hear things.

"You better not tell your Daddy she's your teacher
or he won't let you go to Sunday school any more."

Geraldine was fearful. "Why won't he?"

"He doesn't like Fanny . . ."

"I don't see why. She's nice. She wears bright dresses
and I like her."

Bright dresses? Etta felt a swift pang. The child
had been taken by bright dresses—and maybe it was
because her mother never wore bright dresses any more.
She realized for the first time that she was, after all, a
rather far cry from the debonair girl who had worn
silk stockings and worried about her breasts.

"Well, you'd better not say anything to him about
it if you want to keep on going to Sunday school."

"I want to keep on. I want to be good and go to
heaven, don't I?"

11

Peg had made no effort to see Etta since the day of
the party for her niece—the party to which Charlie
had forbidden Gerry's going. After Peg had sought the
Fraser place as refuge that night she had tried to show
her gratefulness by telephone calls, casual visits, pack-
ages of edibles sent—strangely enough, by Swede himself—to Etta. But when the rebuke had come in the
form of Gerry's refusal, (Charlie had made the child
tell Peg she couldn't come) Mrs. Mongsen became sig-
nificantly silent.

Etta was anxious to see Peg. She was curious, and
from Swede's stolid visits with cake and vegetables she

231

could gain nothing. Charlie said that he had probably beaten Peg soundly and then forgiven her. It seemed that this was plausible enough. Swede was doing excellently, as usual. He had bought a car—a new car that was rather unusual. It was the colour of a smoky sun and the upholstering was maroon leather. He had, Charlie'd learned, paid cash for it, too. The fool seemed always to know when to let go of his wheat; and then he'd sold a piece of mountain land to Joe Key. Swede's harvest expenses never seemed to run as high as Charlie's, though for the life of her Etta couldn't see why.

Swede let Peg drive the car around. He seemed to be really proud to have her seen in it. She looked at home driving it, but he looked sort of silly sitting behind the glass of the windshield wings. But Peg . . . her black hair flying and her lips as red as the car itself, looked like movie heroines Etta had seen at Memorial Hall.

She knew that Peg was going to have a baby, and she suspected that was why Swede was good to her after all that had happened. She couldn't understand it. Why, how could he be sure that it was *his* baby? If she were Swede she'd keep thinking of that man's coat around Peg. It was too horrible, too messy.

If you were absolutely truthful, Peg was a good-for-nothing. Yet Etta always defended her. She'd hated it when Charlie hadn't allowed Gerry to go to the party. Still, Peg was worthless. She'd always been foolish and her mother hadn't helped her any. She was wild . . . crazy. Swede should know better than to let her drive around town in that car. She wore dresses just the same as ever, and when she climbed out of the car you could see clear to her thighs. And her with a baby, too.

But all the time there was something you liked about

Peg. Something elemental about her that took in Etta just as it took in Gerry when Peg had first come into the child's horizon. Swede was always tied by it, no matter what happened. He would go on loving her until the grave, and it was possible for him to do this because his pride was not long-lived. He could knock down Lester Adams, or drive hell-bent to Walla Walla to find her unfaithful—he could do that and it was all over.

Peg treated him with a quiet contempt. She did not love him . . . of that Etta felt sure. She knew why she didn't love him now, why she hated him. He had found her out for what she was and she hated him for that. It was only for this that Etta could not forgive her. Peg should have loved Swede for caring enough to follow her, to beat her and not quite kill her as he would have done if his love were dead.

But a child might settle her.

A child had settled Etta, and she was becoming aware of it, dimly. Whatever rebellion she had held was no longer strong. Whatever interests she possessed seemed focused at last on Gerry. Even her time, her little moments of attention, seemed to be for Gerry.

Well, for whom had they been before? For her mother, at first, and George Dant—and then Charlie. She could not remember any time when she was taken with herself entirely. It was Peg who was for herself utterly. It was Peg who was hard and cruel; and yet, in a crisis, it would be like her to sacrifice. Etta felt sure of that.

Etta couldn't imagine Peg with a child. But, for that matter, there had been a time when she couldn't imagine herself with one. But Gerry, now, seemed as natural as—as natural as she really was.

But Peg with a child . . . only recently had Etta been aware of what Gerry had sensed from the first: that Peg's life was full of high points. Yet most people's seemed to have high points. Hers seemed just to go on. There must be others, too, whose lives just went on. There surely was. But Etta could think of so many to whom things *happened*.

There was Peg up there on Jerry Fleeter's platform . . . Peg wild and drunken at a dance . . . Peg cowed before the wrath of Swede, Peg in another man's coat. No, there'd been nothing like that for Etta. And there was Lester Adams with his crazy talk upon the road that night, and now an aviator at San Antonio. Someone had said he'd married a rich Jewess and she'd left him. That, of course, you couldn't believe even though someone had said they'd seen a notice of the marriage license in a Portland paper. Then there were the tales of the encounters of Fanny Brest—a woman like that in a town as small as Creston. There was always gossip about this and that person. Some of it you believed and some you didn't. A part of it you knew for sure. But there was no gossip about her, nothing glamorous.

"You'll have Charlie's kids," Lester Adams had said. And he'd predicted the same for Peg. What was that he had pretended to believe? Life is a detour on the way to death.

Yes—she'd almost forgotten about that night at Pendleton which had rushed her headlong into Charlie's house. That one moment when convention had eluded her. It seemed nothing now. Certainly she was washed

234

clean by the waters of marriage; and the alarm had proved false anyhow.

She wasn't exactly sorry for the lack of glamour of which she was gradually coming to a realization. She had no desire to be the center of any concentric circles on life's more troubled surfaces. She wondered—as so many women wonder—if she were getting old. Older, that is, than she actually was in point of years. She didn't remember that when she was younger she felt that important things were continually happening to her. She had a chance to observe this in Gerry. How important microscopic things could be to her! But Etta saw this exaggeration diminish in Gerry almost daily. As the child grew older her appreciation grew less, her standards of evaluation grew more marked. Getting old was the act of loading yourself up with good judgment.

Geraldine, however, was an older child than Etta had been. Traipsing around at her grandfather's heels, staying away from other children because the Frasers were ranchers, she had picked up an odd expression of sophistication in her blue eyes. She talked too much like an adult. Her mother had long ago decided that she could give her the benefit of a year's head start in school—provided Laurence Henderson moved on to another town. Etta hoped he would. There was something she didn't like about sending a daughter to the principal who had taught you. It brought home so forcibly the fact that time marches on and institutions and teachers remain forever.

She would wonder what Gerry would be like when she grew up. Surely not at all like her, though people said they resembled each other. But the child had an imperiousness about her, a casual superiority that sometimes broke into a smartness that her parents feared. They punished it as well as they could, and as often as George Dant would let them. But it was a streak that was there to stay.

Would she be pretty? As pretty as she was now? Or would she coarsen under the hot sun; would her skin become red and porous with the sharp winds of an Oregon Fall? Would she broaden too much, mature too woefully early as so many farm girls did—as her mother had?

Etta found herself wondering all this, and the questions seemed incongruous with Geraldine so small. Etta ached for her because of what she must yet suffer, and she would do what all mothers since all time have tried. She would break as many of the falls as possible. And she would succeed in only a few insignificant instances.

III

A baby might settle Peg . . .

But there wasn't any baby. There was some unspeakable *thing*, two months before its time, which might have been a baby had not the gods, rocking with their putrid joke, sent it off unfinished.

And Swede, completing the jest for them, took it up to the cemetery, inglorious in a packing box, in that smashing red car he owned. Charlie went with him. Together they did what had to be done. Together they spent energy forgetting it all.

It was Etta, too, who came to Peg . . . a white, drawn Peg so near to death that she was beautiful. A Peg torn with pain and anguish and the shame of having funked out on what is supposed to be a woman's best job—a woman's one job, some people say. It was Etta who came into a room full of old women who made clucking noises with their tongues and teeth and said it was too bad.

"Do be still . . . she can hear!" she said. What she wanted to say was: "Be still, you damned old fools!" When they were gone she did say it. She said it loud enough so Peg could hear; and Peg tried to smile so that she took heart and it did more, probably, than the doctor.

The thought kept coming up to Etta that it must somehow be Peg's fault. If she'd behaved herself . . . but Etta shut it out. That would be what those old women would be saying, clicking their tongues against their teeth.

Charlie and Etta stayed there at the Mongsen place for two weeks. It was a strange gathering. It had a layer of humour, brittle and cracked, over it. And as Peg came out from under, as she was sure she was going to be all right again, they even ventured a joke or two about the matter. Somebody had to do something, say something to help along. And of the four it was Swede, of all persons, who started it.

"Guess we'll have to try again," he said.

Charlie and Etta had been startled into laughing at him. Peg had smiled, too; a smile that was like a substitute for a grimace of pain. Etta wondered if Peg would be the same again. She had a fear that this might change Peg too much. After all, she didn't want to see Peg Mongsen much different than she'd always been. No matter what people have been, a change is always saddening. Nobody, really, likes to see a sinner repent and become good. There is something depressing about it, something unnatural and strange.

Charlie and Etta stayed there two weeks before they became aware that maybe Swede and Peg would rather have them go.

"We must be getting back . . . Geraldine there with Grandpa——" and she hadn't meant to mention anything about Geraldine at all. She could have slit her own tongue.

"No use goin' on," Swede said. "You two've been great, believe me."

But they got out with relief, wondering if they'd ever been welcome.

"I don't know," Etta told Charlie. "Maybe we shouldn't have stayed there. It's hard to do anything at a time like that. Maybe we ought to have kept away."

"Well, they knew we meant all right . . . That's all that's necessary . . . Do you think she's goin' to be all right?"

"Peg? She's goin' to be well. I don't know what she'll be like."

"It's sure tough on her. She looks kind of pretty now, don't she? Prettier than she was, I mean."

Etta was astonished. Charlie could be so relentless, so smug. She had half expected him to call it justice.

"Yes, she does look different someway."

"It's a damn' shame. And those cracks Swede was makin'. Just like it didn't matter to him."

"I suppose he was trying to cheer her up."

"He's about as cheering as a morgue," Charlie said. "God, if he's as roughshod as that *all* the time I don't wonder she gets fed up."

Charlie's exchange of colours puzzled her for an

answer, so she was silent. It was difficult to talk unless there was a clash. If there were no differences of opinion, what could you talk about?

When they arrived home, met George Dant with Gerry on the porch, they swooped up the child with caresses that were rather frenzied. It was so real, so nice, to have Geraldine—a tangible sweetness, flesh of their flesh, blood of their blood. For them there were no darkened rooms, no odour of iodoform, no sickening travesty of burial. They were, by comparison with Peg and Swede, so richly endowed that they felt fearful of the future. It might well be that they were too richly blessed; there was always the threat of an angry God who might be jealous or capricious.

That night Etta prayed. She did not kneel beside the bed and pray aloud. She was ashamed to do that. She shut her eyes against the darkness to bring herself still more aloof from reality; she said words to herself and to God, words that asked for a happy Geraldine, kept safely always.

IV

Out of things like this there are always changes in a house, a shifting of values, a new tack. It was that way with Swede. He seemed to have taken on a new recklessness, an attitude that the present was, after all, more important than any future.

One of the manifestations of what he certainly wouldn't have called a philosophy of life was his buying of oil stock. Many Crestonites laughed (because they forgot very soon) when he told them what he had done. Their delight came from experience, and it was the delight of the crowd which likes to see one more fool added to its numbers. There had been others who'd bought oil stock. California was dangerously close to Oregon and the state line was no barrier to the glib talkers who drifted into town and then followed up with "attractive brochures" and suave letters on engraved stationery.

They knew what would happen to Swede's money, but they were surprised that he'd fallen for it. You were paid premiums for a while and then presently you learned that the oil had run out, or that the company was patently a fake. There was a general wary notion that oil stock, to be worth anything, must have to do with Signal Hill. Somehow Signal Hill stood for success.

Swede told them good naturedly that "his well" was quite near to Signal Hill.

"The ground's got the same geological formation," he said, quoting from the booklet. "I've got a picture of the well drillin' operations. The picture's been stamped by a notary, too."

"You're stung," they told him. "You better be lookin' around for a place to sell that red car of yours."

Even the promoters may have been astonished at the success of Swede's well. At any rate it was a fact that the company offered to buy his stock or trade other stock for it. Some dogged stubbornness, not unmixed with suspicion, made Swede hang on to what he had. And he eventually learned that the well was a gusher.

It didn't net him much, but it seemed to show possibilities of netting him a monthly income to live upon. He might even be able to disregard his wheat land—which, of course, a Mongsen wouldn't do.

"He has the God damnedest luck," Charlie's opinion ran.

Etta's was a consoling, wifely thought: "I don't know. He seems to go into things pretty careful."

"Careful!" Charlie snorted. "He just didn't give a damn what happened after——" he remembered Geraldine, her fork poised at the table, her shell pink ears visibly ready—"after Peg was sick. He just took a chance and won. I won't gamble any ranch of mine away, luck or no luck."

"No . . . I wouldn't want you to, Charlie."

But she sighed, and as she went on with her eating she felt just a tiny bit futile.

"I bet they go to California," she prophesied, brightening.

"Maybe . . ."

And then Etta remembered what she had meant to say a moment before:

"Charlie, you must stop swearing at the table before Geraldine. You promised you wouldn't, but you're as bad as ever."

Charlie and Geraldine exchanged a glance. She met his sheepish expression with an impish grin that said, "I really don't mind, Daddy. You can swear all you want, and what *has* it got to do with me?"

CHAPTER FIVE

I

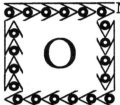NCE again a harvest stole over Creston. There had been so many that they crept up softly on the valley, as birthdays creep up on people who are afraid of them. It was the sun that brought the harvest—and nothing comes into Creston more quietly than the sun. All Winter long you may not realize there is a sun; you think only of fog, of snow, maybe of a day that is lighter than usual, warmer than usual. But you do not think of the sun. It is so remote that you do not even think: if only I could see the sun before April comes again!

And then—some certain day in April—it rises in such splendour that it has you literally prostrate before it has ascended to ten o'clock.

It was such a sun that began to wake Creston to another harvest; and all along the valley of wheat people were stirring. From Pilot Rock, down below Pendleton, clear to Walla Walla, people began to stir themselves. They came out from the houses and were pale with the Winter. But in a month or two their skins would be red or swarthy or freckled. In a month the hot wind and the dry dust and the sun would have turned them all into a virile new race with a new colour.

The snaky highways which led out of Creston into Pendleton and Walla Walla were filled with cars from other small towns like Creston. Some chose the Oregon town, some the Washington; the farmers were loyal to their own choice. The merchants of the little towns

242

decried the easy use of the automobile and preached "home-town loyalty" in vain. Before Henry Ford ever runs for president of the United States he must first make his peace with the merchants of the small towns. People bought the things they wanted, not in Creston, or Acme, or wherever they lived, but in Walla Walla— or maybe Portland or Spokane. It was half because they believed they could do better there and half because they wanted to be going.

There was nothing tangible to hold them to the soil any more. Nothing held them to it but their inherent need for it, their helplessness before anything that didn't have its savor.

There was always to be found someone who couldn't stand it, some sport in the breed who, though he'd come out of it all, didn't belong. Or someone who, like Lester Adams, had been educated away from it or unfitted for it.

Florence Larson, for another, hadn't been able to stick it out. She wasn't of Creston, never wanted it. So she didn't stay. Like Lester Adams, she too had escaped on wings. But they were the wings of her own fear. They were the wings of her own nameless desires which took her into something worse than Creston.

In conquering nature, man was helping her better than he knew. He was helping her to weed out the weak from the wheat lands. The very things with which man whipped nature made it possible for her to get out those who didn't belong. His medicines, his social sanitations, his doctrines—all these had helped to thwart her of the rule that the unfit must go. But, just the same, the unfit disappeared. Instead of meeting death

243

at nature's pitiless hands, the modern age made it possible for them to get away.

The modern age. Every age has invented things, lumped them together as the tangible proof of its "modernity." This age's modernity happened to be radio, aircraft, cheap cars, ready-made everything, and "woman." A woman as new as Ishtar was new; as Cleopatra; as some of Henrik Ibsen's amazons. That new and not one bit newer.

It was this modernity that allowed the weak to get out of Creston and come to the city where the weak may flourish and grow fat. A city likes a weak one; there is something about city Christianity which aids a weak one. But Creston's Christianity was different. In Creston, God was hard and His people could be hard.

But for the city there's a soft side of God. You notice the effect of it everywhere. You begin at the bottom and you see the dirty missions along the street, the Salvation Army playing martial songs and asking nothing from you but faith. You see the five-cent soup joints and the ten-cent flop joints—all instigated by some mortal arm of a soft city God.

And then you go up and see the better churches. You see the offices of the Red Cross, and the community chests, and the poor children's clubs. You see huge edifices dedicated to the care of this sick and that. You seem to sense that the large banks with their savings departments, and the imposing insurance buildings with their unfailing lights on tall towers—they do not want anything to happen to you.

But in the Crestons it's different. Things move on in their appointed way. A man is sick and penniless. He may live awhile on the church, on the sporadic offerings of the townspeople. But there comes that point at which nothing may be done, and he is quickly buried. In Creston, the Reverend Alfred Horliss says relentlessly what he has said relentlessly so many times before. The hard God of the western country places has spoken and had His way.

Yet, on this April when another harvest crept upon it, Creston asked for nothing else. Its people were not less happy than other people. Who would come into Creston with the mind of an iconoclast and say it is hypocritical? Who would enter it with the mind of a poet and call it ugly? Who would dare visit it on the high carriage of smartness and smile at its naïveté? The answers, of course, are obvious enough. Mr. Sherwood Anderson would give these people the minds of Sherwood Andersons. Therefore they would be unhappy in their environment. Therefore they would go through the fields at night and throw clods and wonder what was wrong with them. But they weren't Sherwood Andersons. They were George Dants and Charlie Frasers and Swede Mongsens. Mr. Sinclair Lewis would have been laughed at had he chosen to tell them orally what he eventually wrote on paper.

Harvest was creeping on them and they asked for neither pity nor happiness. They had enough of both. They had their work to do, work they wanted. Out of that can come all the emotions needed by anyone to carry on the business of living. It was enough for them that, once again, there would be yellow wheat to harvest from the rolling hills.

It was during that harvest that Clarissa Hempel, warmed to gossip by another new sun, said to Etta:

245

"I see your family's gettin' along better with the Mongsen's than you did."

Etta had been completely surprised by the remark. She got it for what it was: an innuendo as oblique as Clarissa Hempel could make it. Etta couldn't mistake the tone; but she couldn't, either, catch just what was meant by it.

So when Clarissa, on the steps of the church of which she was a pillar, and, she said, a sacrifice, told Etta of her observation, Etta could only reply: "Well . . . since Peg's unfortunate trouble, you know. I felt we should."

She thought she'd carried it off decently enough. She had picked up the words "unfortunate trouble" especially to describe what had happened to Peg. She had been there all through Peg's sickness and it was natural that people should be asking her about it. You couldn't say miscarriage; and you couldn't say the baby had died, because it hadn't died.

Clarissa glared; it is possible that she felt she was the feminine spirit of God, standing on the steps of the house He had given to Creston. She went on, in enlargement, "I was sayin' to my husband last night—not about the Mongsens, naturally, but about another matter—that people shouldn't try to help others out too much. There's a certain punishment put on them and it's not right for anybody to interfere with it."

It was this statement that confused Etta. She felt Mrs. Hempel's interest was only because the Frasers had thwarted a part of God's wrath at Peg. That must be the reason for her noticing and mentioning it.

But several days afterward, when the thing had simmered down in her mind, it occurred to Etta that they *hadn't* been particularly engaged with them of late. For some time now she hadn't seen Peg or Swede; not, in fact, since they'd come back from California. It rushed over her that this had been a month and a half of time. She traced back as neatly as she could with a mind that held nothing for very long. On the day they'd left the Mongsen ranch, both trying to feel they'd done what they could, and trying to feel, also, that it had been appreciated, they'd ceased to speak of Swede and his wife. It was as if they could help the Mongsens by themselves forgetting. And then, a month and a half ago, Charlie said casually that they were back from California.

Beyond that he had little to say. She'd expected him to remark that the Swede was blowing off all over town.

"Are they pretty stuck up?" she'd wanted to know.

"Not especially, I don't think. Seemed just the same. Both lookin' better than they did after—after she got sick."

Try as she might she could make nothing more of it. Whatever Clarissa had meant must be something she didn't know about.

It was via logic, of a sort, that Etta reached her conclusion. Something she didn't know about—that would involve Charlie. Casually, nicely, did she come to that result. So casually and so nicely that it didn't startle her at first. It wasn't a fact that had popped out of nowhere. Had she caught what Mrs. Hempel meant that day on the church steps, had she got it with no rebound, it might have shocked and agonized her. Coming to it in her own slow way it left her cool.

Not for a moment did she suspect that Mrs. Hempel had been striking in the dark. Her gossip, Etta knew, was unprejudiced and accurate. The whole town was her field and she covered it as dispassionately as a city editor. She wouldn't spare Charlie; neither would she give him more than was his due.

She remembered now that Charlie had said, on that day they'd decamped from their vigil at the Mongsen's, that Peg was prettier. He'd been short with Swede, too, and defended Peg's sensibilities against him.

Etta's mind worked more keenly now. In going back over the trail she picked up shreds that she had missed. Everything Charlie had said, whatever he'd done, took on some new colour. It all focused to the fact that Peg was something to Charlie. Charlie was a conquest of Peg's. Another. He belonged to the rest of them, then, to those unnamed (sometimes) ghosts that hung about Peg like a legend.

If Peg actually loved him, if it weren't just another of her tangents, Etta could forgive them—or so she told herself. She had read enough of the current fiction to know precisely what she must do. She could meet Peg (if Peg actually loved Charlie she would come to Etta) and grandiloquently refuse to give her husband away. She could say that this other woman didn't know what love meant, didn't know how to love Charlie.

Or, she could quietly withdraw for Peg; she could disappear, a martyr, into some black night and leave behind a tragic note to wish them happiness.

She preferred the latter. It seemed to her the bigger way. Yet there were things standing in the way of both these finalities. None of them was Geraldine. Children frequently entered into the situation, making it the more poignant. Etta, of course, would merely take Gerry with her. "Do you think you could understand

Geraldine? You love him, but do you think it's the kind of love that would make you understand his child?"

The things standing in the way of Etta's dealing with it as she knew a wronged wife should deal with it were simply these: she knew Peg too well; and there was Swede to consider. She knew Peg too well to meet her coolly and say what she had to say. There wouldn't be that fear that one would have for a stranger, that certain respect. Etta knew within an inch all the cheap little tricks that Peg possessed. No, with Peg she couldn't do the scene justice; she might become too angry, or she might cry.

Swede—well, Swede was a stolid fact not to be dismissed. He complicated things. Peg should have been a widow, or a professional adventuress.

While Etta viewed the possible solutions, she was still acute enough to realize what a fool she was for anticipating. But she was never struck with the humour of it; the cheap magazines and movies had left their indelible imprint on everything she did or thought. Her very emotions were the reflections of pulp-paper characters.

Earlier, before Gerry was born and there was yet the keen edge on her marriage, she had visioned situations involving something of this sort. Sometimes it would be she who was the sinner, though not often. She loved Charlie and could gain no pleasure from a dream scoundrel. Mostly it was another woman, after her husband. This woman was a siren, a composite of all the slinky ladies she'd ever met, actually or vicariously. It was always a woman of the same appearance: tall, dressed in black. There were long earrings and an exotic hair dress; she was pale as death and her eyes were, of course, a dare into hell. She was *not* Peg Mongsen. She was not short and broad across the hips. You did not see her bare legs at every hectic move, because she made no hectic moves. She did not rely on bizarre and tight sweaters with careless necklines. Her hair, though black enough, was not blown by a dozen winds, some of them yesterday's.

She was a woman eternally beautiful, this creature who—all unknown to Charlie—seduced him from his faithful wife. Somehow, in Etta's mind, her gaunt farmer boy never looked too utterly incongruous in the arms of a Kipling vampire. This dream woman confused whatever purposes Etta might have gathered together. This woman she had pretended to fear, and known she need not fear, had so dulled the blade of actuality that Peg, for the time, seemed an impotent nothing.

When Charlie came in at night for dinner she tried to visualize it, but failed. It was difficult to believe that this fellow across from her could be a lover to a woman like Peg. Charlie . . . Charlie Fraser. Day in and day out she'd seen him. Changing less than most men from day to day. Never up and never down, only a little stubborn and angry at times. But he wasn't flashing or rapier-like. Not daring. He wasn't a man who would wear a coat such as Peg had worn on the night Swede beat her. And Charlie *hated* Peg so. The things he'd said to her that night.

No, it was a mistake. Foolish. Everything was the same. There was Gerry beside him, eating with that grave air of importance that she had. And George Dant, cramming food down his throat, an empty stare in his eyes except when they encountered Gerry's. The four of them eating dinner. They belonged together, were intertwined by flesh and memories.

"Think that Fife is goin' to turn out good, Charlie?" This was Dant.

"Looks good. I was lookin' at it today. Be ready to cut sooner than any, but there's a little mustard."

She could hear them. It was just as always. And Gerry was kicking her foot back and forth as she ate, adding further damage to the worn place she'd made on her chair.

CHAPTER SIX

THERE were things that Etta couldn't possibly know. Charlie wasn't aware of them himself. For instance, on that night he'd cursed Peg in the Fraser kitchen he'd felt her coming over him like the spell she was. Etta couldn't know that seeing Peg there, fearful and half dressed, Peg so truthfully wanton and so frightened, had stirred him more than he himself knew. Charlie's wife wasn't aware that his words had been a shield he had put up in front of him. Neither did she know that he had said them like a cruel, hurting caress to Peg.

Peg going through her pain—all for nothing—when the baby was born, that hadn't helped him either. There in the house with her, watching her white face, he had been snared. He had been ashamed of wanting her there, under her own roof and her so ill. He had tried to believe it was pity but he knew that it was more than pity. Gradually he realized that all his hate for Peg had been a cruelly distorted desire, a masochistic passion to beat her into an idol of his own. She was . . . so different from Etta.

She lay there on the white pillow and her eyes kept saying to Charlie: "This is hell. That's all. I suppose it's sad, too, and useless. But mostly it's just hell."

Clarissa Hempel, on the church steps before Etta, had really lost heart. Once launched on her speech, she hadn't been able to bring it to its conclusion. Etta was so unprepared, and this thing Clarissa had to tell was too direct. It was too much a fact. Clarissa Hempel was an expert at innuendo, at pharisaic subtleties. Had she only heard something, had she only suspected something, she could have told Etta without a qualm.

But this thing she knew for certain. She had got it from her husband, loyal spy to her institution of gossip. She knew that Mr. Hempel wouldn't lie. He was too simple to lie. He had been returning from a lodge meeting at Hermiston. It was rather late (his tale to his wife was by way of being a peace offering, too) and he had encountered Swede's car parked by the side of the road. Mr. Hempel had taken the short cut into Creston, the old road, lined with poplars and alders, and he had seen the red car there. The road was known among the younger hellions of the town as "handkerchief alley." For what reason Mr. Hempel did not pretend to know.

Swede was not in his car. Mr. Hempel had been sure of that; and he was also sure that he'd seen Peg in it. The man with her looked like Charlie Fraser. Mrs. Hempel, when her husband told her, was certain it had been he. After the encounter on the church steps she was angry with herself for not letting Etta know what she felt a wife should have known.

It had been Charlie there with Peg. What other times they had been there, each had forgotten. What other times they had slid down into the deep cushions of the car, thrilling at the fear of detection, while the lights of another automobile went by, they did not know. On the night that Mr. Hempel had passed he had surprised them. They had grown careless. Each knew that they would sense the approach of Swede, if he should chance to be going by in another car. Most of the cars that meandered through the old road contained couples like themselves—perhaps not always precisely comparable, but at least those couples whose desire was not to be

253

seen. The "alley" was not long; if you got into it first the other cars cautiously drove through, saw you there, and went on to seek other havens.

Of course Charlie and Peg didn't know that Mr. Hempel, of all persons, would be cutting through the old lane. Mr. Hempel—had he not seen Swede's red car there—would never have admitted it himself. They sat there, watching his car go down the slight hill, heard the motor increase its noise as the machine hit the paved highway into Creston. They sat there silent for a moment—it was always so deathly still after a car had passed. Along the road were countless shadows that might have been anything in the night. They made Peg deliciously afraid. They were things from which she needed to be protected.

"How long are we goin' on like this, Charlie?" she said. She had asked it before.

"I don't know," he sighed. "I don't know what the hell to say . . ." He let his voice drift off, left the problem hanging as he had always let it hang. He knew very well that the question wasn't too important to her, and he knew that she liked to have him imagine she considered it important. It could always be dismissed, forgotten, by the business at hand.

He drew her to him again, his hand tight against her breast, pressing it cruelly through her thin dress. Craftily he used the gesture to pull her dress above her knees. Her bare legs shot into the corner of his eye and shut out the night and all that it meant . . . The old, old formula along the countless highways. It drew him out of himself, out of the ranch, out of the house with Etta in it.

He kissed her reverently, wholly out of accord with

the position of his paws. It was a holy kiss; it was a kiss as white as Peg's bare legs, and quite as incongruous as that figure.

She began to talk again, and he wished that she wouldn't.

"Remember when we used to go together in high school? I liked you then, too."

She could be so childish, so naïve. Etta hadn't been like that, ever. It seemed as if she somehow always had the upper hand, that she always held something in reserve. His memory did not take him back to the time when she had thrown herself upon her knees asking that he never leave her. "I've nobody but you," she'd said. If Charlie had remembered he would have excused himself by saying that now Etta had old man Dant, that she had Gerry.

"Did you like me then?" Peg was running on, "or were you just wanting to go with somebody, Charlie?"

"I never went with anybody unless I wanted to."

He kissed her again. His hands renewed their explorations, but she bridled them at once.

"Let's don't have to argue any more, Charlie. You know what I told you the last time."

He was petulant, giving up at once, and pouting like a spoiled child. "You make me dam' tired," he said.

"I told you once. I swore I'd be true to Swede, and I am."

Charlie laughed as bitterly as he knew how. "You've sure been true to him all right."

"I have. I've never gone that far with anybody but him."

"I suppose you were playin' chess with that guy up in Walla Walla that time you ran into our place."

"It wasn't like you thought . . . I don't know, but I can go pretty far and not let nothing happen that way."

"Well, you ain't going any farther with me."

Why would she lie so patently? Did she really think he believed her? He felt that she talked partly to convince herself, that she meant each time to wipe out the past with words so that she could begin anew. She tried to face tomorrow and not have yesterday matter.

"You're not," he repeated, "goin' any farther with me either, kid."

"I know I'm not. I've never let you, have I?"

"No," disgruntled. "You're just a goddam teaser, that's all. And you ain't goin' to get the chance to let me go any farther."

"What do you mean?"

He turned upon her. "Just this. Everybody knows what you been doing. It's no secret. I guess people think I been makin' a fool out of myself, too. I'm damned if I know what for. I'm through, that's what I mean."

Wronged and innocent: "You won't meet me any more just because I won't let you do what you want?"

He hated to admit the status when it was put so frankly, but he nodded his head. She began to cry, softly at first, and then, as he drew her head to his shoulder, her sobs became drawn and spasmodic. He softened at once. She must really care a little. He wondered idly what the devil one did to divorce a wife. What would people say about it? Would he and Peg need to move out of Creston altogether?

"Don't say that, Honey . . . but you don't know what you do to me just lettin' me go so far with you and then clamping the brakes. We either ought to

256

not see each other at all, or else—else——" He had to stop. He didn't know himself what the alternative might be. It seemed to offer nothing but a continual furtive sinning in a red car on a vacant roadway.

He felt her pressing against him with a sudden astonishing strength. He felt the steering wheel at his back; it pressed into a vertebra and numbed him. He shifted his position.

"Don't you want me any more at all, Charlie?"

"Sure I do. Why?"

"I love you and you keep pushing away."

"It's this dam' wheel on my back."

She was as practical as woman eternal. "Let's get back in the back seat."

"What if somebody'd come?"

"You can jump over and drive. You just have to let off the brake. It's downhill."

There was something quick and breathless in her voice. He saw that her mind had turned. At what word, at what moment, he didn't know. He did know that it might turn again and he helped her over the seat into the red car's tonneau without enthusiasm.

"It's colder," she said, and he found the robe to throw over both of them.

"It's so black all around, Charlie. It makes you feel like you was away from everything, don't it?"

He grunted an assent. Her voice was dreaming, and he sensed that whatever she was thinking could not be caught by him and thrown back at her.

"Sometimes I wish it was night all the time, don't you?"

Her statement startled him. He told her that he liked

the sun himself, and "you would, too, if there wasn't any."

She giggled. "How could I like it if there wasn't any?"

He was irritable. Damn her, she'd got to talking again now. "You know what I mean. If it should go out all of a sudden and not come up any more."

"Oh, I think I'd like it, Charlie. It's so cool and soft at night. You curl up inside yourself. You can sort of get at yourself. I like the night lots better."

She belonged to it, he thought. She was a . . . a night witch. Should he say that aloud?

"Lester Adams said once that the night was woven with the desires of women wanting to be kissed."

"That's easy," Charlie said, and he demonstrated forcibly, aware of an inferiority before the memory of a Lester Adams who could say things like that.

She told him that pretty soon she'd have to go, and then she was quiet. She became quiescent for a final caressing. He complied with her unnamed wishes. His hand sought her waist, brought her dress above her knees. Under the robe he could not see the bare legs that would have flashed against the dark red cushions of the car. She herself seemed to be unaware of them now.

She surprised him with a swift, "Charlie, would you keep on meeting me if I let you?"

"Sure," he whispered weakly. "Sure I would, Peg."

His throat was dry. His knees trembled as though on a nerve. He half rose from the cushion to relax himself. Looking down at her he saw with sudden panic that she mistook his move, that her eyes were full of nameless wants and her lips were half parted at the night sky.

CHAPTER SEVEN

I

ALIMP sort of help came to Etta finally. She'd thought of everything, even of going to Swede. She thought of a hundred things and did none of them. Her love for Charlie didn't enter in as the days went on. It was all possession now—possession and nothing more.

She wasn't sure that there'd been, lately, what you could really call love. Not since a year or so after Geraldine was born. You sort of got into a rut and plowed along. Love was like everything else; you took time for it or you didn't. It couldn't be all mental. You couldn't keep on loving a man at high pitch and not make some sign. And there had been no signs on either side for a long time now. She'd been busy with the house, with Gerry. Charlie'd been busy with the ranching. Yet not too tired to see the flash of Peg Mongsen against the drabness of his scene.

She'd been happy, though. As Etta looked back over the days before Clarissa Hempel shot her poisoned words from the church steps, those times seemed idyllic. What had he seen in Peg that he couldn't find in Etta? It wasn't so difficult to answer. She forced herself to it: he'd seen a pair of broad sensual hips, he'd seen eyes that promised everything.

That was a man for you. Off on the hunt. They wouldn't stop for Clarissa Hempels who could pierce you with a word. They wouldn't hesitate to tramp across memories and trod them under.

But finally, long after she'd forced herself to face Charlie's infidelities, a limp sort of help came, and it was from the last person from whom she might have expected it. She'd been in The Terminal with Gerry, drinking a "coke." Fanny Brest served them, and she leaned across the counter and whispered, "I'd like to have a talk with you, Etta."

Etta told Geraldine to stay where she was; she and Fanny went back into the "ladies' room," a two-by-four corner screened off from the barn-like back room. It was a little crowded—the two of them and the toilet bowl—but it was tremendously private.

"Will you get sore if I butt into your business, Etta?"

"Why, no . . ." Pretending astonishment. What business? she tried to convey.

But Fanny wouldn't be fooled. "You know what I mean all right. And if it's going to make you sore I'll shut up right now. Will it or won't it?"

"Why, I don't——"

There was a short disgusted laugh from Fanny. "Well, all right then. I mean Peg Mongsen and Charlie. Everybody in town knows it."

"Well?"

"I'm not draggin' it up as a friend. Maybe you know more about it than I do. The fact is, I don't know what it is exactly or how far it's gone. It probably ain't anything much . . . only—I wondered what you were doin'."

"I—what can I do, Fanny?"

The woman nodded knowingly. "I thought you hadn't done anything. You were always like that. Just let things go along. You can't this time. It's liable to be bad. You got to have a showdown. If you make some kind of a showdown he'll come to you. He's got to. He's your husband and you're his wife. You got the advantage all over her. You see, I know what I'm talkin' about. I was on the other side once. But I like you, Etta, and I'm takin' yours this time."

It was funny that she should be in there talking to Fanny, that she should be so near to tears in a place like that.

"What can I do, though, if he likes her better than me?"

"Call him. Ask him which he wants, that's all. You got to. Let him have his choice, and you'd better do it quick, kid. He's ridin' to a fall that maybe might get the whole bunch of you in trouble. Remember there's that prize dam' fool of a Swede. He never pulls the trigger until the rabbit's gone—but he gives it both barrels, then. And there's the kid, too, you know."

Fanny Brest . . . Gerry's Sunday school teacher . . . Creston's bad woman. Etta felt suddenly hot, sweaty. A drop of sweat broke under her arm and ran down in a warm rivulet. Would all this do her any good? She'd known at once what Fanny had wanted; she'd hoped that this woman, out of a mysterious past, might have the formula. But this . . .

"I tell you, Etta, a man'll marry a woman and she'll do her damnedest to please him, run herself all down for him, keep from carin' how she looks. Then he'll turn his head for the first little chippy that looks like she thinks he's something on a stick. But you've always got the edge, Etta. Peg's kind ain't much of an enemy . . . kinda pitiful sometimes. You take my word for it. You got to get a showdown. He'll be yellow. He won't have the guts to stick with her, that's all."

"I'll see, Fanny. Thanks . . . I don't hardly know what to say to him. Thanks, though."

The Brest woman was embarrassed. "I sort of wanted to see if I could do anything. Maybe I was wrong. Maybe it'd come out all right anyhow."

Wordless, then, they returned to the front of The Terminal. Gerry seemed unperturbed by her mother's absence. She was engrossed with trapping the residue of ice in her glass.

11

Etta sat on one of the benches which Pope's store placed out front for the benefit of those who were wearied of the Pioneer Picnic celebration.

It was unmercifully hot. The paint on the bench had weltered up in tiny pimples which exuded turpentine and stained the summer dresses or Sunday suits of all who rested from the festivities. But the corner of the building blotted out the red ball of sun, if not its whole effect, and Etta felt herself gathering enough strength to walk on down the street.

They were holding the street races and people were crowded to the curbing and into the center of the street. It was empty and cooler, now, along the building fronts. She sat there and could follow the swift progress of the runners by the shouts that passed along the lines of spectators, by the turning heads as the racing youths passed. Up at the other end of the street she could hear the sharp snap of a blank cartridge to start the races. It sounded so little different from the endless shots of the children's cap pistols that Etta wondered how the runners knew when to be off.

262

Oblivious to side attractions, the merry-go-round—
a scarecrow portable affair—kept up its ceaseless gyra-
tions and its wheezing music. The barkers at the booths
were quiet while their prospects watched the street
races. As soon as these were over they would begin
again. "Try your luck and win a blanket fer the lady!"
"It's easy—easy—easy! Just ring a cane and get a kew-
pie doll. Get a great big beautiful doll!" "A game of
skill, folks. A game of skill." They were pathetic figures,
these concession owners who made a last stand on the
frontiers of rubedom. They found slender pickings.
Most of them belonged to the carnival era of another
time. Their schemes were antiquated, their equipment
was broken and nailed together. All the barkers were
reduced to following local celebrations. Today it was
the Pioneer Picnic at Creston, tomorrow it would be
the Rodeo Days at Issaquah, or the Strawberry Festival
at Milton. They were not the dapper fellows they may
once have been. They wore dingy caps, greasy clothes,
and many were in need of a shave. They clearly felt
at the mercy of the crowd they sought to bilk. Often
they were forced to stoop to youngsters, or to annoyed
beaux in the company of their chosen maids.

Creston suffered them because their dirty and gaudy
tents lent an atmosphere to the Pioneer Picnic. Ring-
toss, roulette, and the countless other schemes, had no
place in a celebration dedicated to the early settlers of
Oregon. But most of those pioneers were gone. Only
two or three would sit on the platform today when the
program was held beneath the big tent pitched in the
middle of Water Street. And these survivors would be
too deaf to hear the compliments thrown at them by
the speakers of the day. But they would sense what it

263

was all about; they would sit there serenely, secure in the belief that next year would find them absent.

Most of Creston had forgotten what the Picnic was for. It had become a name only; a name which meant an annual two-day carnival. A duo of hot days with ice cream cones, soda pop, street races, a program, a ride on the merry-go-round, the pleasure of seeing people you knew at a time when work wasn't thought of. It was a time of nagging and pulling and bawling of children. It was a time when the walks would be strewn with confetti and paper streamers. The shoe-shining chair would be moved out in front of the barber shop. There would be a dance at the Memorial Hall. On the afternoon of the last day Creston would vie with Athena in a baseball game.

It was in the midst of all this that Etta sat. She found it scarcely less fascinating than always. She had looked forward to it with the same degree of interest as always. The change was only that she found herself less able to take it all in without tiring, a feat which Geraldine performed with ease.

The child was on the merry-go-round now. She'd been able to reach out and snare a gold ring. She had been at a loss to decide whether to keep the ring as proof of her prowess or to trade it for an extra ride. Etta had convinced her that the ring, without its attendant merry-go-round, would be rather useless.

It wouldn't be long now until she would be too big to be interested in merry-go-rounds. Long? Just how long? Etta didn't care to figure it in years. Gerry was going to be tall, maybe too tall. She'd already lost much of that "cuteness" which had so delighted her grown-up friends. As a matter of fact, it would be quite a time.

Etta remembered that she herself had been able to find a carousal exciting even while in high school. But people said children tired more quickly of those things nowadays.

Etta saw Charlie edging through the crowd toward her. He wore a new hat and his best suit. The hat sat rather high on his head—Etta wished he had worn his cap. On Charlie's lapel was the large round celluloid button of the Pioneer Picnic Committee. Hanging from it was a gaudy ribbon—red, white and blue, with a pale orange stripe thrown in for variety.

"Where's the kid, Etta?"

"On the merry-go-round," Etta told him. "She'll be coming back in a minute."

"Think we'd better eat in town?"

Etta reflected on the hot kitchen at home. "I'd have to get some things here before we went out. What do you want to eat?"

"God, I don't know . . ." Charlie wiped his brow and the lining of his hat. "Maybe we better eat a sandwich or something here."

"Papa might expect us, though."

"He can get something. We'll take Geraldine out after dinner, when it gets cooler, and let him know if we decide to go to the dance."

Charlie, very carefully, took a place on the hot bench. They sat wordless. It was too hot to talk. There was too much noise to talk anyway. Charlie sighed. They sat there until Geraldine came back, her face flushed with excitement, her forehead moist and warm, and her hair curled with perspiration against her face.

"Don't run so, dear. You'll be sick."

"I won't either." Mother had told her that before.

You never got sick when you drank soda pop, and ate candy, and played all day in the sun. You got sick when there wasn't any reason to get sick."

"We're goin' to get something to eat."

"I want an ice cream soda and a hamburger."

"You can't have an ice cream soda and a hamburger. I'll be up all night with you. You can have a hamburger and a glass of milk."

"Then I'll just have an ice cream soda."

"No," Charlie chimed in, "you got to eat somethin' hot."

"Maybe," Gerry stated with more diplomacy than assurance, "I can have an ice cream soda after a while."

"Maybe."

Geraldine sighed. Why did older people lie so palpably? You never said you didn't believe them. You pretended to forget what they'd said, and they really thought you had forgotten, too. That made them attempt it again at every possible chance.

She remembered the first time she'd sensed that her father was trying to keep something away from her. It was the Winter that they'd let her go to kindergarten when the weather wasn't too bad. She walked to and from the ranch into Creston, a diminutive and brave figure who found it a rare morning or afternoon when somebody didn't pick her up along the road. Most of the time it was a high school boy named Tod Martin who drove a rattle-trap car of his own.

He called Geraldine "Sailor" and she liked him a lot. He'd stop his car and yell, "Hey, Sailor, want a ride?"

No doubt he'd have continued to give the child a lift if something hadn't happened that Summer. Afterwards, Geraldine knew that Tod wouldn't be along in

266

his car any more. Just by the merest chance she was in town when they brought him in. Charlie had gone into The Terminal for a cigar and Geraldine saw the doctor's car rush by. Several men had seen it too, and they were running along after it because they'd seen Tod inside.

Geraldine forgot about her father. She ran down toward the doctor's office. They'd already taken Tod upstairs. She could hear people talking and could only get snatches of it. Little groups of men and women began to collect. Presently a man came out of the doctor's office. He had a smile on his face, the sort of smile you couldn't describe. It didn't mean the hurt boy was all right. It meant that he was dead and that the fellow with the queer smile was sorry, but that he'd known all along Tod couldn't live.

All the little groups broke up and became one group around this man.

"Is he—how is he?"

"He's gone," the man said, and looked at them with an I-told-you-so expression. There was a kind of victory in his face. Tod who had just died had justified the judgment of this bringer of news.

"I knew he was gone. I knew he was dam' close when he was layin' there and we took him up . . ."

The tools with which it had been accomplished were economical and common; a skittish horse, a rock beneath the soil, the sharp edge of a plowshare. The man had gone on talking while Geraldine stood there. His face was red. "I looked up and there he was standin' on his plow just the same as always. The next time I looked he was right in the air. He kind of slumped down between the first share and the next an' that dam' bay kept pluggin' right on. I ran like hell an' got 'em stopped, but they drug him quite a way. The share got right into his ribs an' he never hollered at the horses or nothing."

Geraldine didn't like the sound of the man's voice, nor what he said with it. She left the crowd and went back toward The Terminal where she found Charlie talking with some men. They were talking about the accident, too.

"What's the matter?" she asked.

"Fella got hurt on a plow," he told her shortly.

"He's dead, isn't he?" She knew that he was. She knew it was Tod Martin, too. And that her father was trying to avoid it.

"Come on, kid. We'll be late for dinner . . ."

That was the way parents did. They lied.

Geraldine didn't want to believe it, though. It was too absurd. It meant that Tod wouldn't yell at her and take her into town. It meant that the road she travelled to kindergarten would be strangely empty now.

One day Kate Nelson had come up to her and said, "You have to walk quite a bit now that Tod's dead, don't you?"

Geraldine looked at Kate as haughtily as is possible for one small child to look at another. But then she turned away and went down into the girls' basement to be alone. It was as if she'd heard of Tod's death for the first time.

III

It was crowded in the Memorial Hall. There were too many people attending from other places. It seemed to Etta and Charlie that most of the dancers were high school girls and boys. These made the dancing difficult;

they shot about the hall erratically. The boys did no guiding, but merely began a mad whirl and let it take them wherever it would. They and their partners ricocheted off older couples and asked no pardon. Some of them were disgustingly drunk, and tomorrow they would be proud of it.

It occurred to Etta that the one sure way to realize you were getting older was to attend a dance. She was a little ashamed of the way she and Charlie meandered around the floor. Charlie picked his way carefully; he was stiff and awkward in her arms. She felt sure she could have followed the intricate steps of any of these high school youths. She remembered how married people had appeared to her at a dance, but she quickly rid herself of the thought that these youngsters viewed her with equal pity. She was positive they weren't viewing anything, much less thinking about it. Their eyes, if not filmed by drink, seemed vacant. Their smiles were empty, half twisted. Sometimes the girls let loose with high, broken throatiness that was laughter.

The music was different, too. She remembered the pieces they had played when she first began going to dances. Japanese Sandman—she had liked that one. She wished they would play it because she had discovered how music can re-create things for the memory.

Of course, it was Geraldine who made her feel old. That was a mean thing to think, but it was true. When you were a mother it changed things. You couldn't go on like these girls did.

Yet there was Trula Cairns. Trula was from Acme, but everyone knew about her. She was here at the Picnic dance, of course. She always came. Tonight she wore a white dress and her hair was long and "done up." The dress had a firm, tight bodice and Trula's pointed breasts were scarcely timid at the mob. Her companion was a dark skinned youth, obviously quite near to the Indian strain.

Etta sought out Trula Cairns and watched her. You couldn't notice anything had happened to her—yet everybody knew that things had. She had suffered an operation once and almost died so that old Doc Grayson got into trouble. And there was a baby living.

But she was youthful. She was only seventeen and she should have been youthful. She'd had children, but she hadn't had the responsibility that goes with them. Trula hadn't had them tugging at her, hadn't worried about them. She'd gone on her way, like tonight. Trula wasn't remembering them tonight—unless that defiant look was a pose.

"I see Trula Cairns is here tonight," Etta told Charlie.

"She's been here every year that I can remember."

"I guess not every year. She's not more'n seventeen."

Charlie grinned. "Maybe. But what she knows would make her sixty."

Somehow Etta didn't like the remark. It sort of made her shrink down inside herself because it reminded her of Charlie and Peg. That remark had been too knowing, too worldly.

Even though she was certain that now whatever attraction Peg had for Charlie was gone Etta didn't like to think of it. But she kept on thinking of it; she couldn't quite forget it because it hadn't turned out as she had wanted.

She had wanted to talk it out with him, but she had tried only once. He had been furious, and she knew perfectly well that his anger had been defense against her questioning. Yet his anger had cowed her, as it always did. She had stopped the querying, and since then she had known nothing. Nothing except that one or the other of the two had lost interest. Or had become frightened and stopped it.

Etta supposed that she should have been relieved and glad. She was neither. The undramatic close to Charlie's extra-marital relations had cheated her of something she felt was hers by right. Her teachings had all pointed toward an inevitable climax which would mean either reunion or stark tragedy. But this was neither victory nor defeat.

So many Creston affairs had been like that. The wife or the husband knowing, and the people of Creston all knowing. And then it would stop, and you would think that nothing had ever happened. You saw the two women, or the two men, talking, smiling, touching hands. And you wondered what was behind the masks they wore—what pain of memory, or what hatred. Now she was one of these, and she felt curious to know whether all such wives just let it pass.

Charlie felt gay tonight, and she wondered if she couldn't approach him about it now. She began to lay a plan that was somewhat extravagant, and she became visibly excited over its possibilities.

"I'm kinda tired, Charlie, but I don't want to quit dancing yet."

This stopped him completely, and his retort annoyed her: "Well? Well, what do you want to do?"

"I thought maybe if we could get just a little something to drink it might pep me up."

For a moment Charlie wavered between the stand of

the puritanical husband and that of a good sport. But
her idea finally shaded itself into the colour of his own
mood.

"Maybe Hank Lovender's got some. You sit down
here and I'll see."

There wasn't any place to sit down and nobody on
the benches ranged along the wall offered her a seat.
She stood near the orchestra, watched Charlie and Lovender go out the door. They were gone the space of
two numbers, and when Charlie returned he'd been
successful in his quest.

"We'll dance around a couple of times so none of
the old hens will catch on," he told her.

"Are you sure it won't make us blind or anything?"

"Sure. Lovender's got a whole jug ditched up in
O'Hara's stubble field. He always gets good stuff. He
gave us a pint."

Involuntarily Etta shuddered. She knew that she
would like the stuff no more than she always had. They
danced twice around the hall, and then merged with
the crowd clustered about the doorway. Someone yelled
at Charlie and borrowed a match. Etta pushed on
through the wide door where she found other couples
and groups of men tipping bottles. It wasn't necessary
to go outside city limits on Picnic. On Picnic the town
was open—in honour of the old pioneers.

Etta and Charlie avoided a group containing people
they knew too intimately and struck out toward the
rear of the hall where a band of high school youths were
holding an exaggerated war dance. Etta passed them a
little fearfully, afraid that they might yell out something that would make Charlie angry.

In the shadow of the building they encountered Peg

272

Mongsen. She was talking with a young boy who tensed himself as Etta and Charlie approached. But Peg called out a greeting, an undercurrent of bravado in her voice. Charlie seemed to hurry on, Etta thought. She was glad they had seen Peg. It would give her a chance to bring up the matter casually.

Charlie halted by one of the alders that lined the walk behind Memorial Hall. He held out the bottle, telling Etta to go ahead. His tone was bantering and he seemed amused at this turn in her. He felt just gay enough tonight not to question it too closely.

Because she wanted to carry it through, and because she still clung to her purpose and needed courage, Etta swallowed some of the white liquor. For a moment her throat seemed to swell and she could scarcely breathe. But pride kept her silent, and at last she felt the white fire warming her breast.

"Had enough, kid?"

She nodded and handed the container to him. Charlie took a stiff drink in a sweeping upward gesture.

"Think you can last the evening now, Etta?"

"Maybe I better walk a little before I go in."

Charlie laughed. "Don't pass out on me." He took another drink from Lovender's bottle.

Etta forced a laugh of her own. "Don't worry about me. I know when to quit."

They flaunted their married recklessness before the gaping high school boys, and walked on past the group arm in arm. Etta noted that Peg had gone.

She imagined that the whiskey had begun to affect her; lights seemed blurred against the night, and the Memorial Hall had a soft, hazy outline. Her voice came easily, and as though from a distance.

273

"I'd like to ask you something before we go back in, Charlie."

He sensed what was coming. His answer was only a grunt, but she kept on with it stubbornly: "I wish you'd tell me about—about you——"

"Listen! Is this the same old thing you're draggin' up?"

"Well, hadn't I ought to know, Charlie? Hadn't you ought to tell me?"

Charlie loosed her arm, stood confronting her. "Ought to tell you what?"

She knew she was losing. She should keep still now, and save what was left of the night they were having together. But some dogged, curious instinct kept her at it.

"You know what, Charlie."

"I know you're always draggin' up some hell." Already the liquor had begun to make him insolent.

"You dragged enough up for me, and I stood it."

"You enjoyed it. You an' the old ladies—mullin' it over."

Etta was nonplussed. He had beaten her in a crude, awkward way. He had excluded her personal interest, made her one of the gossips who had classed him a libertine and added to the filigree of Peg Mongsen's "A." She couldn't cope with his stubborn lack of logic, his hateful knack of placing her in the wrong.

"All right, then . . . We may as well go back . . ."

"Go back?" he snapped. "Who wants to dance now? A fine evening you make for a guy."

She didn't want to dance now, either. "Maybe others," she retorted, "could make you a better one."

"Maybe they could!"

While she climbed into their car which stood in front of the hall, Charlie stormed into the building for his hat. It occurred to Etta that it took him a long time. And that Peg hadn't been in the shadows of the building when they'd returned from their tryst with Lovender's moonshine. Charlie might go back to her now, if he could. It would be like him. He'd want to make it appear as if she'd driven him to it. Well, he couldn't hurt her. She knew it wouldn't be for long. That had all been over for some time now. You couldn't make things like that come back. Etta knew. You couldn't be married and not know. If Peg took him back it wouldn't be beyond tonight. What did tonight matter? The liquor was making her cognizant of the essence of futility.

As Charlie came out onto the walk and into sight of Etta a smile for someone passed like magic from his face. He started the car's engine with an unnecessary feeding of gasoline. It roared and popped, and the hind wheels spun wildly before the machine gained traction and took to the road.

The two were wordless all the way to the ranch. Yet they might as well have been pitching their voices high in mutual bitterness. They were hating each other silently, effectively. If only one had spoken it would have been better.

They approached the drive to the garage, but Charlie kept his course and drew the machine up before the house. Etta shot him a questioning glance.

"I'm goin' back," he muttered.

She disappointed him. Without a word she climbed from the car and went into the house. She knew that had they argued at that moment the quarrel could have been patched. He knew she recognized this; and it meant simply that she was still defiant.

He bent over the wheel, thinking. It would be wearisome, driving back to town alone. It would be wearisome returning. But he'd said he was going, he'd told Etta; and with another noisy demonstration of engine chatter he switched the car around and headed for Creston . . .

Etta did not go to bed at once. She knew that Charlie would be gone for some time, if only from stubbornness. Walking softly so as not to disturb Geraldine and her father she went into the kitchen, made herself a sandwich of bread and lettuce. She wasn't hungry, and the liquor Charlie had got from Lovender was still a turmoil within her stomach. But she felt the nervous need of doing something, anything, besides getting ready for bed.

At length, putting down the half-eaten sandwich on the drain board, she went into the bedroom. She undressed carefully, as though she were planning to arise in the morning for a journey. Each little act that she had done mechanically so many times became a thinking move . . . I must wind the clock and place it here so that we'll wake in the morning . . . I must see that Geraldine hasn't thrown her covers off . . . I must make sure that the front screen door is hooked back so that it won't bang against the house if the wind comes up. Mechanically and slowly, just as always—but with thought this time. As if she'd never done those things before. Finally there was nothing more to do but climb between the sheets. All of it was done. And now to bed. She closed her eyes but did not sleep.

She could have slept had she known that she and Charlie were through. It would be the ending of something, the beginning of something else. But she and Charlie weren't through. They would go on and on until one of them died—with always this thing between them which didn't make it easier.

Fanny Brest had wanted her to "have a showdown." But the thing had ended before she'd had the chance for a showdown. There was nothing tangible now, nothing you could handle. It was a fact of which you had only the memory. And no chance to ever know, really, what had happened. A secret between Peg and Charlie.

Would he go back to her tonight? Well, if he did, it would be only for tonight. Something made her sure that he was done with Peg. It would be only for tonight, if at all. And he would be doing it to hurt Etta; as long as she possessed that knowledge he couldn't hurt her as much as he might like. There was the possibility, too, that he wouldn't go near the dance again. It would be like him to play cards all night and then come home to say nothing of where he had been.

What he did tonight didn't matter. It was the idea of going on with him, getting old with him, and always knowing that he and Peg Mongsen had a secret between them. It was . . . it was . . .

Sleep crept in at last and shut her off from communications with her own troubled brain.

Hours later. Or minutes? The front door opening, a vague form in the doorway. These things in her sleep, and the muffled thought: "He's come home now." And then a jagged voice splitting into the darkness, through the darkness and into her sleep. Charlie's voice unlike it had ever been before, unlike it would ever be again.

He was calling her name, and she could see now that his face was unbelievably white.

"My God, Etta!" That was all; over and over, until she had to hush him, to lead him into the front room away from the hearing of Geraldine and old Dant. She saw his shadow groping in the darkness of the room. It was the outline of blabbering fright.

She was thinking: He must be drunk. Crazy drunk. Or hurt some way. No, not drunk or hurt. Something's happened. He won't tell me. He's killed somebody . . . *killed somebody.* I won't turn on the light. He'd never tell me then. Anyway, it would be too horrible seeing him like this. I've never seen him like it before.

She put out a hand to his shoulder, oddly fascinated by his strangeness to her.

"Charlie! . . . Charlie, what's wrong? *Please . . .*"

"God . . ." he kept saying, without meaning. "Oh, Christ . . . " until there was nothing to his words but sobs that petered into quiet.

She pushed him down gently onto the old living room couch.

"Charlie, you got to tell me. Tell me, please."

The touch of her hands seemed to draw him out of the nightmare he had been living, to bring him back into the room. Presently she heard his voice again in the darkness, a little sane now.

"I only went to her because I was mad. Honest to God, Etta, that's all the reason why I went to her. I was mad and I guess maybe Lovender's stuff made me a little crazy. I met her up by the high school when I went back to town——" He broke off and stood up in the darkness, started to walk back and forth, half sobbing.

278

"*Charlie* . . ." It was as she would have spoken to a hysterical child.

He turned to her again. "Etta, I got to tell you. They'll tell you all kinds of things an' I got to tell you how it was."

"I know, Charlie. But I won't believe them. I'll believe you."

The words seemed to reassure him and he stammered on with it. "We sat in the car a while and then she got scared somebody would see us. She was the one that wanted to go up the cemetery road. She was the one. It wasn't me . . . I guess I was drivin' pretty fast. I guess I ought not to have driven so fast. When we went by Keys' place there was somebody on the porch and she squatted down on the floor so they wouldn't see her. I didn't know she was goin' to. She was crazy for doin' that because it was too dark to see. I didn't know she was goin' to. Somethin' happened. I turned too quick or she leaned against that goddam ol' door or something. She—she just kind of slipped out and into the road and she had the goddamnedest look on her——"

"Charlie! Didn't you go back? Don't you know how bad she was hurt?"

"Hurt?" Charlie's shadowed figure stood stolidly in the middle of the floor. "Hurt?" he repeated, as though the thought hadn't occurred to him.

"Yes . . . you don't think she——"

His words came from a fear-tightened throat. "She's dead, I tell you. She couldn't hit like that and not be dead."

"And you never went back?"

"God, I couldn't!" he sank down again upon the

279

couch. "I kept tryin' to go back an' I couldn't. Besides, there was somebody came runnin' off Keys' porch."

What was making Etta so calm? What was holding her so securely now? She put her hand against Charlie's shoulder again. "But it wasn't your fault, Charlie. She fell——" Etta broke off in a sudden intake of breath. "Charlie, you sure she fell? You wasn't——"

"I swear to God she did. You got to believe me. Oh, Jesus, Etta, you got to!"

"Hush, Charlie . . . you'll wake Gerry . . ."

The mention of Geraldine seemed to strike him afresh with horror. He sank against the lounge and sobbed like a woman, cried loudly into a pale restless drowse that gave Etta time to think.

There was fear in her heart for what might be done to him, and there was instinctive dread at Peg's death—at what she felt as surely as Charlie had been her death. Yet the meanness in her kept singing that Peg Mongsen was gone, that she was no longer a reality.

She roused Charlie. "You've got to get in bed. You got to be in bed if they come . . . Charlie, was Peg drinking?"

He nodded. "I gave her some of Lovender's stuff. She wanted some. She——"

"You sure nobody saw you up at the school house?"

"I——I don't think so . . . Etta, what the goddam hell can I *say* to 'em?"

"You go to bed, Charlie. You go to bed now."

Like a sick child he let himself be put to bed; but he stared wide-eyed through the windows of the room and more than once shot upright to live again that helpless second during which Peg had seemed to be poised above the rough, speeding roadway.

Etta, too, was awake. All night she listened for the footfall of old Dant on the stair. Just at the first gray-pink streaks of morning it came.

"Papa?"

Dant shuffled into the doorway of the bedroom.

"I wanted to know what time your watch said, Papa. I think this is stopped."

"It's five-ten, Etta."

"In the excitement of the Picnic we forgot to set the darn thing, I guess." She fussed with the cheap alarm.

"Have a good time?"

"Pretty good. The dance was dumb, though. We got home pretty early."

When old Dant had gone into the kitchen, Etta avoided Charlie's eyes. They were pitiful eyes, fawning eyes looking on her with a gratefulness that made her feel uncomfortable.

While they were dressing, the telephone rang. Etta had expected it before, yet her heart rose and whirred like a scared pheasant within her. Charlie, drawn and white, his work shirt shaking in his hands, stopped to listen.

It was Clarissa Hempel. With news of Peg Mongsen.

Charlie heard Etta's voice utter meaningless words of pity and astonishment, and then: "Isn't that terrible! . . . We saw her, you know, outside the dance hall last night with some man . . . No, I couldn't tell. She waved and said hello . . . What—what does Swede think? . . ."

Etta listening for Clarissa Hempel's words; Charlie listening for Etta's.

"Thanks awfully for telling me . . ."

She hung the receiver and then started back toward it with a jerk.

"I didn't say I was sorry. I should of said I was sorry."

Charlie kept standing there, his hands frantic and helpless. Etta walked into the dining room, to the sideboard. She took out the breakfast cloth and began smoothing it onto the table. She began talking to Charlie as though he'd just come in, as though she didn't remember last night.

"Clarissa says they found Peg last night on the road. That the Keys' hired man found her. They said she'd been with some boy from Pendleton. It's probably the one we saw last night outside the hall with her. Clarissa says they aren't looking for anybody because Swede don't want them to. She says she heard he's had letters from Florence Larson, but I don't believe that. I think he don't want them to hunt for anybody because he loved her . . ."

She began setting the table, carefully—more carefully than usual.

"The man at Keys' place don't know what kind of a car it was." She straightened. "Charlie, you got to go over to Swede's and offer to help him this morning. Like as not he'll kind of want somebody."

Old Dant and Geraldine naturally wanted to know why Charlie wasn't at breakfast.

"He went over to Swede Mongsen's. Peg———" Geraldine had to be considered, and Papa could be told afterward. "Swede wanted Charlie to come over and help him store his machinery in the new shed."

282

When Geraldine had gone outside Etta told her father.

"It's what I expected some time," she said smugly. She felt sinful for the remark, and secretly withdrew it from the annals of heaven.

But it did seem like God had got tired of watching Peg forever breaking His commandments.

THE END

This book was set in 11 point Garamond
on the linotype, printed and bound by
J. J. Little & Ives Company,
New York